the linen god

by

Jim O'Shea

the linen god

Copyright c. 2013 by James O'Shea
Published by Wayside Press,
an Imprint of Written World Communications
PO Box 26677
Colorado Springs, CO 80936
Written-World.com

All Rights Reserved. No part of this publication may be reproduced in any form, stored in a retrieval system, or transmitted in any form by any means—electronic, mechanical, photocopy, recording, or otherwise—without prior written permission of the publisher, except as provided by the United States of America copyright law.

This is a work of fiction. Names, characters, organizations, and incidents are either the products of the author's imagination and/or are used fictitiously, and any resemblance to actual persons, living or dead, organizations, events, or locales is purely coincidental.

All Bible verses are taken from the King James Version of the Bible.

Brought to you by the creative team at Written-World.com:
Kristine Pratt, Dale Hansen, Normandie Ward Fischer, Robin Patchen, J. Christine Richards, & Melissa Alicia

Cover Design: Lynda K. Arndt

Library of Congress Control Number: 2013939888
International Standard Book Number: 978-1-938679-06-3

Printed in the United States of America

Author's Note

The Shroud of Turin is very real, as is much of the history and science portrayed in "the linen god". For more information, please visit **www.jimoshea-author.com** where I have links to several excellent sites that delve into more detail on the most studied religious relic in human history.

"Why seek ye the living among the dead?"

Luke 24:5

Chapter 1

The gaping wound in her side made every movement, every breath, more painful than the last. Crimson stained her bare feet, and the remnants of her screams echoed, but no lights beckoned from the shuttered buildings she passed. Not a single soul responded to her pleas for help. Rain beat a tattoo on rooftops and into puddles, drowning out all other sounds, so that only she and the feral-scented pursuer seemed to exist this night. Someplace behind her, his heavy boots slapped the cobblestones.

From a dark street, she slipped into an even darker alleyway and behind trash bins. The rain intensified, pounding the metal cans and pouring from the downspout by her feet. A red neon sign overhead made the discharge look like a river of blood.

She crouched down, wiped her face with her sleeve, and tried to still a shiver, but it wasn't the bitter night that iced her bones. It was as if the cold were a living thing, seeping in through her thick, black tunic. "The Lord is my rock and salvation," she whispered, her shallow breaths hanging in the rancid air. "In whom should I fear?"

Her whole body jerked at the sound of clinking glass and slurred voices rising above the rain's steady drum. The silhouette of two young men swayed down the alleyway, no more than fifty meters away. Hoping to get their attention and beg for help, she slid out from behind the metal bins, stopped by something both sinister and familiar that passed through the darkness between them. She recoiled and then turned and ran, the wet fabric of her tunic clinging to her burning thighs.

Out of the night, church bells tolled, and the rain stopped. She spun toward the familiar sound. Storm clouds had scattered to reveal an open piazza at the end of the dark and narrow street. She gathered her tunic above swollen ankles and hurried toward it, pausing at the entrance to the open space. Across the piazza, a dim light filtered out through stained glass windows. *Grazie, Dio! Thank you, God!*

As she cowered in the darkness of the street, trying to control her ragged breathing, she looked left and right. She could sense him out there, lurking, somewhere. The bell tower's shadow reached across the moonlit space, beckoning. She clenched her teeth, swallowed hard, and forced her body to move. "The Lord is my light and my salvation," she said, as she ran toward the shadow and church steps. "In whom shall I fear?"

At the top of the stairs, she looked back and saw no movement, heard no sound. Her arthritic hands fumbled with the door's iron latch. As it gave way, thunder rumbled. Startled, she peered over her shoulder to see plumes of warm breath that wafted from a still black form lurking in the shadows. *O Dio, O God.* She quickly leaned into the heavy wood door. The rusty hinges gave way, and she stepped through, slid the bolt in place behind her, and slumped against the door, her breath coming in halting gasps.

The air inside, redolent of oils and incense, felt thick and damp. In the distance, a small rack of votive candles interrupted the shadows, giving the space an unearthly glow. Her wrinkled hands guided her along the wall toward the flickering light as her eyes struggled to adjust. Instead of the flat surface she expected, her fingers traveled over an odd jumble of smooth contours and rough edges.

The walls came into slow focus, and her heart skipped a beat. A desperate scream lodged in her throat, choking her. She tried desperately to sort shadows from reality as her gaze darted back and forth. It couldn't... Those couldn't be human remains. Skulls . . . bones . . . thousands of them lining the walls.

She spun away, knelt, and folded her hands in prayer. "Yea," she began. Her throat was dry, but the words were soothing. She swallowed and tried again, her voice now barely above a whisper. "Yea, though I walk through the valley of the shadow of death, I will fear no evil."

Where was she? What horror had she come upon? She could almost hear the wails of the souls trapped deep inside. She turned back toward the horrific vision, because she remembered it now. Santa Maria della Concezione, the storehouse for the bones of Capuchin friars dating back to the fifteenth century.

"*Dio Mio.*" My God.

She lowered her head and hurried toward the candlelight, her calloused fingers traveling along the worn rosary beads. The candle's light revealed the base of a circular staircase. She climbed into the nave and, thanks to a flash of lightning, avoided knocking over a holy water font hidden in the darkness. Her fingers dipped instinctively. Closing her eyes, she made the sign of the cross, invoking the *Father, Son, and Holy Spirit*, before stumbling into a pew to catch her breath.

In the stark silence of the church, a tiny noise coaxed her out of her trance. She fell to her knees between the pews, ignoring the rush of pain from the hard marble floor. Faint footsteps advanced. A man hummed, random notes that soon merged into a familiar melody, one whose lyrics she had known since her childhood.

"Amazing Grace," he sang softly. "How sweet the sound." Both footsteps and words grew louder. "That saved a wretch like me." Then silence but for the steady throb of her heartbeat in her ears.

She peered over the top of the pew and spotted a confessional across the aisle. She crept forward, struggling to silence the creak in her bones and the sound of wet fabric swishing along the marble floor. The aisle was empty. She eased forward into the penitent's side of the confessional booth, pulling the door behind her and sliding the privacy latch quietly in place.

As she stood, waiting for her heart to find its normal rhythm, a whisper sounded, as if someone exhaled, and muted words drifted in from the far side of the wall that separated penitent from priest. "Would you like to make your confession, Ana?"

She stumbled and fell, hitting her head against the back wall. The privacy door slid open from the priest's side of the booth as she lay crumpled in the corner.

Her mouth tried to form words but all she could manage was chattering teeth.

"Your sins, Sister Anastasia," came the familiar voice again. "Would you like to confess them?"

She pulled herself up, struggling against the shooting pain in her side, and knelt on the padded kneeler. She stared into the blackness behind the privacy screen, unable to control her tremors. "My . . . my sins?"

"Come now," the oily voice replied. "Who would know them better than I?"

"I have sinned against God and against man." She felt a single tear track a course down her cheek. "I have nothing to confess to you."

The voice hesitated and spoke slowly. "Perhaps then you can forgive me for what I have done?"

"No," she said without hesitation. She sucked in a deep breath, released it, and said, "Nor can I forgive you for what you are about to do."

Without warning, the metal privacy screen between the two booths exploded outward. She tried to shout, struggling to unleash a scream that would wake the dead around her. But a powerful hand muffled her cry as it squeezed the life from her frail body. His eyes flared into a fiery red.

"I choose not to forgive you, woman. Salvation shall elude you this day."

Her world slowly faded from gray to black as he whispered, "You shall pay for your transgressions."

Chapter 2

With each step, the line narrowed, the crowd pressed in, and the velvet rope edged closer. Elbows jabbed his back, his sides, his front. He gagged at the sour medley of cologne and sweat. Voices blurred until the background noise sounded like the scratch of a needle at the end of a record.

Why had he picked a Saturday to see the exhibit? As he pressed his fingers to his temples, Immanuel Lusum whispered a prayer under his breath and felt Grace slide her hand up his spine. At her touch, the muscles in his back eased slightly.

"Breathe," she said. "Just breathe."

He closed his eyes, focused on the movement of her fingers, and sucked in a deep breath even as he counted the beats. In, one. Out, two. In, three. Out, four.

"Where are you?" Grace asked.

"Five."

"Good. Nice and slow." Her soft voice helped him center. Her fingertips felt silky as they reached up to his neck. "How about now?"

"Seven."

Grace counted with him, "Eight . . . nine . . . ten," and waited a few more beats before wrapping her arm around his waist and squeezing. "Feel better?"

Manny inhaled and exhaled once more for good measure and then opened his eyes to the bright lights of the museum lobby. As soon as Grace removed her arm, he started bouncing on the balls of his feet. Another deep breath, another touch from Grace, and he was able to still his body. Her breath blew on his cheek, and gooseflesh flared. She didn't move away. His heart sped as she brushed her fingertips across his jaw. He should have shaved. "Did you find your happy place?" she asked.

"I'll be happy when we get out of this lobby."

"The line's moving now." She slowed, allowing distance between them and the man ahead. "We'll be in the exhibit in less than five minutes. Read your book. It'll take your mind off the crowd."

Oh, right. His book.

"*Another* Shroud exposé?" she asked.

Manny pulled a large, leather-bound volume out of the crook of his elbow and stared at it as if for the first time. It looked much older than the elderly man selling tickets. It looked older than New York City for that matter.

"A Bible?" Grace said. "What's up with that?"

Manny hushed her. "Not now."

Grace arched an eyebrow.

As they approached the ticket booth, he reached for his wallet. "Let me get this."

Grace leaned over to peer at his wallet, at her picture under plastic. He'd taken it in Battery Park over a year ago.

She turned away as if she'd been caught trespassing and shook her head. "Forget it," she said. "This isn't a date."

"Seriously, I talked you into coming, so the least I can do is pay

13

your way." The *very* least. "You can buy me an expensive coffee. How's that?" He leaned toward the clerk. "Two general admission tickets, please. And passes to the Vatican Art Exposition."

Thanking the clerk, he steered Grace up the wide center staircase to the second level. Moving, focusing, he could deal with the close spaces and the masses of humanity. But it wasn't until the crowd thinned at the top of the stairs that his heart began to find its normal rhythm. They followed an elderly couple down a wide corridor lined with abstract artwork.

"Wow." Grace's mouth gaped as she pulled off her coat to reveal the NYU sweatshirt he'd given her for her birthday three years ago. Her blue eyes swept a wall of paintings by Pollack, Picasso, and Dali. "These weren't here the last time I brought my class. They're so beautiful." She pointed to a painting entitled *Woman in an Armchair*. "I should stick to painting houses."

"Give me a break, Gracie. Your work is awesome. Besides, your students are crazy about you."

"Yeah, she who can't, teaches. Still, I'm way better than this guy." She nodded at the Picasso. "At least I can stay inside the lines."

"You kill me sometimes," he said, suppressing a smile. "Come on."

"Not yet." Grace pulled him down a hallway that led to the telephones and restrooms. "Now tell. What's with the Bible?"

"It was my dad's," he said in a low voice as he bent next to her ear. "He kept it, even in its damaged state. Anyway, I hollowed it out."

"Manny!"

"Shush." He scanned the area.

She grabbed his arm and pulled him close. Speaking to his neck, she said, "What do you have in there?"

"Camera."

"Are you crazy? Why would you risk getting us tossed out of here? This exhibition comes to New York once every million years, and you risk it for a picture of an old rag, when you can buy one anywhere? And what was wrong with your phone's camera—even though that's not allowed either."

"For some reason," he said, trying to ignore the subtle scent of lilac wafting up at him, "the Vatican doesn't allow the public to photograph the Shroud. Ever. I want to know why."

Squinting up at him, she said, "Couldn't your dad get you access? With all the money he gives the Church, he must have connections."

He sighed. He respected the man who'd raised him, perhaps even loved him. "I didn't want any special treatment."

"Okay, fine, so you risk this. Tell me why you need a photograph of your very own?"

He leaned against the wall so that he could watch in both directions. This probably wasn't the best time for a lecture, but if he wanted her help, she'd need to understand. "An amateur photographer named Secondo Pia took the first photo of the Shroud of Turin in 1898. He—"

A young boy scampered into the alcove, turning only at a sharp command from his father. Manny waited until they were alone again and turned his gaze to Grace's familiar blue eyes. They sparkled, even under this recessed lighting.

What had he been talking about? Oh, right.

"As the story goes," he continued, "Pia was stunned when he saw the exposed plate in his darkroom. The negative gave the appearance of a positive image, like this one." He pointed to the Shroud picture on a poster. "Although the Shroud had been around for hundreds of years, no one had seen this image prior to 1898. The positive image implies that the Shroud itself is effectively a negative of some kind."

"How did the image get on the cloth?"

"That's the hundred-thousand-dollar question. There are lots of theories, but I'm pursuing one I believe holds some serious water."

"Which is?"

"Later." Manny stole another glance toward the hallway and back at Grace. "Suffice it to say, I'm convinced the Shroud is not a forgery."

"Again, why the camera? I know you have a whole box of photos."

"For one," and he said this with a grin, "original photography would give me a bit of an edge with the committee."

Grace sighed. "I still cannot believe you're doing your doctoral thesis to prove that old piece of cloth is anything more than an old piece of cloth."

Her words made him bristle. "If I had a million dollars, a particle accelerator, and a piece of the actual linen, I'm sure I could prove the Shroud of Turin was the very cloth they buried Christ in two thousand years ago."

Grace flashed a quirky grin. "Yeah, and if my aunt grew a beard, she could be my uncle."

Manny couldn't help but smile back. "Any time somebody doesn't want you to do something, for no good reason, it's usually a good idea to find out why."

"You're a rebel."

"No, Giordano Bruno was a rebel. I'm just a curious worker bee, wondering what Rome is up to."

She raised her brows, but he stopped himself from diving into the history of the seventeenth century scientist and Dominican friar. "Later."

He led her back into the gallery area and gestured toward a

corridor on the right and an arched entryway, taking her hand as they passed the placard announcing *The Shroud of Turin*.

Again, there were too many people in too small a space. "There's no way I'm going to be able to sneak a photo without someone noticing."

"Not to mention the enormous security guard." Grace gestured over his shoulder.

He turned to see the big man in blue wearing a shiny security badge. "Let's take a closer look." Concentrating ahead and not on the crowd, he edged into the room and squeezed past the curious to within ten feet of the famed artifact. The Shroud was mounted horizontally in a glass case on the wall and separated from the crowd by another velvet rope, this one thick and gold, supported by shiny gold stanchions.

The Shroud of Turin. Manny felt an instant communion with the infamous relic. Whether the feeling was real or self-induced from years of research, an itch that bordered on déjà vu caused him to tremble. He focused on the display pedestal and the words in front of him.

The Shroud of Turin, the most controversial and studied religious artifact in history, is believed by some to be the actual burial shroud of the Christian deity, Jesus of Nazareth. Although carbon dating places the origin of the linen cloth in the sixteenth century, many Christians believe the Shroud is much older, dating back to the first century.

Manny bristled. "Believed by some," he muttered under his breath. "Sixteenth century. No mention of all the issues associated with the flawed carbon dating tests. So typical."

"I guess the Met wrote their own display cards, eh?"

"Probably the Vatican. They've never actually vouched for its legitimacy. Maybe that'll be different in a few years." If he had anything to say about it, it would.

"I have no doubt, my obsessed and brilliant friend," Grace said. "Now, what's your plan?"

"I'm thinking."

"Take your time. Except for the long hippie hair, you blend in well with your outfit."

"How many times do I need to tell you, it's not an *outfit?*" He adjusted the white Roman collar around his neck and smoothed wrinkles out of his starched black shirt.

"I know. But I don't think I'll ever get used to your priest uniform."

"It's called a cassock, and I'm a seminarian, not a priest."

"Oh, right, your priest *trainee* uniform."

Even when she made fun of him, Grace was still a delight. He shook his head. That familiar rush washed over him. He pushed it away. Soon-to-be priests weren't supposed to have those kinds of thoughts.

Stop it, Manny. Focus.

"Well," Grace said, pulling him toward a corner, out of the way of other ears. "No matter what you're wearing, it's not going to help you with the gazillion people in the room and Goliath over there."

"I've got an idea."

She squinted up at him. "I don't like the way you said that, Lusum."

"I need you to do me a solid, Gracie."

"Solid?" She folded her arms across her chest. "How solid?"

"There's only one way I'm going to get this shot. If we can divert the crowd for a second."

"We?"

"Okay, you."

"Sure, no problem," she said. "Would you like me to run

naked through the world-famous Vatican Art Exposition or just set myself on fire?"

"Well..."

She straightened, not relaxing even when Manny wrapped his arm around her. "All right, I know the stink eye when I see it. No fire, no flesh. Trust me. It'll be simple and easy."

One of her brows hiked.

He leaned closer. "Look, all you have to do is move back by the entrance and fall down. Just lie there and pretend you fainted. Everybody will turn to look, and I'm sure the guard will come to your rescue. It'll only take me a couple of seconds to whip out the camera and get a couple of shots. You can just say you were overheated. Simple as that. We might even get some free drinks out of the deal."

"Simple as that?"

"I'll owe you huge, Gracie. Name your price. How about I throw you a pizza party at a bowling alley?"

"It's about time." Grace flashed a smile that made him suck in another deep breath. "Okay, *Mr. Bond*, here's my price," she said. "I do this for you, and you owe me a favor, a big one. I get to use that favor whenever I want. Deal?"

Manny nodded. He would go to the ends of the earth for her anyway, deal or no deal.

"Say it."

"Deal." He bit back a smile. "Ready?"

"I was born ready."

He watched the sway of her hips as she threaded her way toward the entrance. She fit her hair into a ponytail as she walked, looking over her shoulder as she got in position. His King James was in his hand, ready to go. He made a show of looking at his wristwatch before glancing at the guard. And then he nodded toward her.

Grace immediately let out a gasp and fell to the floor. An elderly woman screamed. The entire crowd parted like the Red Sea, providing Manny with a front-row view of the show. Rather than following his simple script, she writhed around for a few seconds, let out a loud groan, and wilted into a mound.

Manny fought the urge to laugh. After the burly guard did a quick assessment, he grabbed a walkie-talkie from his belt and lumbered towards the commotion. Manny removed the camera, raised it to his eye, and snapped several photos before rushing to see how he could comfort the poor, helpless woman.

Chapter 3

A loud ringing pulled Cardinal Anthony Lombardi from the depths of a nightmare. He struggled to focus, swiping at the sweat on his forehead as his free hand dragged across the nightstand to the telephone. *"Pronto?"*

"Vi prego di scusarmi, Sua Eminenza," said the familiar voice of his aide. "Please forgive the unusual hour, but it is quite urgent."

Anthony sat up, yawned, and swung his legs out from underneath thick, woolen blankets. The tile felt cold on his bare feet. "I trust it is, Roberto. What possesses you to ring me at . . ." He glanced at the red glow of the clock radio on his nightstand. "Four a.m.?"

"It is the Carabinieri. They are here, in the Palace."

The Carabinieri? Why would the military police be within the walls of the Vatican at this hour? "Is it Michael?"

"No, Your Eminence. Two officers, accompanied by the Swiss Guard. They wish for you to go with them."

Fully alert, he asked, "Go with them? Why?"

"It seems there has been a murder."

Ω

Mud slurped under Anthony's shoes. Father Roberto Carlo followed, muttering as they approached a floodlit Carabinieri Senior Investigatore Phillipe Sansone. Sansone's hand rested on a holstered 9mm Glock, and his warm breaths plumed in the cold night air. In the dark expanse beyond the artificial lights, walkie-talkies squawked and flashlights hopped around like fireflies, as a dozen of his officers and several members of the Vatican Swiss Guard scurried about in the night.

And then Anthony saw them. "*Dio mio*," he whispered, turning his face away and toward the rain. His fingernails dug into his palms. He took a deep breath as the cold water trickled down his cheeks and dripped past his collar. "*O Signore*, help us, I pray."

Anthony knew the instant his aide saw the bodies. Roberto jerked once and darted toward the dark recesses of the stone walkway. Hiking up his own robe, Anthony lifted his feet out of the mud and followed the young priest, arriving just as the man dropped to his knees on the stones and expelled the contents of his stomach.

"Roberto." Anthony crouched and wrapped his arm around the other man.

"I am very sorry, Your Eminence," Father Carlo said, his voice barely a whisper. "I have never witnessed such a sight in my life. It is worse than what they did to our Savior."

Anthony tightened his hold momentarily and brushed back dripping hair from Roberto's forehead. As the light rain intensified, he glanced again toward the grisly scene—and again recoiled. It hadn't gone away. This wasn't another nightmare. The two naked men still hung on either side of a wooden cross, crucified upside down with their tongues cut out.

Signore, have mercy, have mercy.

"We must be strong," he said, speaking as much to himself as to the younger priest. "They are with our Heavenly Father now." Using his robe's sash, he wiped a tear from Carlo's cheek. "We must do our best to help find their killers."

He extended a hand as they rose and an arm to steady his assistant. "Come. We must speak to the investigator."

As they approached, Sansone dismissed a subordinate and gave them his attention. "I apologize for pulling you from your warm bed, Cardinal Lombardi." His sympathetic tone and expression softened the harsh lines of his ashen face. "A security guard found them a little over an hour ago. I am very sorry you had to see them like this."

Anthony tried to speak, but the words stuck in his dry throat. He coughed to clear the way and to give him a moment to collect himself. "As . . . as am I." He crossed himself. "I believe the devil himself was in this place tonight."

"You do not need to go looking for demons. There are plenty out there in human form. Since the time of the Caesars, this place has been used for their work—as it was also this very night."

Anthony looked around, at anything but the bodies of his friends. "We are in the Hypogeum, are we not?"

Sansone nodded. "This is where the contestants in the day's entertainment awaited their fate, both men and animals." He pointed toward a stone arch at the far end of the circular structure. "At the conclusion, the bodies of the unlucky ones were dragged through the Porta Libitinensis."

Anthony shuddered as Father Carlo sucked in a sharp breath. Unlucky ones indeed.

"You know it was named after the goddess of funerals," Sansone said. "It has always been called the *Gate of Death*."

Anthony braced himself before stealing another quick glance

over his shoulder, checking the shadows that surrounded them. The rain stopped. The clouds seemed to stand still, as if nature itself paused to observe the extraordinary sight. "Can you bring them down?"

"I am very sorry, Your Eminence, but the crime scene must not be altered in any way until we complete our initial investigation."

As a young officer scraped dirt into a plastic bag, Sansone ran his fingers through his hair. "Both victims carried Vatican security passes. At least one was a priest. We found a note inside his black cassock with your name and a phone number. He has been identified as—"

"Father Genovese Ceste." Anthony pressed clenched fists into his thighs as he spoke the name. "He is . . . he *was* a very respected member of our Congregation for the Doctrine of the Faith." He could barely say the next words. "He was also a very dear friend."

"My condolences."

"The other is Doctor Francis Adakem, Professor Emeritus in the Vatican's Pontifical Academy of Science."

"The Academy?" Sansone's brows arched. "What is the nature of your relationship with Dr. Adakem?"

"He was . . ." Anthony tried to draw spit into his dry mouth so his tongue would work. "He was one of Pope Peter's five senior advisors, his only lay advisor. I am one of the remaining four."

Sansone opened his lips as if to speak. Instead, he gestured for them to follow him away from the team of forensics personnel. Anthony pointed Carlo toward a large rock where he could rest and wait before he followed the Inspector.

As they entered a narrow walkway in the stone maze, the dark seemed overwhelming. Anthony had so many questions. *God, where are You? Why has this happened?* But the heavens remained silent as they had for too many years. He swiped at tears before they fell.

Sansone stepped into a tiny, dim space that centuries ago had housed a hungry lion or a frightened Christian. The Inspector lit a cigarette with shaking hands and set the glowing butane flame on a stone outcropping for additional light. Looking up and pulling a long draw, he exhaled slowly. "I have seen much death over the years, Cardinal Lombardi, enough to haunt me the rest of my life. However, in over thirty years of police work, never have I seen anything like this." He hesitated for a few moments before continuing, his voice softening. "I must ask you some difficult questions."

"You have a duty." Anthony shivered from the cold damp and from the smell of blood, the odor of death. "Is my brother aware of this situation?"

"He has been alerted." Sansone paused. "Do you have any idea why Father Ceste would have your name and phone number on his person?"

Anthony hesitated. It was a good question, one he'd like answered. "Father Ceste and I go back many years. However, I do not know why he would have my contact information in his pocket unless he planned to give it to someone."

Sansone waited.

"He would have no reason to give it to Francis," Anthony said. "I saw Dr. Adakem on a regular basis."

Sansone pulled a pad from his breast pocket and scratched notes using a pen that had been lodged above his ear. "When did you last speak to Ceste?"

"Not for many months, perhaps a year."

The Carabinieri officer continued probing, his questions methodical yet thorough. Finally, he replaced the cap on his pen, removed his glasses, and cleaned them with his shirtsleeve. "Very well." He flicked away ashes, put the cigarette between his lips, and extinguished the blue flame of the lighter.

The detective's eyes were now hidden behind blue smoke when not lit by glowing tobacco embers. Anthony studied him. Finally, he said, "Am I a suspect, Investigatore?"

Sansone's eyes widened, and he coughed. "Absolutely not, Cardinal Lombardi. You are merely a person of interest in this case, nothing more. Standard procedure. I only ask that you please make yourself available for further questioning should the need arise."

"Of course."

Sansone flicked the cigarette butt onto the muddy stone and stepped on it. "Do you have any idea who would be capable of such an act? Why anyone would perpetrate a crime such as this?"

Anthony folded his hands in front of his chest as if in prayer. "I do not. However, I am certain the Vatican Gendarme will get to the bottom of the matter, considering that both Genovese and Francis were citizens of the Vatican."

Sansone stiffened. "We have every reason to believe the crime was committed at this location, Cardinal Lombardi. We believe both victims were abducted outside of Vatican City and were alive when they were brought here. There is evidence of a struggle across the floor of the Hypogeum, and the only blood we have found is in the ground below their bodies. This, I believe, is sufficient evidence to assume the crime was committed on Italian soil. The Carabinieri, therefore, would have jurisdiction."

Anthony nodded. "I see. I would like to help you in any way I can, Investigatore."

Sansone extended his hand. "Thank you, Your Eminence. We will, of course, work closely with your authorities. We are hopeful the Vatican's video surveillance will shed some light on what transpired as they left the Holy City. I am confident we will find the guilty parties very soon."

"I trust you will," Anthony said. "This crime cannot go unpunished. An eye for an eye, as Scripture says."

"Yes, indeed," Sansone replied, his lips curled. "And a tooth for a tooth."

Chapter 4

Grace squirmed in the hard wooden pew. She loved everything about *Becka's Beans,* all but this remnant from its former life as Brooklyn's oldest Catholic church. Here, she could partake in scrumptious scones and green tea instead of consecrated bread and wine, and Grace much preferred the smell of freshly ground coffee to that of incense.

She turned at the familiar sound of high heels clacking on the worn hardwood to see her friend Becka Long dodge a tray-toting waiter. Holding a bagel and mug of steaming coffee, Becka slid in across the table, pulled back long dreadlocks, and gestured toward a young man ready to take Grace's order.

Grace looked up. "Rum and coke, please." She flashed a feeble grin before adding, "Hold the rum." And to Becka, "Hey, lady."

Outside, lightning flashed and thunder rattled the leaded glass windows. "My mom used to say thunder was just angels bowling in heaven."

Becka tapped a single green-painted fingernail on the mahogany table. Another flash and crack, and she said, "She still MIA?"

Grace sighed. Her mother still hadn't returned her call from the night before. Kellen often went off on sudden trips to points unknown, but this silence felt different.

"You're worried."

"She's fine." Grace turned her eyes toward rain-soaked windows and shivered.

When Becka reached across the table, Grace slipped her fingers into her friend's warm palm.

"Her job's demanding," Becka said. "You know that."

"I know. She just hasn't been answering her phone, and I wish she'd call."

"She will."

The waiter set a can of Coke and glass of ice in front of Grace. She thanked him. Pouring half the can into the glass, she watched as the cola fizzed into a brown cloud before it slowly melted away. "We did the Met thing this morning."

"Well, that explains the denim-colored spandex." Becka's smile widened.

Grace folded her arms across her chest, frowned, and looked down at her jeans. "They're not *that* tight."

"Whatever." Becka picked a plump raisin from her bagel and popped it in her mouth. "How did Manny handle the crowd?"

"He worked through it," Grace said. She leaned forward, tucking stray hair out of her way as she recounted the day's adventure. "After we got his precious photos, we spent the next three hours seeing the most *amazing* art. It was awesome."

"Speaking of Manny, where is he? I thought he'd be here with you."

"He had some film to develop first."

"*Develop* film?" Becka's eyes grew large and round.

Grace grinned. "He says he needs photo negatives to compare with the originals. For his thesis."

"That boy ain't right." Becka drained her cup and nodded at the waiter, who whisked it off the table. "So you had fun at the exhibit?"

"Does the Pope wear a funny hat? It was incredible, but, you know, Manny sure took his Shroud compulsion to another level today."

"So he's passionate."

"Trust me. He gives OCD a bad name."

"You're as bad as he is, girlfriend. You're obsessed with your art. Not to mention your teaching."

"Teaching is what I do, Becks. Artist is what I am, or at least what I wish I were. You should've come with us."

Becka quirked a brow. "I'd rather leave you two lovebirds alone."

Where had that come from? Grace smoothed her palms along the table top, brushing at non-existent crumbs. "Manny's a great guy. Committed to his calling. We're just friends, and we both intend to keep it that way."

"Sure."

Grace couldn't let herself think about Manny that way. Instead, she stared at the street.

"I know you, Grace. And I know how you really feel about him, even if you're not willing to admit it."

"That's insane."

"Just don't come crying to me when some pretty NYU co-ed convinces Manny the priesthood's not for him. Especially when one of them finds out his dad is the CEO of some humongous corporation. There's some rich blood in those veins."

"There's not," Grace said.

"Well, some day he—"

"I thought I told you. Manny was adopted."

"I think I would have remembered that."

"His adoptive parents have been divorced for a few years now," Grace said. "But his dad still lives in the apartment where Manny grew up. He hasn't seen his mom for quite a while."

"Seriously?"

"It's a sensitive subject." Grace sighed. "So I don't bring it up much. I can tell he really misses her."

"Well, he's solid. They obviously did a great job while they were together."

"Manny says they got a little help from the parish he grew up in. Like free therapy sessions when he was a kid."

A nest of hair fell to one side when Becka cocked her head. "Why?"

"To help him adjust as an adopted child. He doesn't remember much of it."

"Whatever," Becka said. "The guy grows up in a penthouse overlooking Central Park, yet still chooses to live in a tiny apartment in the Bronx. Then attends seminary instead of joining his dad's company and becoming wealthy."

"I suppose there's more than one way to be rich."

"Touché. He's one-in-a-million, Gracie. I understand why you feel the way you do."

Grace winced. "I don't feel—"

"Ah, ah, ah." Becka wagged her index finger. "Don't you know it's bad manners to lie to your best friend? Beneath that black robe and white collar, he's a man, Gracie, a handsome man with far more character than most of the losers in this city."

Flushing, Grace traced her finger around the edge of her glass. It was true. Everything about Manny made her world better, warmer, safer. His breath against her face, his arm, strong and sure, when he offered it to her. "It's not that simple." She leaned closer. "Manny's my friend, period. Besides, he's in *seminary*."

Becka flashed her white teeth. "So? He hasn't made any vows. You owe it to the both of you to see if this is right or not."

Taking a long sip of her Coke, Grace lamented the absence of rum. "I'm having a tough time with the whole vocation thing. It feels so awkward to think of him romantically, especially when he wears *the collar*, like he did today in the museum."

"Forbidden fruit? Or maybe just a convenient excuse to avoid the risk of opening up your heart?"

Grace didn't answer, but fortunately the soft ringing of old church bells dangling from the front door drew her friend's attention. "Well, well, well," Becka said, waving toward the entrance. "Speak of the devil."

Manny held out a manila envelope as he bent to kiss Becka's cheek before sliding into the pew next to Grace. No kiss.

"Ladies." He pulled out two large sheets of paper, set them face down on the table, and paused. With a flourish, he flipped them over and revealed photonegative images of the Shroud of Turin. "Tight focus, no glare, absolutely perfect."

"Congratulations," Becka said. "Now what?"

"We compare them to Pia's original photonegative."

"We?" Becka asked.

Grace didn't get it. "If you and that Pia guy each took a photo of the same thing, wouldn't the negatives be identical?"

"They should be," Manny said. He flashed the same grin that had Grace prone on the floor of the Metropolitan Museum of Art just hours ago. She knew instantly how she would spend the afternoon.

"I've got two magnifying glasses, a six-pack of beer, and the rest of the day," he said. "Would you beautiful ladies care to join me?"

Becka ran her fingers around the edges of the photo paper. "What got you so spun up about all this Shroud nonsense?"

"Please. Nonsense? You can't say that yet."

"Sure I can." Becka winked at Grace.

"Give it a chance," he said. "I've been really into the Shroud since I was a kid."

Becka grinned. "Instead of t-ball?"

He ignored her. "My dad first told me about it. Then a priest at St. Williams really got me curious during a fourth grade science class." He glanced from Grace to Becka. "Keep in mind it was a Catholic school, so the Shroud study was considered legitimate science. Father Baggio noticed I knew a lot about the subject, so later on he gave me some books to read."

Grace winked at Becka. "Is he still corrupting little kids at that school of yours?"

"A year after I left St. Williams," he said with a smirk, "the Brooklyn archdiocese transferred him to my prep school to be headmaster. Back then, St. Terrance was the only Catholic prep school in the New York area."

A waiter appeared. Manny ordered water and turned back to them. "There was always an air about Father Baggio, almost mystical, like he was in constant contact with God. You know, privy to His thoughts."

"Sounds creepy," Becka said.

He shrugged. "He got promoted to archbishop not long after I graduated. Now he's in charge of the entire Brooklyn archdiocese. We kept in touch over the years, but I think it's just because my dad's such a big contributor to the Church."

Grace picked up one of Manny's photos and studied it. "Okay. I'm in."

"Sorry, guys. I've got to stick around here for the afternoon rush," Becka said. "Besides, I've got my parents coming to stay for a week, and the apartment's in chaos."

"That'll be fun," Grace said. "Well, you've still got me."

"You don't have to do this, Gracie," he said. "I just thought . . ."

She set the photo back down on the table. "Relax. Spring break means I have time. Besides, I'd like to help."

He gathered his hair that had come loose and stuffed it back into a rubber band. "As Sir Arthur Conan Doyle so aptly put it, 'When you have eliminated the impossible, whatever remains, however improbable, must be the truth.' You can help me find it."

Grace suppressed a smile. He was so cute, *especially* when he wore normal street clothes like these.

"I still don't get what difference it makes if the Shroud is real or not," Becka said. "The world's full of religious artifacts. What's one more to add to the collection?"

Grace shook her head. "Don't go there."

"I believe it's much more than that. Think about it." Manny leaned forward and lowered his voice. "What if I could actually prove it's real?"

"Well, that and three bucks would get you a great cup of java at the best coffee house in New York," Becka said, winking at Grace.

"We know it's a big deal to you, Manny." Grace wiped the water that had pooled under her glass. "But how can a thirty-year-old physics major at NYU prove something nobody else in the world has been able to?"

Manny's lips thinned. "Doctoral candidate."

"Manny, honey," Grace said. "I've seen you struggle with the lids on childproof containers, and you're going to single-handedly prove conventional scientific wisdom wrong?"

"It can be done."

"As my grandma once told me, 'Knowledge is knowing a tomato is a fruit. Wisdom is not putting it in a fruit salad.'"

"Deep, real deep, Barden." Manny turned to Becka. "If you

haven't noticed, our friend here is a big fan of clichés."

Grace poked him. "We artistic types have our moments."

"And we science-types have our theories. Mark my words, ladies, this could change your life. It could change everyone's." Manny grinned. "Trust me. I'll be famous for this someday."

"Boyfriend." Becka pointed a fingernail at him. "All you've got is a cloth with a lot of blood on it in the shape of a man's body. Plus, you don't even have access to it."

Manny shook his head. "There *is* some blood on the linen, Becks, but that's not the source of the image, despite what most people think. In fact, there's no evidence of any pigment of any kind on the linen. It's been tested. The coloration on the Shroud comes from a substance thinner than a bacteria cell."

"Substance?"

"Officially, it's a dried carbohydrate mixture of starch fractions and various saccharides."

"Of course it is." Becka arched her eyebrows. "Back to my original question. Why . . . does . . . it . . . matter?"

"If I can prove the image came from the first century and was formed the way I believe it was, the truth will rock the world unlike anything since Christ Himself was here. You can say you knew me when."

"Not to mention, you'll be famous for changing the social fabric of the entire planet."

"Yeah," Manny chuckled. "That too."

Chapter 5

Two members of the Vatican Swiss Guard flanked Cardinal Anthony Lombardi as he entered the foyer of the Apostolic Palace, but he barely noticed their presence. He shook rain from his overcoat and peered into the private residence of the current Bishop of Rome, Pope Peter II.

Something seemed out of place. Not the ornate furniture, priceless artwork, or colorful tapestries lining the walls, but something. He nodded to Cardinal-Carmerlengo Tarcisio Marini, the Pope's personal assistant and long-time confidant. The thin man with salt-and-pepper hair and deep-set eyes sat expressionless in his motorized wheelchair.

"Thank you for seeing me on such short notice, Tarcisio," Anthony said, surprised by the tremor in his own voice. He cleared his throat and tried again. "I am sorry to disturb you at such an early hour."

Marini began to speak, stopped, and nodded dismissal to the Swiss Guard. In his mid-fifties, Marini was young by Vatican standards, yet he looked much older. In fact, he'd aged in the week since Anthony had seen him last. His constant attention to the ailing pope must have produced the drawn face and inky shadows under his bloodshot eyes.

When the door closed, Marini turned to him. "I am confused," he said, his clear baritone betraying a Sicilian heritage. "Did you not receive the message I left you this morning?"

"Message?"

Marini released his grip on wheelchair's joystick and clasped his hands in his lap. After a slight pause, he said, "Why are you here, Anthony?"

"I have grave news that concerns Peter."

Marini's expression blended curiosity and concern but also a sense of purpose. "Very well," he said, as he maneuvered the wheelchair down the hall away from Lombardi. "You can share the news with everyone. Please join us in Peter's study."

"Everyone?" Anthony said. "What I have to share is highly sensitive, Tarcisio. I am concerned . . ."

Marini's sudden stop caused him to lurch forward in his chair. He spoke without looking back at Anthony. "Our colleagues are here. Peter's illness has taken a turn for the worse."

Anthony made the sign of the cross with sweaty fingers.

"It happened very quickly," Marini said. "His Holiness is being cared for in the medical quarters upstairs. He requested an audience with his advisors, so it is very fortunate you came when you did. When Francis arrives, you can share your news with the entire team."

Anthony blinked. Oh, God. *Francis. Genovese.* "Tarcisio," he said. His voice was barely above a whisper, but loud enough for Marini to lift his hand from the controls. "I just came from the Colosseum."

Marini turned slowly toward Anthony, his face expressionless.

"The Carabinieri found Francis there early this morning," Anthony said. "Murdered."

Marini's eyes widened and his mouth gaped open, stretching all the wrinkles from his face. But he didn't speak.

"Two hours ago. I was summoned to the murder scene by the Carabinieri. Because of my relationship with the other victim."

"Other victim?"

Anthony winced. That was wrong. His old friend Genovese was not just *another victim*. "Father Genovese Ceste. An associate from my days in America. The Carabinieri alerted me this morning because they found a piece of paper in his pocket with my contact information."

"I cannot believe what I am hearing, Anthony. What happened?"

He saw again the brutal murder scene and could barely speak. "Suffice it to say that our brothers died in a horrific manner."

Marini spun his chair a quarter turn and stared at the blank wall next to the entrance. His voice sounded harsh as it bounced against the stone. "Peter will ask about Francis. I am not sure what we can tell him in his frail condition."

"I will leave that decision up to you," Anthony said, inclining his head slightly in a deference he did not feel. "There were reporters at the scene when I left, and I did not want His Holiness to learn of the murders through the press."

The shadows in the hallway seemed to settle in around Marini as he spoke. "As improbable as it may sound, I sense His Holiness' agenda may supercede the news you bring."

"His death?"

"He is near, but I do not believe he fears dying. However, there is something of great urgency on his mind. Please follow me."

Crystal sconces cast a tawny light on the walls and ceiling as they neared the ornately paneled and gilded elevator. It took them to the top floor where velvet drapes held back the waking sun in the pope's private quarters. Dozens of medical and security personnel had been present for weeks, but a heavy silence now permeated the candlelit rooms. Anthony peered over Marini's head into the Papal Study. He had been in the room a hundred times, but dark shadows and an odor of decay seemed to rest on the familiar hush, as if the room itself had taken on a pall.

"Anthony." Cardinal Lucius Capello glided toward him. A slim, normally handsome man in his early seventies, Capello now appeared pasty and drawn, his eyes empty. Anthony raised a brow but said nothing as the other man embraced him. "It is good to see you," Capello said, "in spite of the circumstances."

"You as well, Lucius." Anthony looked from Capello to the large man next to him. "And you, Patrick."

"Aye." Cardinal Dougherty's somber tone held a hint of Irish brogue. His freckled face reflected concern. "It is good to see you too, Anthony."

"I am afraid Cardinal Lombardi brings us additional bad news," Marini said. He approached the group slowly and added, "Francis has gone to be with Our Lord."

Capello stepped back a pace.

Dougherty whispered, "Saints preserve us! What happened to him, Anthony?"

"He was murdered," Anthony said. He couldn't talk about it. He wouldn't. "I would prefer we not discuss the details at this time. May our brother rest in peace."

In the fading echo of three amens, Marini ushered the men to a U-shaped cluster of four leather chairs in front of a massive fireplace. Anthony realized how tired he was as he eased down into one. A fire blazed, but its leaping flames did little to dispel the mood. Lombardi leaned forward in his chair and held his hands up to the fire.

"Time is of the essence," Marini said, sliding a red leather notebook from a side table onto his lap. He rolled close to the group, his gaze directed at the empty chair. "I would like to thank you all again for coming on such short notice. His Holiness is anxious to speak to you. Our medical team indicates his time is short."

"Days?" Anthony asked.

"Perhaps hours."

Capello sighed. "Has the Bishop of Ostia been notified?"

"Of course," Marini said. "Bishop Gregorio has been aware of the situation for quite some time and has been making preparations to preside over conclave. Messages have been sent to all cardinals around the world, and most should be en route soon."

"En route?" Dougherty asked. "The electoral cardinals have fifteen days to prepare for the election after a Pope's death. Peter is still with us."

"His Holiness has requested this, Patrick," Marini said. "Peter summoned Gregorio here late last night to meet with him. I was not present in the room, but he told me Peter insisted *all* cardinals be gathered in Rome immediately."

"The entire College of Cardinals?" Dougherty asked.

Marini nodded "Even those too old to vote. When I asked him why, Gregorio had no answers. I am as confused as each of you, my friends."

"I am sure Peter will shed light on the situation," Dougherty said. He leaned forward in his chair toward Marini. "What do you believe is the purpose of our gathering this morning, Tarcisio?"

Marini folded his hands in his lap. "I believe His Holiness has something of great importance he wishes to pass on to the Church before his death. I assume he intends to do this via the five—"

Marini brought a fist up to his mouth and coughed. After taking a deep breath, he said, "I suppose he intends to communicate his last wishes to his Senior Advisors."

"What leads you to this belief?" Anthony asked.

"Peter has been troubled lately," Marini said. "He shared dreams he has experienced in recent weeks, visions similar to Pius VII. I have personally witnessed him reading the prophecies of Saint Malachy."

Dougherty's brows rose. "The Archbishop of Armagh?"

"You know of these writings?" Marini asked.

"*Ar ndóigh, Maolmhaodhog ua Morgair,*" Dougherty replied in his native Gaelic. "I am sorry," he said, clasping his hands in front of his face. "Malachy was canonized in 1190 as the first Irish Saint. He is not well known in the church these days, but I am very familiar with his writings."

"Perhaps you should enlighten us, Patrick," Anthony said.

The room became silent as Dougherty recounted the life of the obscure Irish cleric from the northern part of the Emerald Isle, a monk who eventually became a Bishop. Malachy had traveled to Rome in 1139, where he had a vision of every Pope who would preside from that point forward until the end of the Church, one hundred and twelve in all. He had written a series of Latin phrases describing each of those Popes, descriptions that had been extremely accurate for almost nine centuries.

Anthony considered the implications of this unfamiliar revelation. As well versed as he was in Papal history, he knew nothing of Malachy. He stared at Patrick. "Peter is the one hundred and twelfth?"

Dougherty nodded. "Malachy's writings refer to him as *Petrus Romanus.*"

Anthony dropped his head and whispered, "Peter of Rome."

"Remarkable," Capello commented.

Marini cleared his throat. "The prefect also said that Peter had withdrawn the original transcripts of the Fatima prophesies from the Vatican Archives just last week and has them in his private lockbox, refusing to return them. I am not sure what this means, but my instincts tell me it is not simply his interest in Church history."

"Mary's appearance to the children of Fatima is the most well-known miracle in the modern Church age," Anthony said. "But the last of Our Lady's three prophecies was fulfilled over thirty years ago. What possible interest could Peter have in these documents?"

"This, I do not know," Marini said. "I wanted you all to understand his state of mind before we visit with him." At the sound of a beep, Marini glanced down at a visual display mounted on his wheelchair. He looked up with wide eyes. "He is awake. Unless there are any further questions, we should proceed immediately."

"Peter has always had a flair for the dramatic," Anthony said. "Perhaps he simply wants to be remembered?"

"Perhaps," Marini replied carefully. "And perhaps not."

$$\Omega$$

The Pontiff's private medical suite, unlike the rest of the Papal Apartment, was plain. The carpet was a dull tan, the walls an even more dreary brown. State-of-the-art medical equipment stood alongside priceless medieval paintings, creating a bizarre blend of technology and art.

The four men surrounded the Pope's hospital bed, two on each side. Pope Peter II shifted back and forth under a white sheet that came up to his waist, his arms twitching, his pillow heavy with sweat. His granite-gray eyes were half closed, but steady, and his silver hair, which had not been trimmed in recent months, gave him an almost leonine appearance. A black leather folder with a fresh wax crest emblazoned across its metal clasp lay beside him on the bed. The crest bore the coat of arms of the Holy See surrounded by four words in a circle, *Archivum Secretum Apostolicum Vaticanum*, The Vatican Secret Archives.

Anthony watched the Pope as the pontiff's expression changed from a look of peace into what seemed to be a grimace. A Benedictine nun, the only member of the Pontifical medical staff still in the room, wiped the old man's forehead with a cool towel. Peter's eyes fluttered and his lips opened slowly. "Brothers." After the single word, he took a long, labored breath.

"Sister," Marini said. "Please leave us for now."

The old woman nodded and hurried toward the door, shutting it quietly behind her.

"We are here, Your Holiness." Marini leaned forward and took the Pope's wrinkled hand in his. "We are here to do your bidding for the sake of the Holy Mother Church."

Peter's dim eyes focused as he surveyed his surroundings. "Francis," he said, his words barely audible over the rain pounding at the window. "Where is Francis?"

Marini leaned forward. "He is unable to be here, Your Holiness. However, the rest of your council is present."

The Pope closed his eyes. When he opened them seconds later, they seemed sharper. "I have a message of the utmost importance to share with you, my brothers in Christ. Information that will have tremendous impact on the Church."

The elderly Pontiff coughed and held an open palm out in front of his face to keep his advisors at bay. After a few seconds, he continued, his voice regaining its fervor. "I had intended to share this revelation myself with the world via a public pronouncement, but my health will not permit it."

They waited. No one spoke.

After several more ragged coughs, the Pope said, "Therefore, I gather you all here today to be my witnesses. To ensure my decree is heard and felt across all Catholicism, across all of Christendom, throughout the world."

Anthony laid a hand on the thin fingers of his old friend, the former Father Lorenzo Agostini of Naples, now Pope Peter II. "Lorenzo, my friend," he whispered into the Pope's ear. "Your faithful and loyal servants are here, praying for you. What burden do you carry on your heart?"

The outline of a smile formed on the corners the Pontiff's mouth, and his hand turned in Anthony's.

"Anthony," he said. His grip was stronger than Anthony had expected. "We have guarded many secrets within these walls over the past two thousand years, including the words of Our Holy Mother Mary to Lucia of Fatima."

Anthony exchanged a quick glance with Marini across Peter's bed but remained silent, squeezing the Pope's hand gently.

"However," Peter continued, "secrecy is a luxury the Church can no longer afford. In an absence of truth, lies run rampant. I intend to shine light into a darkness that has plagued us, on a truth that must see the light of day. It is time, my brothers, time to pull back the veil."

A stark chill returned, making Anthony shudder. Tears spilled from the corners of the old man's eyes.

"I am near the end of my time in this earthly dwelling. Although the world will mourn my death, it will anticipate my replacement soon after. It will expect the Church's leadership to gather to elect a Pope as it has done for two thousand years. However . . ." Peter paused, pulled a rattling breath into his failing lungs. "There shall be no conclave."

Anthony leaned back. He and the others shared confused stares.

"Your Holiness," Marini said into the silence. "Last night, you asked Bishop Gregorio to assemble the cardinals. We assumed—"

"The time for mankind's corrupt rule over Christ's church on Earth has ended," Peter stated with surprising force. "As foretold by Saint Malachy . . . as revealed by Holy Mother Mary herself to the children of Fatima . . . my reign will be the last. As instructed in my final decree to Christ's church on Earth, I speak the following words *Ex Cathedra*. There shall be no conclave."

Pope Peter II lifted both arms and held trembling hands in the air, drawing a deep breath. "I shall be the final Pope."

Chapter 6

The rain had cleared, and bright morning sun seeped around the edges of the closed draperies in the Papal Study. Cardinal Anthony Lombardi held one aside to gaze at the pinks and purples that contrasted sharply with the dark shadows inside the room.

Near the fireplace, Cardinals Capello and Dougherty mumbled prayers, their bodies swaying, their hands clasped at the waist of their crimson robes. Anthony could make sense of nothing. First, the gruesome murders, and now this insanity. Surely the old man had not gone mad. He'd been a rock for as long as Anthony had known him. No, they must all have faith in the Holy Father. They must all *show* faith.

"Brothers, please." Marini's voice interrupted the silence. "The Church is depending on us. We must discuss this logically. We must decide what to do."

"I am not sure we have a decision to make, Tarcisio." Capello merely stared with one brow raised. "Peter invoked *Ex Cathedra*."

"He is right," Daugherty said. "Peter demanded the decree be presented to the world seventy-two hours after his death. There is no way to overrule the decree of Papal infallibility."

"Understood." Marini shifted his gaze from them to the Pontiff's closed door and then back. "What Peter has decreed does not make sense. We must slow down and discuss this rationally. Please, take a seat."

Anthony joined Capello and Daugherty as they returned to the chairs in front of the fireplace. In the hearth, a log cracked and hissed, and the flames grew. Marini wheeled to the front, leaning forward in his wheelchair. His fingers trembled slightly as they brushed across his forehead.

Gazing at the leather portfolio on the table before them, Anthony focused on the unbroken Papal seal. He asked what they must all be thinking. "What madness lies beneath that seal?"

Marini lowered his voice. "Other than what he said to the four of us, I do not know, Anthony. I was with him every day, yet I am stunned by his words. Obviously, it will address his claim to be the final Pope, but beyond that?" Marini paused. His shoulders lifted in a shrug. "Perhaps we should discuss what we *do* know."

"Agreed. If we are to believe Peter . . ." Dougherty's voice trailed off, and he shook his head. "I am sorry, brothers, but this is difficult for me to accept."

"It is for all of us, Patrick," Capello said. "You are among friends. Say what is in your heart."

Dougherty planted his elbows on the arm of the chair and clasped his hands in his lap. "According to His Holiness, the Church lied to the world."

Anthony bit his lip. For a moment, no one spoke.

Finally, Marini nodded. "For the record, Peter refused to accept pain medications since early yesterday morning. He told me he wanted his mind clear when he spoke to us."

"Therefore," Dougherty continued. "The third prophecy received in the miracle of Fatima was not, in fact, what was revealed to the public in 2000."

"That is also what I heard," Capello said. "The prophecy to Lucia was not what the Church claimed it to be, the 1981 assassination attempt on John Paul II."

Anthony sighed, agreeing. "That is clearly what Peter said."

"Are we to accept the fact the Church lied to its flock?" Dougherty asked.

"This is not a truth I wish to embrace, Patrick," Capello said. "However, I must admit I have carried a burden on my heart for many years when it came to Mary's revelations. I have always found it extremely disturbing that the Church elected to ignore her instructions to the children of Fatima, Our Lady's clear directive to reveal the third prophesy in 1960. The Church was in possession of the prophecy since 1941, and the entire world knew it. If they can ignore the Blessed Mother's wishes for almost forty years, is it so difficult to believe they also withheld the truth?"

Capello was right. Anthony felt fear mounting as he tried to comprehend the incomprehensible. "I believe Peter," he blurted out. "I have known him for many years, and his word is one we can trust. We are all familiar with the rumor about John XXIII."

"That he fainted when he read the third prophecy," Capello said.

Anthony nodded. "Apparently, it was more than just a rumor."

"This is insanity." Dougherty shot up, his eyes now round, horrified. "We represent the senior leadership of the largest church on Earth," he said. "Yet we, apparently, do not know the true content of the most famous prophecy of the modern Church era. If that is not bad enough, we do not even know the specific content of Peter's declaration. One that he insists must be revealed to the entire world within seventy-two hours of his death."

Seventy-two hours. Anthony bit his lip until he tasted blood. "The *third day*," he mumbled.

Marini nodded, as if he had been contemplating the concept for hours. "The Church was formed three days after the death of Jesus when He died and rose from the dead. It would be more than ironic if the Church were to fall on the third day after the death of its final Pope."

As Marini and Capello dropped their heads in unison, Dougherty fell back into his chair. After a few seconds, Capello looked up, his hands clasped, his knuckles white. "What do we do without a Pope?"

Marini picked up the leather portfolio, set it in his lap, and stared at it. When he looked at each of the others, his eyes were focused and intense. "I am afraid," he said. "This announcement could rip apart the entire fabric of the Church. A body without a head cannot survive."

"We must have . . . faith." Capello's voice cracked. He cleared his throat and tried again. "Faith that God is truly speaking through his servant on Earth. Peter knows he has stepped out on a thin limb."

"And there are those who will want to see it snap behind him," Marini said.

Anthony's frown tightened. "Or to cut it."

Marini sighed. When a knock sounded on the door of the study, he wheeled over to answer it and tilted his ear toward the opening.

"I wish Francis were with us now," Anthony said. "Perhaps he could have made some sense of Peter's words."

"Perhaps, it is why he is *not* here," Dougherty said.

Capello shook his head. "In any case, we shall know soon."

"Very soon, I am afraid," Marini said from the door as it shut quietly behind him. "Peter has gone to his heavenly reward."

Chapter 7

Comandante Generale Michael Lombardi rubbed at the heavy stubble on his chin and stared at Senior Investigatore Phillipe Sansone, who stood at attention on the opposite side of his desk.

Michael nodded. "Investigatore Sansone, please be seated." He leaned back in his well-worn black leather chair and took a cigarette from his coat pocket. He lit it and cradled it carefully between his fingers. "It has been a long morning, no?"

"*Si,* Comandante."

"I am anxious for your report on the Colosseum murders."

Sansone placed an inordinate importance on protocol, which, of course, now made him squirm. Michael tried not to smile. His eyes may have betrayed him.

"Should we not wait for Capitano Merida?" Sansone asked.

"Merida is detained. We will proceed in his absence."

Sansone's shoulders sagged. "As you wish, Comandante."

"I am not happy, Investigatore." Michael did not make eye contact. His bumbling subordinate did not deserve it. "The press is aware there has been a murder. It is *very* difficult to suppress this fact when a Crime Scene Investigation van is parked right outside one of the most popular tourist sites in the world."

"I am sorry, Comandante," Sansone said. "I should have—"

He raised his hand to stop the man's excuses. "Yes, you should have." Michael spun his chair to face the window behind his desk, but nothing outside could erase his certainty that things were beyond his control. "Details are not yet available from the Vatican, but I have heard troubling rumors concerning the health of His Holiness. Peter's death would bring the international press to Rome like flies to a cadaver. I would like to get to the bottom of these murder cases before that happens, before the details of this crime become public knowledge."

"I also, Comandante," Sansone replied. "However, the perpetrators were very careful. They left little physical evidence behind. Security cameras at the Colosseum had been disabled and footage from the past two days is missing. However, the Vatican Gendarme provided video surveillance of the two men leaving the Holy City."

Michael spun back around, dragged deeply on his cigarette, and waited.

Sansone stole a quick glance at his notes again. "They left via different exits Tuesday morning," he said. "Father Ceste left via the main employee gate at 1:55 a.m. Dr. Adakem left from the North security gate at 2:35 a.m. The security system at the Pontifical Academy of Science indicates that Adakem left that building precisely at 2:26 a.m. It is not far from there to the northern border of the city."

"And the murder site?" Michael asked.

"In addition to the bodies and the wooden cross, we also have many footprints plus small strands of hair and fabric that are being analyzed. So far, physical evidence has yielded very little."

That was not good. Michael tapped the ash off the end of his cigarette and glanced quickly at the stack of papers and photos on his desk. "Have you confirmed your suspicion that the murders took place within the Colosseum's walls?"

"We are now very confident that is the case, Comandante. There are no traces of blood in the grass leading up to the site of the murder, and the footsteps in the mud of the Hypogeum seem to indicate a struggle. We believe they were bound, gagged, and dragged alive to the location."

"The cross?"

"Consisted of two pieces, designed to be assembled quickly. It was hand-carved from what appears to be a unique type of cedar found only in parts of Lebanon. We also now believe the operation was carefully planned ahead of time. Preparations had been put in place, which implies the perpetrators must have had access to the site prior to the murder."

Michael leaned forward. "Explain."

"When we removed the cross for analysis, we discovered a hollow metal sleeve planted in the floor of the Hypogeum. Our theory is the components of the cross were carried in last night after tourist hours or perhaps hidden somewhere within the Colosseum. They were then assembled and slid into the sleeve just prior to the murder. We also discovered a small patch of grass the exact size of the metal sleeve hidden within one of the Hyogeum's smaller stone rooms. We believe it was used to cover the opening so it would not be noticed by Colosseum security."

The cigarette had grown tasteless. Michael ground it out in the ashtray. "This is not just a murder, Investigatore. Someone went to great lengths. Perhaps someone with a vendetta against the Academy or its scientists."

"He was not merely a scientist, Comandante."

"Adakem?"

"*Si*," Sansone said. "In addition to being one of Pope Peter's senior advisors, he was also a high-level member of a group within the Academy that was responsible for a special area of research. I inquired officially as to the nature of the research and was told it is considered confidential by the Vatican. We have no jurisdiction within their walls to investigate further."

"I am aware of the Holy See's political status."

"My apologies," Sansone said, bowing his head momentarily. "However, we *have* established a personal connection between the two men."

"As opposed to professional?" Michael could feel the corners of his mouth curl up. "Go on," he said.

"Doctor Adakem and Father Ceste worked together at the Academy over thirty years ago," Sansone said. "Our investigation has revealed that they were once friends."

"Am I to understand that *both* Doctor Adakem and Father Ceste were members of the Academy?"

"Ceste was not. He was a staff biologist working *for* the Academy, but he was never a member. As you know, membership is limited to a very select group."

"Of course."

"We know Father Ceste worked with Doctor Adakem on some projects in the Life Sciences division." Sansone glanced down again at his notes. "Specifically, in the Molecular Biology group."

"You said they *were* friends."

"*Si*. Apparently, Ceste and Adakem had some differences regarding on-going research. Ceste left for what were termed 'philosophical differences'."

A potential motive? "Please elaborate."

"We have not been able to ascertain the specifics yet,

Comandante, but are pursuing several potential leads with our contacts within the Vatican. At this point, we believe Adakem's group may have been conducting experimental research involving stem cells or perhaps in-vitro fertilization."

"Are not those practices in clear violation of Church teachings?" Michael asked, tapping a pencil point on his desk. The rat-a-tat rhythm sounded loud in the room until Sansone's voice drowned it.

Sansone cleared his throat. "They may have been. Which is why we believe information about the projects has been difficult to extract. We also theorize that this is why Ceste ceased performing experimental work for the Academy and why he ended communications with Doctor Adakem. As far as we can tell, the two had not spoken since that time."

Michael's gaze shifted to the city outside his window. What evil lurked behind those facades? He twirled the pencil between thumb and forefinger and spoke without turning. "Yet, we find the two crucified upside down. On either side of a single wooden cross, in one of the most popular historical sites in the world."

"Perhaps—" Sansone began.

Michael spun back around and cut Sansone off with a raised palm. "Have you looked into phone records?"

"We have found no evidence of any cell phone or email contact between the two men in the weeks leading up to the murders," Sansone said. "If there were any communication prior to the crimes, it must have been in person or via landline. There is no record of such a meeting in either of their personal logs, but this does not mean they could not have met secretly. However, we did discover a call that originated from Ceste's phone less than an hour before the estimated time of death and another that was incoming shortly after. Both were the same number."

"After?"

"Yes, we believe the second call came in approximately thirty to forty-five minutes *after* Ceste was murdered. It was answered."

Michael pulled twice on his ear lobe. It did not make sense. Why would the murderer answer Ceste's phone? "No prints on the phone?"

"None."

"You have the name and address of the person connected to this number?"

Sansone nodded. "Ceste placed a series of calls to this same number during the weeks leading up to the murder."

"I want an officer on this man's doorstep within the hour."

"We cannot do so."

"Excuse me?" The pencil broke between his fingers as he glared at Sansone.

"The call was placed to a number in the United States," Sansone said. "I have already contacted the phone's owner, one Signora Barden."

"Signora?" Michael folded his arms across his chest. "And?"

"She was quite upset when she learned of Ceste's death. I attempted to ascertain the nature of their relationship, but she was not forthcoming. All she would tell me was that they were friends from Ceste's time in America as a visiting priest. I inquired as to who had answered the call she placed, and she confirmed it was not Ceste. She said she hung up immediately when she did not recognize the voice, which implies the call would have lasted three seconds, perhaps five. The phone's records indicate the call actually lasted forty-three seconds. I believe she is covering something up, but I did not want to press her at this point."

Two brutal murders, a mysterious woman in America, a potential cover up. And yet, no obvious connections or motives. "Go on."

"After his brief period with the Academy, we know Ceste participated in the Vatican's exchange program with the American Church. We have records of him spending time during the eighties in the states of Ohio and Massachusetts. After that, he returned to the Vatican."

Michael nodded once.

"Our preliminary investigation also indicates that Signora Barden is a member of the American media. A radio station, we believe, but with no known connection to the Vatican. Perhaps she was investigating something within the Holy See, and the men were—"

"You are drawing lines where no lines exist as yet," Michael said. "There is no reason to make those assumptions. Make no more calls to Signora Barden at this time. We do not want to risk her involving American law enforcement."

Sansone scribbled in his notebook. At least the man knew how to take notes.

"We must pursue what evidence we have in our hands. Only if necessary will we involve U.S. authorities. We cannot help the involvement of the Swiss Guard or Vatican Gendarme, but we must try to limit further leaks to the press. This task will be virtually impossible if too many external law enforcement agencies become part of the investigation."

"*Si*, Comandante."

The press would swarm. Michael swiped a hand down his face. "We have a priest and a Vatican scientist brutally murdered. One of them had my brother's name and phone number in his pocket. Both were associated with the Pontifical Academy of Science and yet, to our knowledge, had not spoken in over thirty years. Plus, contact was made with a seemingly unrelated media person in America. No suspects, no clues, little physical evidence." He stared at his subordinate. "Anything else?"

"No, Comandante."

Michael turned to his computer screen and brought up a streaming video of the crime scene.

Sansone interrupted the grisly replay. "We are examining the forensics and should have something on the footprints and fabric soon. Now that it has stopped raining, we are dusting the area for fingerprints, but we don't expect much from that exercise." After a brief pause, he added, "I would like to interview Church and Academy leadership, with your permission."

"Absolutely not," Michael said, pointing at the other man. There was little room for error on a case like this, and Sansone was an error waiting to happen. "Whatever Adakem and Ceste knew, it was worth killing them to keep them quiet. Whoever is guilty of these murders wants the truth buried with them. If the chain of command needs to be rattled, I will do it. And only I. Is that understood?"

Chapter 8

Grace twisted the cap off a second beer, stifling a giggle as Manny leaned forward until his nose almost touched the photonegative. How could he stay so focused? After helping him compare these things for two hours, her neck hurt, and her eyes wanted to cross.

Look at him, all that character, commitment, focus, and intelligence. That and *so* much more, all rolled into one incredible man. An incredibly handsome man who suddenly looked up and interrupted her stare.

"What?" he asked.

"Uh . . . nothing." Blood rushed to her face. She tightened her fingers on the bottle instead of fanning the heat. "Just taking a break."

"You look like you just ran a marathon."

"The beer. Does it to me every time. You know that."

"Ah. Any luck yet?" he said, turning back to his project with a wave of his hand toward the pictures in front of her.

"Nothing but a couple of minor variations."

"Excuse me?" Manny's head shot up. "They should be exact,

Grace. Like we discussed at Becka's. *Zero* variations." He quickly circled the table. "Show me."

"Relax, they're not much. I put little pieces of sticky note where I found them." Grace didn't move back fast enough, and he almost knocked her over. She pointed at a tiny piece of yellow paper stuck to the forehead of the figure on the photonegative with a handwritten arrow pointing down. "Check out the right eyelid."

Manny hunched over the image with a magnifying glass in hand. "What do you see?" she asked.

After a few seconds, he said, "An eyelid."

She pursed her lips. "Right, but the stock version has very slight marks on both eyelids." She pointed at the photonegative in the middle of the table. "Traces of blood, I assume."

"Leptons. Small coins from the period." Manny slid the magnifying glass over the image and stared for a few seconds before looking up slowly. "That's not blood." He repositioned the magnifying glass over Grace's version of the negative. "You've got great eyes, Barden." He circled to the other side of the table. While hovering over his version of the negative, he added, "Most people don't notice those."

"What, those things you said? Coins?"

Manny's thin lips curved in the shape of a smile. "Back in the time of the Caesars, people often placed Roman coins over the eyelids of the dead when they were buried, Some researches believe the faint marks on the Shroud eyelids match coins in circulation at the time Jesus died. The right eye coin appears to reveal a curved staff and a few Roman letters that formed part of a word."

He positioned his thumb just under the arch of the right eyelid of the man in the stock photo. "An Italian numismatics expert named Mario Moroni identified these as coming from a lepton coin minted in AD 30 or 31 during Pontius Pilate's governorship of Judea. The letters were part of the inscription *Tibepiou Caicapoc*, or Tiberius Caesar."

"That's incredible."

He shrugged. "Over the left eye, Moroni identified what looks like a *Juolia* lepton, known by its distinctive sheaf of barley design. The Juolia lepton was only struck in 29 AD in honor of Caesar's wife, Julia."

Grace turned the magnifying glass at an angle so she could see the eyelid markings again. "Wouldn't that shoot a hole in those people claiming it's a medieval forgery?"

"Not really. It doesn't really prove anything, other than the fact that the man might have been buried sometime after 29 AD. Those who consider the Shroud a forgery think the images could be the result of photographic enlargement or computer processing. Not to mention, the Jews didn't put those coins on their dead. Only the Romans. Right now it just falls into the general category of evidence that could support a first century burial."

"Why don't they show up on yours?"

"Maybe I just wasn't close enough. Or maybe it gives credence to the photo enhancement theories. Bottom line, it's not worth pursuing." Manny pointed at a yellow sticky note. "What's this one?"

She slid the stock photo next to the photonegative she had been studying. "Look at the pinky fingers on the left hands." His head bounced back and forth between the two images. She asked, "See anything different?"

Angling his head, he brought the third photo alongside and snatched the magnifying glass to study each of them. "I must be blind," he said, shaking his head. "Both little fingers look the same. Length, width, shape."

"They are, but look again." She placed her hand gently over the tight muscles in his back. "Check the angle between the two pinky fingers."

He remained virtually motionless as he stared through the magnifying glass. Standing abruptly, he dashed down the hall toward his bedroom.

"What?" Grace called out.

He returned with a clear, semicircle-shaped piece of plastic in his hand and a fiery zeal in his eyes. "Protractor from high school geometry," he said with a sheepish grin. "Couldn't bring myself to throw it away."

"You are *such* a nerd."

He ignored the comment. Placing the protractor over her version of the photonegative, he carefully aligned the zero degree mark. "Okay, the angle established between the two digits is approximately ninety-one point six degrees.

After performing the same exercise on the stock photonegative, he began mumbling unintelligibly before tossing the protractor on the table. "That can't be right." He repositioned the protractor on the stock photo. Then he grabbed a pencil and notebook from his book bag. After scratching notes and a crude drawing in the notebook, he shoved the pencil into the crook above his ear.

He returned to the other side of the table, placed the protractor on the second photo he had taken at the museum and performed the same series of measurements. "Eighty-nine point one degrees." His voice sounded like someone much older. "There's no question about it. The angles are off by two and a half degrees. How did you pick up on that?"

"It's a gift. Trust me, if a painting on a gallery wall isn't level by a millionth of a degree, I'll know it."

He slumped into his chair, leaned forward, and propped his elbows on his knees. Sweat dotted his forehead.

"You okay?"

He nodded and pressed his index finger on the third yellow sticky note. "There's another one?"

Grace circled the table and stood behind him. "See these lines on his legs?"

"The scourge marks?"

"If you say so."

He bent over until his face was just above the faint white line on the image. "Researchers believe the man in the Shroud was scourged by at least two executioners," he said. "They stood on either side of him and used a Roman flagrum, which was a whip with spikes on the ends. I don't see anything in any of the markings that's inconsistent with that."

Sliding her fingers under his ponytail, she massaged his neck gently. Then, removing the yellow sticky note, she placed her finger next to the shadowy image.

"Check out the *length* of this scourge mark."

He bent low over the photo again. His head bobbed back and forth between the three photonegatives, before he suddenly looked up, his eyes large and round. "They're different lengths."

She nodded. "I don't think anybody would ever notice it unless they were looking for it." She ran her index finger along the scourge mark on the stock photo and on each of Manny's versions. "Yours shows them just a bit longer than the stock photo."

Biting his bottom lip, he stared and said, "Do you know what this means, Grace?"

"It means your negatives and the original are a little different. This is what we were looking for, right?"

"Yeah." He wandered toward the window and stared down at the street. "But we weren't supposed to find anything. They're photonegatives of the same object. I took the photo dead on, no angle. By definition, they have to be exactly the same."

"Couldn't it just be the same issue as the coins?"

"No way," Manny said, turning back to face Grace. "Photo processing techniques *could* explain the variations in shadows, but not the position of the thumb or a longer scourge mark. And I know for sure there's *no way* the actual Shroud was altered in any way. There's only one possible explanation."

"This isn't the same cloth photographed by that Pia guy?"

"Bingo."

"Somebody made a copy."

Manny paused and rubbed the beard on his chin. "I can't think of any other plausible explanation. An *almost* perfect copy, down to the size, material, coloration, and markings."

"Why?"

"Exactly. Why?"

"How is it nobody has ever noticed this before?"

He sighed. "Who would think to look?"

"Only someone as obsessed as you."

"Right," he said. "With the Church's hard line on photography, it would have been tough to do what we did today. The big question is why. Why would the Vatican go to such elaborate lengths to dupe the public, especially when they own the real deal?"

"What was the name of the family that gave the Shroud to the Catholic Church?"

"The Savoys," he said. "In 1983. Why?"

Grace moved several books from the futon and plopped down. "Maybe the Savoy family gave them a copy instead of the original."

"No way. I know the Vatican did their own carbon dating when they took ownership, and it matched the original tests. In fact, my dad's company donated the equipment because the Academy didn't have a mass spectrometer at the time. I'm positive they got the actual Shroud from the Savoys. The real question is, why the farce? What reason does the Church have for tricking everyone? Most importantly, what do we do about it?"

She tapped one finger on the futon's black metal frame, staring over his head out the window. Clouds had slipped toward the setting sun when he finally spoke over his shoulder. "Do you think your mom would talk to me?"

Her eyes misted at the mention of her mom.

He approached and sat beside her. "What?"

She forced a smile. "Nothing."

Taking both of her hands in his, he said, "Is there something wrong with your mom?"

"No. I mean I don't *think* so. I'm sure she's fine, I just haven't been able to reach her for the past few days."

"This isn't the first time."

"You're right. Of course." She related the details of the past few days.

The gentle squeeze of his hands on hers eased some of her tension. His voice sounded confident. "She'll check in soon. Then we can get together and talk about all this." At her nod, he wrapped an arm around her, pulling her toward his chest.

She leaned into his embrace. "After I give her a hard time, I'll talk to her about what we found. Maybe her producer at the station will be interested."

"That's exactly what I was thinking."

Grace pulled free and kissed his cheek. "I'm going home to get some rest, boyfriend. I'm beat, and I told Becka I'd help her tonight."

"Let me take you home." He stood to follow her.

"No need," Grace said, grabbing her purse.

"At least let me walk you to the subway."

"You're sweet." Grace cupped her hand under Manny's chin. "But it's not even dark yet. I'll enjoy the trip."

"All right. Call me when you get home."

She nodded.

"Thanks for helping, Gracie. I owe you one."

"Actually, you owe me *two*."

As she stepped onto the streets of the South Bronx, the encroaching clouds smudged the city's skyline. She turned up her collar and headed east, trying to keep ahead of the storm.

Chapter 9

Grace stirred in her bed, staring out at the remnants of night and shivering. The atmosphere inside her tiny apartment had grown frigid since she'd fallen asleep. But why? Had the furnace quit on her again?

Moonlight emphasized shadows, revealing an open door. That was odd. She never left her bedroom door ajar. And what was wrong with her walls? Why did they seem twisted out of shape?

She slammed her eyes shut and tried to slow her breathing. This was just a holdover from a dream. It had to be. As she looked again, the shadowy dark seemed to shift and breathe as if the room itself exhaled.

O God, O God, help.

A mantel clock on her dresser began to chime, and Grace almost swallowed her tongue as she turned toward it and a dark corner.

O God.

Although far more geometric than any other shadow in the room, this one first appeared as nothing but vapor tangled in darkness. Then it coalesced into a vague, glowing silhouette.

Hollow openings appeared instead of eyes, and its joints seemed to bend at impossible angles. The entity moved in and out of focus like a holographic projection, emitting its strange white light in pebbly bits, so different from the moon's soft glow through the bedroom window.

Grace pulled the blanket over her head. "One Mississippi, two Mississippi," she whispered. She wiggled her foot. Yep, it still hurt from standing all evening at Becka's. But foot pain or not, this *had* to be a nightmare. But could a dream attack all of the senses at once?

"Three Mississippi."

Her heartbeat seemed to speed, sounding impossibly loud in her ears. Thud, thud, thud.

"Four Mississippi."

The entity reeked, its odor sour, sulfurish.

Her teeth clacked. She bit hard to still their chatter. "Five Mississippi."

She hid and counted. At the twelfth Mississippi, Grace peered out from under her blanket. It had gone. Her door was closed. Only remnants of a thin red mist remained. *God. Please.*

She ducked back under and squeezed shut her eyes. The bizarre imagery, the detail, so much more than the gray diffused edges of normal nightmares, wouldn't go away.

Her cell phone vibrated almost off the nightstand. She released a breath and reached out from under the blankets. The phone's display read Unknown Caller. She didn't want to talk to anyone, but there'd be a voice at the other end. Some tether to reality. Still, who would call at this hour?

"Who are you and who do you want?" she asked, more loudly than she'd intended.

"Gracie?" The subdued female voice stopped her.

Anger warred with relief. "Mom? Where have you *been?* I've been worried sick."

"I know. I'm so sorry, honey." Kellen Barden's voice hesitated. "It was unavoidable."

"You couldn't even call?"

"It's complicated."

"Are you all right? Where are you?"

"I'll explain it all soon, but I can't stay on the phone right now. I think I'm being watched, and I need to get off before they can trace this call."

Watched? Traced? Grace felt her nightmare shakes return. "What have you gotten yourself into?"

"I'm not sure yet. All I know is, I've been put in the middle of something that could get a little hairy, and I'm trying to make sure you don't get involved. They don't know much about me right now, so you should be safe."

"*They?*"

"This is going to sound strange, Grace, but I need you to do me a big favor."

The line went silent, but Grace could hear shallow breaths. Before she could say anything, her mother continued in a voice that sounded both familiar and frightening. "I need you to go see your father."

Grace stiffened instantly. Her mother had to be kidding. "Why would I do that? Does that loser have something to do with this?"

"Grace, don't. Please. He's not the man you think he is."

"You've been saying that since I was a little girl. I didn't buy it then, I'm not buying it now, and I don't think you do either. There's not a single photo of him *anywhere* in the house."

"You don't understand. He's—"

"I don't care how good of a person you *claim* he is. The bottom line is, he left you. He left *us*. Period, end of story."

"Not quite." Her mother sounded not only determined, but also a bit sad. "I don't have much time." A sense of urgency crept in to Kellen Barden's voice, which brought Grace into alert mode. "There are things you need to know, things I'd rather you heard from your father. Tell him Father Ceste is dead. Ask him to tell you what happened in 1987, that I said it's okay."

Grace wanted to swat away this whole mess. "What's okay?" she said. "Who's this Ceste character? *You* tell me. I don't need to see your ex-lover."

"I haven't been able to reach him yet, but I'll keep trying. Either way, you must see him, first thing. After you do, I'll fill you in on the details."

Grace hated that her biological father could reach across twenty-plus years and still affect her life. "I don't know if I can do that."

"You *can* do it, Gracie. You're a strong woman. I know exactly where he will be at seven. Promise me you'll go."

Grace sighed, trapped by the quiver in her mother's voice. "All right. Fine. If it means so much to you."

"Thank you, Gracie. I'm very proud of you. I'll call you later and explain everything, but I've got to hang up now."

After Kellen provided Grace the meeting location, the line disconnected. Her gaze drifted to the empty corner of the bedroom. It had to have been a dream. What did Ebenezer Scrooge call it, undigested lamb?

More importantly, why had her mother sounded so frightened? She had always been the rock in her life. Steady, reliable, trustworthy. Loving unconditionally. Why had she asked this of Grace now?

Still, it came back to the fear. Both hers and her mom's.

Grace dialed a familiar number. When Manny's groggy voice answered, she said, "It's me. Remember the favor you owe me?"

Ω

She frowned at her empty travel mug. The flowering pink dogwoods probably hated the cold morning as much as she did. She just wanted to sleep for a day . . . or maybe a month. To click her heels together three times and return to Kansas. She shoved the mug into her coat pocket.

Keep moving. She had to keep moving.

As she crossed the street, a strong wind gusted light snow against the dogwood petals, spawning an enormous pink wave down Central Park South. Half a block ahead, a lone figure sat atop the stone steps leading into St. William Catholic Church. His green hoodie poked out from underneath a heavy black coat, and his breath plumed up as fog. Soon, recognizable facial features emerged as he lowered the cell phone. Manny's clothes looked disheveled, but he smiled at her in spite of the dark circles rimming his eyes.

Grace forced herself to return his smile as a rush of warmth pushed back the pervasive cold. "Morning," she said.

"Yes it is." Manny looked her over carefully. "You okay?"

"Yeah, I'm fine." She eased down onto the cold steps next to him. "Who was that?"

"Becka. She's worried about you."

Grace shook her head. Too many people, too many worries. "You couldn't go back to sleep either?"

He shrugged.

After her mother's call, Grace had stood in her apartment's shower until the hot water had turned cold. But she hadn't wanted to risk her bed—or sleep—again. "I'm sorry. I shouldn't have woken you so early. It could have waited."

"Relax, Gracie, it's no big deal. I don't sleep much anyway."

Her eyes blurred as he moved closer to comfort her. "Nervous?"

"That's a complicated question."

He stared into her eyes, as if taking her emotional temperature. "No, it isn't. He's your father."

"He's not my *dad*."

"Gracie."

On the subway ride in from Brooklyn, she had pretended this meeting was merely a task to be checked off her to-do list. It wasn't. "I don't think nervous is the right word," she said. "Mom met him in college and said he was an accounting major. I'm imagining some loser with a white shirt and pocket protector."

He frowned.

"So, meeting him is just something I have to do before the morning shift at Becka's."

"I know you, Barden."

She lowered her eyes momentarily before smiling up at him. "I can't thank you enough for being here."

"No worries." He pulled the hoodie down around his neck, slumped his shoulders, and sighed.

"What?" Grace said.

"Nothing, just…"

"Just what?"

"It just has me thinking about my mom, that's all."

Grace felt her anxiety drain away, replaced by something much softer.

Before she could say anything, Manny stood and offered his hand. "Ready?"

She considered pursuing the subject further and thought better of it. "Maybe when my skin stops crawling."

"It's best to just pull the Band-Aid off quickly, Gracie."

"I know, I know." But she couldn't go in yet, so she asked, "Will that Baggio guy be saying the Mass?"

"No, he moved on years ago."

"Oh, right. You said that yesterday."

"Father Dan says the early Mass every weekday."

"Father Dan?"

"Father Daniel Neumann. He's the pastor now, but he was just a new priest when I was a kid." He led her up the stone stairs toward massive wood doors. "The Mass should be over soon. I'd like to catch communion."

Like most Catholic churches Grace had been in over the years, St. Williams had massive arches, burning candles, and porcelain statues with longing eyes that gazed into heaven. And, like so many others, it smelled of incense and history.

As she slid into a back pew, a handful of faithful filed into the aisle for communion. Manny joined the procession.

She surveyed each middle-aged man as he returned to the pews, checking for facial features that might seem recognizable from her own mirror. Of the few potential candidates, none even glanced her direction. Ten minutes later, they sat in the back of an empty church.

"Are you sure you got the time and place right?" Manny asked.

"She was very specific. The 7:00 AM Mass at St. Williams Catholic Church in Manhattan, across from the park."

"Well, we're in the right place. Sure you had the day right?" His words echoed in the quiet of the large church.

"We talked just a few hours ago. She said this morning and that he'd find me. Only a couple of men in the crowd were even in the right age group, and they walked out without paying me any attention."

"Maybe he chickened out?"

Grace frowned and looked over her shoulder at the vacant pews. The coward.

As a black-robed priest approached from the front of the church, Manny's face lit. "Maybe Father Dan can help." He patted Grace on the knee before stepping into the aisle. She eased from the pew as the two men approached.

"Grace Barden," Manny said, his arm around the priest. "I'd like you to meet Father Daniel Neumann. The man I told you about."

"Pleased to meet you, Father." Grace extended her hand.

The black-robed man stared into her eyes for a long moment before he seemed to catch himself. "My pleasure, Ms. Barden. Manny has mentioned you frequently over the past few years. He speaks very highly of you."

"Ah." Yes, well. Should she thank Manny?

He adjusted horn-rimmed glasses and coughed nervously. "I understand you're here to meet your father."

"My mom told me he would meet me here after the Mass, but I guess he didn't get her message. She said they were in college together, so that would make him in his late fifties. He was an accounting major, so maybe a CPA? You know anyone like that?"

The priest's expression stilled. He took off the thick glasses, wiped them with the sleeve of his robe, and returned them to his nose.

When he spoke, his voice had a raspy sound, full of emotion. "Well, I used to know someone who fit that description."

Used to? Grace stole a glance at Manny, whose expression mirrored her confusion.

"Before I left for seminary," Father Neumann said, "I was an accounting major in college. I'm your father, Grace."

Chapter 10

Grace clutched Manny's hand on the way to the priest's office. To say she felt stunned would be a gross understatement.

Could this priest, this Father, actually be *her* father?

Manny eased down next to her on a worn leather sofa as the black-robed man—her father?—went to find coffee. Heavy drapes covered a lone window, and dark wooden shelves lined the walls.

Black robes. Dark office. It fit. The room appeared only a few lumens brighter than the church's sanctuary, making it hard to discern titles among the dusty books.

Neither of them spoke as they waited. This man who claimed to be her father was the same man who had mentored a young Manny. A sharp pain hit her chest. She tried to slow her breathing so she wouldn't scream.

Manny tightened his hold on her hand. It didn't help. "You should at least hear him out."

"Why?" Her chin trembled, making her voice quaky. "He abandoned us, Manny. Now he's out there pretending to be a holy man. Why should I listen to anything he says? I can't even believe I'm sitting here now."

His thumb traced across her knuckles. "I know him, Grace. I've known him most of my life. He's a good man. I'm not sure why he left you, but he must have had a reason."

"Yeah, a good man." She struggled to contain tears.

Father Daniel Neumann pushed the office door open with his knee. "Sorry it took so long." He set three unmatched mugs on the desk and pulled open the drapes. The dirty glass exposed a pale brick wall thirty feet across an open courtyard but added little to the light in the room. "Had to go all the way to the convent to find hot coffee," he said, his lips trying to form a thin smile. "I hope you can handle it black."

His casual words annoyed her. She stifled an expletive and said instead, "I can handle black coffee, Mr. Neumann. What I can't handle is your—"

"Black is fine, Father Dan. Thanks." Manny glared at her. She withdrew her hand from his.

"My pleasure." Father Neumann closed the door before sitting down behind his desk and sipping his coffee. Slowly, he inhaled the steam.

Grace gripped her own mug in silence, releasing her tight hold when the heat burned. She sipped the black liquid as if it were a magic elixir that could wake her from this latest nightmare. Her entire life seemed like a prologue to this moment. Yet now, sitting in a dim office outside an even darker church, she wasn't sure she wanted to know what came next.

Manny broke the uneasy silence. "Father Dan, maybe we should get to the reason why Grace came here this morning."

Father Neumann nodded. "Your mother left a number of voicemails, but I've been away and in meetings for the last two days and didn't check the phone until this morning."

His mention of her mother grated like fingernails on a

blackboard. Grace ignored the apology in his voice. "Are you speaking of the woman you abandoned twenty-three years ago?" She hoped her tone matched her disgust. "That mother?"

Father Neumann lowered his head. When he looked up, his eyes glistened with moisture. "I'm so sorry, Grace," he said softly. "More than anything, I'm sorry that I wasn't there for you. To be your dad." He raised his hand and coughed.

They waited in silence for him to recover.

Finally, he said, "I can't expect you to understand how much I've missed you over the years, especially knowing you were only a subway connection away the entire time."

Grace focused her gaze across the courtyard on a brick wall that was gray like a tombstone. A shiver passed through her, and she hugged herself. But she didn't speak.

"I watched you play in St. Mary's schoolyard many times when you were in elementary school," he said. "But I . . . well, I eventually found it too difficult. I finally quit going, but I never stopped thinking about you, praying for you, loving you."

That was too much. "Loving me?" Grace spat the words. "You don't abandon someone you love. I don't care if you didn't want to marry Mom, you should have at least stayed around for me."

"I never stopped loving your mom either, Gracie."

"Please." She dug her fingers into her upper arms and stared down, unseeing. He had no right to use her nickname. "Just tell me what I need to know so I can get out of here. I don't care about anything else."

"Grace." Manny touched her shoulder.

She shrugged him off.

"I'll make a deal with you," Father Neumann said, maintaining a calm she couldn't. "Tell me what you do know, and I'll try to fill in the blanks."

She didn't respond.

"I was hoping your mother would have explained the situation." Father Neumann pinched the bridge of his nose and sighed. "I never abandoned you, Grace, because I never knew about you. I didn't even know you existed for the first six years of your life."

Grace turned toward Manny, but his gaze was still fixed on the priest, his expression mirroring her shock.

"I met your mother during my last semester at the University of Akron," he continued. "She was a freshman English major, and I was studying accounting. I fell in love with her while I was still struggling over my vocation. We talked about it, agonized over it, and yet she supported me when I made the hard choice to enroll in the seminary." He paused, obviously overwhelmed by the memories. Finally, he met her eyes again. "It was the toughest decision of my life to leave her, but I believed I had a true calling. We'd agreed that seeing each other would have been too hard, so I never contacted her again. I swear I didn't know she was pregnant with you."

She bit the inside of her cheek. A would-be priest who'd impregnated a girl and then walked away. The brave new world of sainthood.

Father Neumann leaned forward as if he hoped for something from her, but Grace didn't change her posture. When she sensed Manny's stare, she turned to see another pair of haunted eyes.

Boy, oh, boy. The priest and the almost-priest.

"Your mother mentioned Genovese on the voicemail she left this morning," Father Neumann said. "She also described some of what's been happening recently. She asked me to explain the past so you can put things in their proper perspective."

Grace tried to refocus. "She's afraid. That's why I'm here,

because I want to know who this Ceste guy is and why I had to meet you after all these years."

"You don't remember, but this isn't our first encounter. We met twenty-three years ago."

Grace exchanged a curious glance with Manny.

Clasping his hands under his chin, Father Neumann said, "Genovese Ceste was a parish priest who helped you and your mom when you were little. He was a very good man."

Grace decided to swallow the sharp words she longed to say. "What do you mean, he helped me?"

Father Neumann circled his desk slowly and perched on its corner, balancing with one foot flat on the floor. His words were barely audible. "This is not going to be easy to accept, Grace. Once you hear what I have to say, you can never un-hear it. Are you sure you're ready for that?"

She tried to focus on dust motes spinning in the gray light as black clouds hovered outside. "I'll tell you what I'm ready for," she said finally. "The truth. Let's try that one, shall we?"

Father Neumann rubbed his face with both hands. "When you were six years old." He paused to clear his throat and take another deep breath. "On the evening of March eighth, 1987, your mother contacted me for the first time since we'd dated in college. We met the next day at your home while you were at school, and she told me the whole story."

Whole story? Grace shivered. "She told you about me?"

"Yes," Father Neumann said. "About you . . . and about what was happening to you."

Grace stole a glance at Manny. His face held the blank stare of a mannequin. It was not reassuring.

"She said you'd been acting strangely," Father Neumann said. "Actually, way beyond strange. You were saying and doing things that should have been impossible."

"Like what?" Grace wanted to take back the question before the words left her lips.

The hesitation in the priest's voice was now gone. "Your mother said you were speaking in a language she could not understand. You were incredibly strong—too strong—and at times violent."

"It could have been a medical condition," Grace stammered. None of it seemed real, but she could almost feel it. The realness of what he said.

"She'd heard about *glossolalia*, speaking in tongues, but she was pretty sure you weren't manifesting a spiritual gift from God, not with the violence and contortions. So she tried doctors, psychiatrists, counselors, drugs. Nothing worked. She was at her wit's end when she reached out to me." He paused, looking stricken. "Needless to say, I was overwhelmed by the entire situation. That I had a daughter and that she . . . she . . . "

Grace could feel her throat muscles contract. "What?"

"I met you for the first time that afternoon. I went with your mother and picked you up at school. Kellen introduced me simply as Daniel. You never knew who I really was." He broke off and sipped from his coffee cup. His next words were halting. "But when you looked at me, you said . . ."

"What?" Grace clenched her hands until her fingernails scored her palms. She concentrated on the pain to distract herself. Because she didn't want to know. And yet she repeated the question. "What did I say?"

"I was wearing street clothes, Grace." His soft words whispered over her. "You said, 'Father, help me,' even though you couldn't have known I was a priest—or that I was actually your father."

Manny placed his hand on her fist, uncurling and holding

it. Grace barely felt his caress.

"Your mother seemed as confused as I was. Then I looked at you." He steepled his fingers in front of his chin. "This isn't going to make much sense."

As the priest hesitated, time seemed to slow for Grace. She tried to think of pleasant things, but all she saw were the images from her nightmare.

Father Neumann dropped his hands and stared into her eyes. She looked away. She wanted to cover her ears.

"Your feet weren't touching the ground."

The beating of her heart sped along with her breaths. She tried to slow them both as she shook her head.

"We met with Father Ceste that night, and he called in an expert, Father Lombardi from the Vatican, who was visiting a monastery in upstate New York. He drove right down."

"An expert in what?" Manny asked, his voice unsteady and his expression cautious.

Father Neumann nodded at Manny. When he spoke to Grace, his voice had gentled even more. "You know, don't you, that counterfeit gifts exist? The enemy mimics the things of God, always trying to deceive and destroy. God's gifts are to enlighten and bless the Body, His church." He glanced from Grace to Manny, pausing for this to register. "Father Lombardi had experience with both the blessing and the curse."

Grace clutched Manny's hand, shivering from a deep cold. Manny drew closer. "You're not saying . . .?" Manny began.

Father Neumann shook his head. "No. Remember, there's a difference between possession and oppression. We're not talking *The Omen*." Father Neumann knelt in front of Grace and looked up into her eyes. "Father Lombardi determined that you were under attack by demonic forces. You were not possessed. Late that night, we performed the Rite of Exorcism to cast them away and to protect you."

Memories surfaced, as if a long-forgotten nightmare had suddenly become real. Her limbs weakened, and the last thing Grace saw was a red haze behind her eyes. And then nothing.

Chapter 11

Demons?

The word echoed in Grace's ears as she struggled to focus on Manny and keep up with his longer stride. She wanted to hear what had happened after she'd regained consciousness and fled the church, but staying focused was proving a challenge.

"Let's get you out of the cold." He pulled her across the sidewalk and reached for a glass door with an orange plastic sign hanging on the inside that simply read Open. "You'll feel better."

The warmth hit her as she stepped inside. They found a quiet spot in the back of the small café, near a brick fireplace with a deer head over the mantle. The fragrance of strong coffee and fresh bread wafted over her. Perfect.

Grace had gone into the church longing for answers, but had run from memories of something she didn't want to explore, a monster threatening to swallow her whole. She accepted the hot chocolate Manny ordered. The first sip helped warm her. Some.

"Feeling better?" he said.

"I'm fine." Maybe she wasn't exactly fine, but curled up on the café's overstuffed brown leather sofa with one leg folded under the other and her hands around a warm cup, she could admit to feeling less awful. "I'm glad you came after me . . . eventually."

Manny squeezed her hand. "I knew you were going to want to hear the rest of the story."

"I had some weird theories on the way over to the church this morning," she said with a sigh. "Like my biological father had turned gay or was a secret agent. I would never have came up with this scenario. Does that crazy priest expect me to believe all his nonsense?"

Manny stared at the floor between his feet. "I realize you have issues with Father Dan, but you should try to understand he...." The background din drowned his words.

Understand? She'd love to understand. In fact, she'd love to find anything even remotely explicable about the whole thing. "How could he not know about me for all those years?"

"Your mom knew how committed he was to the priesthood," he said, sipping his own drink. "She didn't want to get in the way of his calling when she found out she was pregnant. After you were born, she thought it would be too embarrassing for everyone if the truth came out."

"So, instead, I didn't get a father."

"When your mother moved from Ohio to New York, she hadn't a clue he was a parish priest in the city until she tracked him down through the diocese when she needed his help. No one else knew of your relationship."

"Until now."

"Grace, listen to me." His voice grew serious. "Think about how tough it must have been for Father Dan to return to his regular duties after meeting you. Especially after he learned you lived right across the East River. I can tell he loves you, and I know he has no doubt about what he said to you. He believes you were being attacked by demons. Apparently, so does your mom."

"Do you?"

Manny hesitated, studying her face. "The Church today doesn't really acknowledge demonic attacks as it once did. They tend to—"

"You do, don't you?"

"Look. I know that there are forces beyond what we can experience with our five senses. Dark forces that have been waging war against God and man since well before human history. Obviously, your mother believes this, too."

"Well, maybe she's crazy, along with the rest of you." Grace took a sip of her hot chocolate, which wasn't so hot anymore. "Really, Manny? The devil? Come on! I've got news for you. Demons are like vampires, they don't exist. They're all inventions of Hollywood, just figurative scapegoats for the evils in our world. Have you ever seen a demon? How can an educated person like you be so naïve?"

She sighed and turned to gaze out the glass door of the café. She wouldn't think about it any more or the *thing* in her room this morning. She'd forget the whole story and that feeling—the cold, the vapor, the odd sensations. She would *not* remember the fear.

Large flakes of snow fluttered across the late morning sky. So beautiful. So far removed from all this ugliness in her life, from all this craziness.

Manny looked up from the floor, but his eyes did not meet hers. "I've never seen a black hole either. But I know they're real. I know from scientific evidence that black holes are out there, including one in the center of our own galaxy. I don't have to see a demon to know they exist." He paused, massaging his temples in slow circles. "Jesus spoke of Satan more often than he spoke of heaven. He wasn't warning us about some figurative scapegoat. The difference between vampires and demons is that vampires don't exist."

Grace felt her eyes brimming again and blinked back tears. It wasn't fair. What had she done to deserve all this? "Why me?"

"I don't know." Manny's words again drifted into the background noise. "I . . ."

"There's something you're not saying. I can hear it in your voice."

He cleared his throat and looked intently at her. "I believe, Grace, that the devil always has a plan, one that may not be obvious until things unfold. I don't think these happenings are random."

Manny brushed back wisps of her hair, and his gentle fingers wiped away tears she didn't remember shedding. His touch felt so good.

She made a lame attempt at a chuckle and said, "I'll bet you wouldn't have agreed to that favor exchange if you had known what you were in for."

"You know me better than that."

She nodded. She did know him better than that, and he deserved a lot more respect and appreciation than she was giving him. "I was kind of in and out while you were bringing me up to speed," she said. "What was all that Vatican stuff about?"

"Father Dan talked more about the two priests who . . ." Again, he cleared his throat. "A priest named Anthony Lombardi assisted Ceste with the actual Rite. Lombardi returned to Rome after they met with you and has been there ever since. Believe it or not, he's a cardinal now."

"So?"

"That's a big deal in the Catholic Church. Anyway, Lombardi knew your dad. Well, I always knew Lombardi was an old friend of Father Dan's. I just never knew why until now. Rumor has it, he's potentially in line for a big promotion. The big promotion."

She sifted through her knowledge of Catholic Church hierarchy, making mental connections in her head. Priest. Pastor. Bishop. Archbishop. Cardinal. Whoa... "Are you saying this

Lombardi guy could be the next Pope?"

He shrugged his shoulders. "That's what I heard at the seminary, but you never know. The Church is as much about politics as it is religion."

"What about Ceste?"

"I would have loved to meet that man," he said, a note of wistfulness in his voice. "After he left the States, he went to work for the Pontifical Academy of Sciences."

"So?" she said carefully. "The Catholic Church still believes the Earth is flat, doesn't it? Their science people can't have much credibility in your world."

"On the contrary," Manny said. "The Pontifical Academy is one of the most respected scientific organizations in the world. They're all about discovering scientific truths, from subatomic particles to galaxies. Although they fully expect science to prove the existence of God some day, they aren't under the thumb of the Pope. In fact, they have openly acknowledged the validity of many controversial theories such as Darwinism."

Her eyes widened. "They agree with evolution?"

"Not the way most people understand it. Christianity is made up of very diverse individuals. Although we all believe God created the universe and everything in it, many Christians believe creationism and evolution can peacefully coexist. In other words, God created the building blocks of life, and His divine finger used His evolution process to guide creation over the—"

"Six days." The words came out laced in sarcasm, and Grace wanted to kick herself. She made a conscious decision to adjust her attitude as Manny shifted position on the sofa. She prefaced her next words with a slim smile. "Sorry, but I can't even finish a painting in six days."

"A day was often used as metaphorically in the Bible. A verse in

Second Peter says, 'With the Lord, a day is like a thousand years and a thousand years are like a day.'"

"Wow, sounds like there's some pretty bright people in that Academy of yours."

"Many lynx," Manny said.

"Links to what?"

"L, Y, N, X," Manny said. "It's a wildcat with incredible eyesight and is the official symbol of The Pontifical Academy of Science. They use it to represent the observational prowess required by science to discover the truth in God's creation."

"Ceste was a member?"

"No," Manny said. "He assisted with some of the Academy's research as a staff biologist."

Grace pulled her jacket over her shoulders, trying to get warm. "Why would my mom be so secretive about all this?"

Manny shrugged. "I guess she'll have all the missing puzzle pieces when you talk to her later. Right now, I just want to get you back to your apartment so you can get some rest."

"Will you stay with me for a while?"

"Of course." He patted her hand gently. "Are you going to be okay?"

"I think so." But she wasn't sure, especially when tears blurred her world again. "I'm just anxious to be done with all the mystery. To know why some dead priest has her in such a panic. I did my part. Now I want to know."

She felt overwhelmed by a desire to retreat to a world of soft pillows, warm blankets, and fairy tales, where none of this horror existed. As if he could read her thoughts, Manny drew her into his arms. His embrace felt like more than a hug, and when Grace looked up, she froze. His face was only inches from hers, betraying a depth she had only dreamt of seeing in a man's eyes. She stared back.

"Ah, Gracie."

He wanted her. She could see it in those trembling lips, in the light in his eyes. And yet, she knew his greatest strength was also his greatest weakness. She understood his analytical mind and could almost see those internal scales tipping back and forth. A lump rose in her throat as he looked away and said, "Never mind."

Two simple words. With two simple words that took no longer to say than an "I love you," he'd retreated from the narrow chasm that separated friend from lover. With two simple words, Manny Lusum proclaimed his devotion to his Church, as her father had done so many years ago.

Grace bit down on her lip. Manny Lusum was not Daniel Neumann. Manny was the finest man Grace had ever known—or ever would know. A man who loved her, cared for her. A man who deserved her faith. She snuggled against him, finding a fast heart beating against her ear. "Thanks," she said.

"For what?"

"For finding me."

Chapter 12

Manny watched as Grace slept next to him on the couch of her tiny Brooklyn apartment. Her chest rose and fell rhythmically, and her full lips seemed almost pouty. A stray blonde curl lay across one cheek.

She was so beautiful.

And he was so stupid. Why was it so hard for him to admit the truth? Everything about her filled up his world. He yearned to touch that soft skin, those lush curves. She needed him, which was the most seductive tug of all.

She stirred against him as her cell phone buzzed. He should have turned it off. If only it were as easy to turn himself off. He eased away from her sleeping form to grab the phone, which registered an unknown number. Moving quickly toward the bedroom, he clicked the green Call button and whispered, "Grace Barden's phone."

After a slight delay, a ragged voice said, "Manny, is that you?"

"Ms. Barden?"

"Where's Grace?" Kellen Barden's voice sounded urgent, worried. "Is she okay?"

"Yeah." Manny returned to the couch and gently caressed Grace's hair. "She's right here," he said as he handed over the phone. "It's your mom."

Grace sat up slowly, taking the phone with shaking hands. After a series of "Uh-huh's," she returned the phone to the coffee table and pressed Speaker.

"Manny's here with me," she said.

There was a noticeable pause on the line before Kellen spoke. "This is very personal, honey. Do you think . . . ?"

"He was with me all morning, Mom." Grace patted Manny on the knee and left her hand there. Her smile was crooked. "Whatever you have to say to me you can say in front of him."

"Actually, I'm glad he's there." Kellen paused briefly. "So, you met your father?"

"I met *a* father."

"Grace, you—"

"How could you do this to me? You're my mother!" She let the tears flow, hiccupping over a sob. "How . . . how could you keep this from me for so long?"

No one spoke. Grace dabbed at her face with her shirt sleeve, and indistinct sounds came from the phone.

When Kellen finally answered, her own voice was less than steady. "Oh, honey, I'm sorry. So sorry. It's just, I thought it best for everyone. For your father, for me, especially for you."

"How? How could it be best for me not to know who my father was? Not to know if he was even alive?"

"Oh, Gracie, honey, I wish I could do it all over again. I'd wish none of it had happened in the first place." Another pause. "No, that's not right. I could never regret having you as my daughter."

Manny longed to channel his best Dr. Phil, but he came up

empty. He felt like an interloper, listening as Grace and her mother exchanged words not meant for his ears. He ducked into the hallway outside of her apartment door and leaned against the wall, his hands on his knees. But he couldn't stand it, couldn't stand leaving Grace alone and in pain. He peeked back in and heard Grace say, "I know, Mom. I just need a little time. It wasn't Father Neumann's fault. It was nobody's fault."

Returning, Manny lowered himself next to Grace just as Kellen said, "He told you about . . . . He told you what happened?"

Grace jerked, as if the word alone might conjure a legion of evil spirits. She mumbled, "Yes," and he watched what little color she had left in her face drain away.

"I'm so sorry it had to be this way. Daniel and I both wanted to spare you, but had you witnessed what . . . " Kellen's voice trailed off into a symphony of traffic and sirens outside Grace's apartment.

"He told me the whole story."

A muffled noise over the phone, and, "Oh, God," which sounded very much like a plea for help. At the sound of Kellen's tears, Grace grabbed a tissue and fled to the kitchen.

"Can you hang on a minute, Ms. Barden?"

Kellen didn't answer, but he could hear sounds of distress. Grace stood with her back to him until she finally blew her nose and returned, her eyes swollen and bloodshot.

"Mom." Her voice sounded much stronger than Manny had expected. "I just need to know why. Assuming any of this nonsense is true, why was it so important I know it now? After all these years?"

"Because of what's happened," Kellen said soberly. "I felt compelled to help Father Ceste because of what he'd done for us, and he seemed so worried. He said he was struggling with something very important."

Grace pulled a throw off the back of the sofa and wrapped it around her shoulders. "But why did he call you? And what does it have to do with me?"

"He wanted someone outside the Vatican to know whatever this thing was. He trusts—trusted—me. And you're affected because of my involvement. If I'm forced to go public with whatever he sent me, I could be the next target, which would mean the media might then go after you as they dig into my relationship with Father Ceste. It's all hypothetical at this point, but I wanted you to hear the truth from your father and me, not from the Internet."

"Father Ceste sent you something?" Manny could feel Grace's muscles tighten. "What did he send?"

"I don't know. He was very secretive about its contents, so I won't know until I receive it. I do know it originally came from someone named Adakem and that Father Ceste forwarded it to me right away. Maybe it will explain everything, or at least as much as Father Ceste knew." A sigh came through the phone. "Even though we spoke many times over the past two weeks, I'm not sure he ever uncovered the whole truth himself." A momentary pause, and then, "Or maybe he did, and that's why he was murdered."

"Murdered?" Grace's voice rose an octave.

"His last call came the night of his murder."

Grace clutched his hand. "You told me he d . . .died. You didn't say anything about murder."

"I know. I didn't want to dump too much on you at once." Kellen said. "Maybe now you can understand why I felt you needed some background information."

"I don't like the sound of this." Grace's leg began to bounce. Manny scooted closer so his thigh touched hers, trying to share body heat and still her jitters. Her fingers tightened on his. "I don't like you being messed up with something dangerous," she said.

"That's why I'm being as cautious as possible."

Grace stared at the phone in silence, as if the inert piece of metal and plastic were to blame. Manny used his free hand to caress hers. She didn't seem to notice.

"We actually spoke twice on the night of his murder," Kellen continued. "He said he had a meeting with an associate he hadn't seen in years and hoped it would help fill in the blanks. He told me he was certain someone was watching him. The second and last call came later that same night."

Grace shot him a quick glance.

"He phoned less than an hour before he was murdered. He'd met with this Adakem person, and he was extremely upset. He told me he was trying to come to grips with what he'd confirmed."

"Confirmed?" Grace asked. "Confirmed what?"

"That's it. I don't know. He wouldn't tell me over the phone, but he was very upset." Kellen paused to clear her throat.

Manny had intended to remain silent and supportive. But Grace was scared, and it sounded as if the journalist might be hunting a story. Or making one up? "I still don't understand why you think you're in danger because this priest was killed," he said. "Or why it should affect Grace. What has it got to do with the two of you? Other than peripherally, because you knew him years ago."

He waited, watching the silent phone along with Grace, who had released his hand and now twirled a lock of hair between nervous fingers.

"I called him back later that night," Kellen said, and he heard real fear. "Someone else answered the phone."

"And?" Manny asked.

"I can't really describe the voice except to say that it freaked me out. Whoever he was, he threatened me and told me to mind my own business."

Grace's hand found his again. He squeezed gently and spoke to Kellen. "Did he ask about the package?"

"No, he must not have known about it. I think Father Ceste may have died protecting me. I panicked," Kellen said.

"Mom," Grace pleaded.

"The Italian police called me an hour later. They had found Father Ceste's phone and wanted to know who I was, but I made them tell me what was going on first. Even then I didn't say much because I don't know who to trust. I wasn't even sure it was the police. That's when I learned about Father Ceste's death. He came to me for a reason, Grace. Unfortunately, that pulled both of us into the mess."

Grace leaned into Manny. "All I know is, you've flipped my world upside down, and I don't like what I'm finding underneath."

"I wish I knew how to pray this whole thing away," Kellen said. "Or pretend none of it ever happened. But I can't."

Manny pulled Grace closer to him when he saw the tears pooling in her eyes.

Kellen continued. "I need to tell you a few more things while I have a chance."

"Oh, geez," Grace said. "There's more?"

"There is. I don't have a lot of time right now, so please just listen."

As Grace turned toward him, her expression tugged at his heart. What was she picturing? A murdered priest? Her biological father? A demon?

"When Father Ceste worked with this fellow Adakem at the Academy over twenty years ago," Kellen said, "Adakem tried to recruit him into a group within the Church called The Evangelists, named, it seemed, after St. John of Patmos. Without providing Ceste with any specifics about their work, Adakem referred to extremely valuable relics smuggled out of the Vatican Archives by the Prefect, a high-ranking member of the clandestine organization. Ceste refused. He also left the Academy after the group began to dabble in reproductive research that violated Church law."

"Okay. So?" Grace said.

Her mother continued. "Fast-forward two decades, and Adakem again approached Ceste, this time remorseful over his role in the Academy's research, which he described as well beyond what Ceste could imagine. At a second meeting, which took place on the morning of the murders, Adakem provided Ceste with evidence verifying his incredible claims."

"So you think that's what Father Ceste sent you?"

"I do. I think that before Ceste ventured outside the Vatican walls on the night of his death, he forwarded this evidence to the one person he felt he could trust. Me."

Manny watched Grace's face to make sure she wasn't going to fall apart. He was having a hard enough time himself, imagining covert organizations and strange discoveries, but he was one step removed from the process. This was Grace's mother.

Kellen continued. "I don't have any answers, honey, but I'd really like it if you could go stay with Becka for a few days until I get back. Just to be on the safe side."

Grace glanced at him. He shrugged. "Back from where?" she said.

"I'm in Rome, honey," Kellen said. "I just got off the plane."

"Rome?"

"I packed a bag and went straight to LaGuardia after I heard the news. I plan on attending the visitation and funeral, maybe see the crime scene if I can get up the nerve. Your father . . . Father Neumann is also trying to help me get an appointment with Cardinal Lombardi."

"Mom, this is insane. Rome is the last place you need to be."

"I'm sorry, Gracie, but you're going to have to trust me on this. I'm being very careful."

"Trust you on what? That you won't get yourself killed?"

"I won't. But you'd be helping me a lot if you'd just lie low until I know more. I'm sure I'm only being overprotective, but it would really ease my mind. Then, when I get back, I'll look over what Father Ceste sent and decide what to do with it."

"Mom, I don't—"

"I've got to go now, honey. Please help me here, will you? Stay with Becka? When I know more, I'll call again."

"Mom—"

The phone connection ended abruptly. Manny drew a finger to his lips and pulled her to him, stroking her lightly. "There's no room at the inn," he said. "Remember, Becka has her folks there this week. You'll stay at my place." She sat up, but he smiled at the question in her eyes.

"I'm not sure that's a good idea," she said, shaking her head.

"The futon's very comfortable. You can take the bed. I'm so tired I could sleep standing up."

"That's too much to ask," she said. "You're so busy with all you've got on your plate right now."

"It'll give us a chance to look into some of the nonsense your mom was talking about."

"The murders?"

"No. Unfortunately, they're true. While you were talking to your mom, I checked my phone for articles." His voice trailed off.

"What?"

"It was awful."

"Mom's there. I need to know."

He made the sign of the cross. "There were two men. Both were crucified."

Her face blanched. Of course it did. He bent over to tie his shoes, his hands trembling as he fumbled with the laces, hoping she wouldn't ask for details.

She did. "Is there more?"

He hesitated, taking a deep breath. If he didn't tell her, she'd find out soon enough on her own. "They were crucified upside down, with their tongues cut out. On the floor of the Colosseum."

"I know you didn't want me to hear that. Thank you." Her voice was barely above a whisper.

He nodded. At her shiver, he headed to the kitchen to nuke some water and grab a tea bag and spoon. "Drink this. It'll warm you."

She dipped the bag up and down a few times, stirred the green liquid slowly, and sipped the hot brew. "You're too good to me."

"Pack up some things. If you come over to my place now, we can do a little research tonight and see if we can find out anything about stolen relics or these Evangelist characters. Who knows, it could save her some time and trouble."

Her smile barely registered as a change of expression. "I haven't been sleeping well lately. Maybe a change of scenery will help."

He knelt down in front of her. "Tell me."

A hand flutter seemed to dismiss the issue, even when she admitted she'd been having a few nightmares recently. He wasn't buying her, "Nothing to worry about." Not even when she said lightly, "You go ahead. I'll put together some things to bring over."

Yeah, right. "I can wait."

"No, really. Spend the time cleaning up your apartment." She leaned over and kissed his cheek. "You can't expect a lady to sleep in a pig sty."

"Sorry. Your mom is afraid for your safety, and it sounds like she has a right to be. I'm not leaving you here alone." He rose and crossed his arms, waiting.

Seeming surprised by his vehemence, Grace paused. Eventually, she nodded. "Okay, give me a minute."

Chapter 13

The town of Poggio Mirteto Scalo overlooked the Tiber River valley, fifty kilometers north of Rome and far enough off the beaten track to insure anonymity for Cardinal Anthony Lombardi and his brother. Dressed in gray wool pants and a black windbreaker, Anthony sat at a tiny table in the corner, listening to the rain pound the clay roof shingles.

As he waited for Michael, he sipped a steaming cappuccino and remembered their childhood in Sicily, when they'd roamed hills and fields not unlike the landscape before him. They certainly had chosen different paths. Anthony smiled at the thought of how perfectly Michael's aggressive and physical nature fit the military, while his own thoughtful and introspective personality made him perfect for the priesthood.

He smiled faintly as a dark, hulking figure approached the café. The man's wide-brimmed hat diverted the rain as well as any prying eyes. Carabinieri Comandante-Generale Michael Lombardi stepped beneath the roof's overhang, removed the hat, and shook off the rain before he entered.

The café's huge oak door swung open on squeaky hinges, and

a bell jingled. Anthony watched his older brother's gaze sweep the room before settling on an ancient black and white TV, where Michael's surly face stared at them from a late-night interview on the local news.

When Michael turned his way, Anthony could see that the television hadn't lied. Deeper wrinkles surrounded his brother's familiar green eyes. Their mama used to warn a younger Michael that his constant frown would age him, and it seemed she'd been right, as usual. Anthony whispered a quick prayer.

Michael's thin lips stretched, and he extended open arms to pull Anthony into a bear hug and aim kisses at each cheek. "*Fratello mio,* it has been far too long."

"It is good to see you as well, my brother."

Michael draped his wet overcoat and hat on an empty table. He chose a chair with its back against the wall and groaned into it. Pulling a single cigarette from his shirt pocket, he lit it and then stared at his brother intently. "You look as if sleep has eluded you in recent days."

Anthony shrugged. "As always, your eyes do not miss much. Perhaps it is why you are so good at your job?"

"Keen observational skills can keep one alive."

Anthony interlaced his fingers on the wooden table and nodded.

"Thank you for meeting me here." Michael drew deeply on the cigarette as he waved away a waitress. "As you can see," he said, gesturing toward his TV voice still droning in the background, "the Colosseum murders are big news, and some are even linking them to the murder of the nun at Santa Maria della Concezione last month. I am trying to keep a low profile as we sort truth from fiction."

"As am I," Anthony said. "With the murders, the death of His Holiness yesterday, and his announcement scheduled for tomorrow, there are many eyes on the Vatican right now. I was happy to escape for an hour or two."

Michael tapped his wristwatch and carefully set his glowing cigarette in the groove of a plastic ashtray. "I am afraid I must get immediately to the matter at hand," he said. "There are many demands for me in Rome at this time. Security issues are greatly magnified with the College of Cardinals arriving early. Do you have any idea why Peter made this specific request before his death? Why he did not wait the traditional length of time for conclave?"

"I am not certain." Anthony stared down at the remaining froth in his cup and up into piercing eyes. "I was in Peter's chambers the morning he died, along with Carmerlengo Marini and his other senior advisors." He bowed his head. "Except for Francis, may God rest his soul." Looking up, he added, "Peter made a very unusual proclamation before he died."

"That is the one to be released tomorrow night in St. Peter's Square? His final words to the Church?"

"I fear it will be much more than that," Anthony said. His chest tightened on the words. "Much more."

"You worry me." Michael's eyes narrowed to pin points. "I have enough on my plate right now, yet I sense I have yet to see the main course. What is this *more* you allude to?"

He shook his head slightly and sighed. "Peter declared . . ." Still, he hesitated. "This is between us?"

"Of course."

"This is difficult to say, but His Holiness . . ."

"Yes?" Michael said, a faint note of irritation in his voice. His fingers drummed the table.

Anthony leaned forward and said in just above a whisper, "Peter declared he would be the final Pope."

His brother grew still. Then his lips curled. "I do not have time for such absurdity. It is important I know the contents of the declaration for security reasons. We must be prepared. I can consult the Vatican Gendarme if necessary."

"I understand your skepticism, but I tell you the truth. His Holiness said the time for man's corrupt rule over Christ's church would end. I can assure you, the Gendarme and Swiss Guard know nothing of what I have just spoken. Nor are they aware of any specifics in Peter's declaration. Its contents are hidden behind the Papal seal." Anthony clasped his hands together in his lap. "I prayed for guidance in this matter, Michael, and shall trust in your discretion."

"He was dying and on pain medication, obviously. Under the influence, so to speak."

"To the contrary. His Holiness had his pain medication cancelled several days before we met. According to Carmerlengo Marini, he did this so that no one would think his judgment clouded." Anthony paused as he did a quick sweep of the room and lowered his voice even further. "He spoke ex *cathedra*."

Slowly, Michael leaned back in his chair, obviously trying to process this strange business. Anthony had seen such an expression and posture many times. "*From the chair of Peter*," Michael said.

Anthony nodded. "Are you aware that the doctrine of Papal infallibility has not been invoked in over fifty years?"

Michael shook his head.

"The declaration was made and sworn to prior to his death. This means that the Church is bound by holy law to obey whatever is in the decree."

Michael picked up his cigarette, tapped off the ash, and set it back down without taking a puff. "Which begs the obvious question," he said. "Who shall preside over the Roman Catholic

Church? Does he intend to disband the largest religion on the face of the earth?"

"Peter said his intention would be fully revealed in his declaration. As I said, no one knows the exact contents. Not I, not the Camerlengo, nor any of his other senior advisors. *No one* is permitted to see the declaration before it is read publicly. The world will find out at the same time as the leadership of the Church."

"Then why bring the cardinals in early? Or at all, for that matter? If there is to be no Pope, there is no need for conclave."

"Agreed," Anthony said. "However, his other advisors and I believe the declaration will propose some form of legislative approach to Church leadership, as opposed to the Papal autocracy."

Michael rubbed his scarred chin. "Yet, it remains a mystery."

"As I have said, no one knows the precise content of His Holiness' declaration." Anthony leaned in closer. "Peter wrote it with his own hand. The Papal Seal cannot be broken until it is read to the world. It was Peter's final wish."

Michael raised his hand and brought his fist down hard on the wooden table. "This is absurd," he said. Then, apparently realizing he'd drawn attention to their quiet corner, he leaned forward, lowering his voice. "The death of a Pope . . . three murders . . . a mysterious proclamation. Tell me everything you know."

"I have told you what I know."

"Not everything." Michael picked up his cigarette again, drew deeply, and said, "There is an American. A woman."

Anthony's heartbeat quickened.

"I understand you know a Signora Barden, Signora Kellen Barden from New York City."

How had Michael made the connection? Anthony reached into his coat pocket for a stainless steel flask, unscrewed the cap, and poured a tablespoon into the last of his cappuccino.

Sipping, he studied his brother.

"Our friends in the Vatican Gendarme provided a dossier on Father Ceste," Michael said. "My investigatore was surprised to discover such a long-standing relationship between you and the murder victim."

Anthony whispered a prayer as images flashed, unbidden.

"The file revealed that you and the murdered priest assisted the Barden family in some way during your time in America. Is that not true?"

"It is."

"You have kept in touch with her over the years?"

"Somewhat. However, Genovese kept regular contact."

"Ceste?"

"Yes," Anthony said stiffly, before adding, "I have nothing to hide, Michael."

Michael squinted at him. "I trust that is the case," he said softly.

"How did you make the connection with Signora Barden?"

"Ceste placed numerous calls to her in the weeks leading up to his murder," Michael said, "including one less than an hour before his death. In fact, she called Ceste shortly *after* his estimated time of death, and the call was answered by someone at the murder scene. Are you able to shed any light on this very confusing sequence of events?"

Anthony shook his head.

"I am very disappointed you did not come to me."

"I had nothing to tell you and saw no connection that needed reporting. You obviously know more than I." This was so typical of Michael, hotheaded and swift on the trigger. Anthony sighed. "As I said, Genovese kept in close contact with Signora Barden over the years, but my contact was minimal. I had not heard from her for many years until she called me yesterday and left a message. I had no idea she had been in contact with Father Ceste."

"Interesting." Michael directed a cloud of blue smoke in his direction.

"She wants to meet with me," Anthony said, folding his arms across his chest. "Although I missed Signora Barden's call, I spoke to an American priest by the name of Daniel Neumann, a close friend of the family's. He said that she has concerns she would like to share with me."

Michael pursed his lips. "What *concerns?*"

"I do not know for sure. According to Daniel, she is in Rome to attend Genovese's funeral and asked if we could meet. Apparently, she is in great distress, so I agreed to see her."

"Distress over the death of Ceste?"

"I have no way of knowing. Once I meet with her, I will have a clearer picture."

Michael stared for a moment in silence. "Very well," he said, snuffing out the cigarette stub and grabbing his coat and hat from the chair. "We will leave it at that for now. My *investigatore* will reach out to Signora Barden, now that I know she is in Rome."

Anthony stood also, but remained on the opposite side of the table. "I am certain she would be willing to have a word with the Carabinieri. I can't believe she has anything to hide from you."

Michael paused halfway to the door and looked back over his shoulder. "For now, we will assume that is the case."

Chapter 14

Grace stood at the door of Manny's spare bedroom. Like the rest of his apartment, it was cramped and dirty, but unlike the rest, it resembled a sophisticated research facility. The stale air was tainted by the smell of photographic chemicals, burnt coffee, and—thank heavens—the vanilla-scented candle she had given him for his birthday.

Stacks of books, printouts, maps, and diagrams covered a large table in the center of the room, and he'd tacked a huge periodic chart of elements on the right wall. Above hung a wooden crucifix gilded in brass. Three desktop computers occupied tables along the left wall, each featuring large, high-definition color monitors. A nuclear physics textbook sat propped open next to one on religious history, and a Bible rested on a thick book entitled, *Theories in Quantum Mechanics*. Manny Lusum…to a tee.

"Impressed?" Manny asked as he set her suitcase on the floor.

Grace spun around. "Sorry."

"No worries." Manny winked. "You've got *Top Secret* clearance around here."

She returned her gaze to the crowded room. "What *is* all this?"

"I like to call it my war room."

"Who are you at war *with*?"

"The scientific establishment." He took on a more sober look. "With anybody who thinks the Shroud of Turin is a clever forgery. With everyone who looks at it as just another pointless religious relic."

"Good luck with that."

"I don't mind being the underdog. Makes it more fun."

"What's this?" She picked up a spiral-bound stack of paper, the word *Draft* scrawled across the blank cover page in bright red.

"That's what I've been working on now for almost a year. Actually, twenty years is more like it."

An aching shoulder reminded Grace she still carried the gym bag she'd hauled up the stairs from the taxi. She dropped it on the floor with a thud and fanned the pages of the thick document with two hands. "Your thesis?"

"The one and only."

"How close are you to finishing?"

"Very." He shoved his hands into his jeans pockets and rocked back on his heels. "Just working on all the reference data. That's what all this is about," he said as he tipped his head toward the maze of technology.

"I can't believe it." Her gaze tracked across the room again. "So you think you can really *prove* it?"

"I believe so, or at least prove it's a valid theory." Manny's brow knit into tight lines across his forehead. "I love that you're interested in my work, but we should be focusing on your mom's issues."

He was right again. Now was not the time to be immersing herself in Manny's world of strange energies and exotic atoms. She shrugged and nodded.

He plopped down in front of one of the monitors. "Let's check this out."

Grace perched on the corner of the table as he began typing. Her thoughts wandered away from the background sound of keystrokes and mouse clicks until her phone signaled the receipt of a text message. The CNN news update scrolling across the screen seemed surreal: *Pope Peter the Second, dead at 81. Details to follow.*

Grace tried to speak, but Manny interrupted her. "Wow, I was assuming it was a bunch of conspiracy theory nonsense. I'm not so sure now."

Grace decided the news could wait. "My mom's not a liar," she said.

"Didn't say she was. But Ceste's story sounded like something out of a John Grisham novel."

"And?"

"Well, there's no mention of any missing relics on the Vatican website or in any news stories that I could find. At least none in recent history. But if an important relic *were* missing, I'm not surprised they would keep it a secret. Especially something of a sensitive nature like Ceste mentioned."

Grace shrugged, waiting for more.

"However, according to the Academy's website, this Adakem guy is the real deal. A *big* deal, actually. For one thing, he's . . ." Manny paused. "He *was* a full Professor Emeritus in the Pontifical Academy of Science. But, get this, he was also one of Pope Peter's senior advisors. Guess who else is?"

She shook her head.

"Your mom's friend, Cardinal Anthony Lombardi."

Grace dry swallowed the lump in her throat. "The guy in line to be the Pope?"

He nodded. "That means they definitely knew one another."

"So far, I don't like how this is going." She sat in a chair next to Manny's and scooted closer to the screen. "What else?"

"Well, I *know* the Academy's biology group began studying molecular genetics in the early sixties. By the eighties, it was a well-established discipline. So, Ceste's claim about the Life Sciences group doing morally questionable science is at least in the realm of possibility."

"How could they get away with that sort of thing?"

"Remember, the Academy operates independently," Manny said. "They could easily have had secret research going on within Life Sciences, projects the Vatican could have been totally unaware of."

"What about the Archives guy?"

"Guys."

Grace tilted her head.

"Look at this. Your mom said Ceste referred to the prefect who smuggled out some relics in 1983. Turns out, he died mysteriously in 1985, and the man who replaced him at the time was named Capello." Manny pointed to a photo of a distinguished looking man dressed in a red robe and skull cap with a large silver crucifix hanging from his neck. "I recognized his name because he's a big shot in the Church now. Another cardinal and *another* personal advisor to Pope Peter, like Adakem and Lombardi."

"He died," Grace said.

Manny cocked his head at Grace and turned back toward the monitor. Repositioning the cursor, he said, "I don't think so. I just saw Capello referenced recently in an article on—"

"I mean, Pope Peter. He's the one who died. I just got a text a few minutes ago."

Manny closed his eyes. His lips murmured something, probably a prayer. Grace waited in silence. When he looked up, she stroked his forearm.

"I'm sorry. I know you thought very highly of him."

"He was a good man," Manny said with a deep sigh. "But he was very sick. He's in a better place now."

"I'm sure."

He pulled the rubber band holding his ponytail until it broke. Tossing it in the trashcan next to his desk, he ran his fingers forcefully through long, dark hair before turning to her. "Lombardi and Capello definitely know one another, and your mom needs to be aware of that before she speaks to Lombardi. I wouldn't be surprised if Capello was a member of the Evangelist group, too."

"Why do you think that?" she asked.

"Check this out." He turned back toward the computer screen. "Capello's background. In addition to being a cardinal and Prefect of the Archives, he was the Archbishop of Sicily at one time and President of the Pontifical Council for the Family."

"Is he a member of the Academy?"

"He's not a scientist. But here's a reference to him in an early document being called John of Patmos after ordination. Most priests don't change their names, and he obviously didn't continue to go by that. I mean, he's Cardinal Capello now."

As Manny's fingers danced across the keyboard, Grace clasped her hands beneath her chin. There were too many coincidences. Too many connections. Something nudged at her subconscious, but it was far too deep to locate.

"Maybe it's just coincidence," Manny said, interrupting her thoughts. "Maybe not. But it seems the Academy came officially under the protection of St. John the Evangelist in 1836. Seems like a pretty big coincidence to me."

Grace sighed.

"It gets better."

"How?" She asked the question calmly, but she didn't feel it.

"I saw a familiar name in the list of the early Academy members. Turns out, a key scientist with the Academy in 1870 had the same last name." Manny clicked on the link. "Look at this," he said. *Benedetto Capello, Biologist* appeared on a screen entitled, *Academy History*.

Grace grabbed the mouse and tried to click to find the biologist's background. Nothing happened. "That's weird," she said, leaning back. "What about the Evangelists themselves? Can you check them out?"

He hammered away on the keyboard for a few seconds. "Nothing," he said, staring at the screen. "There are a few obscure references to religious groups around the world with similar names, but nothing about the group Ceste mentioned to your mom. If they *do* exist, they've managed to keep a pretty low profile."

"So, as far as we know, everything Ceste told my mom was true." Grace stood, walked back to the room's only door, and leaned on the frame. From behind her, bright sunlight shone through the living room windows, but the small apartment felt cold. Grace rubbed her arms. "Mom's really upset about all this."

"Sounds like she might have a reason to be," he said. "I don't know whose toes got stepped on, but we're talking about some very powerful people. Stealing from the Vatican Archives took some major chops. If your mom got caught up with those people—" Manny stopped abruptly.

Those people? Her mom knew Ceste well, probably more than she was letting on. He was sending her a secret package. She knew Lombardi. Lombardi seemed to know everyone. "I'm going to call her," Grace said.

"Good idea, but you'll probably just get her voicemail."

"Maybe, but I can at least make sure she stocks up on holy

water." Grace feigned a thin smile and took a deep breath, before releasing it slowly. She dialed her mom's cell and absently scanned the periodic chart of elements for anything familiar as she leaned against the wall. H, Hydrogen . . . yep. C, Carbon . . . no doubt. AL, Aluminum . . . that's an element?

Voicemail. Again.

After the beep, Grace tried to think of what to say. She forced her lips to move, relaying as much as she could before being cut off by a second beep. She redialed. After getting voicemail again, she finished the bizarre story. "Please be careful. Oh, and call back soon?"

As Grace slid the phone into her purse, she felt a single tear in the corner of one eye. She didn't want to start crying—she might never stop. She took in a deep breath, hoping the special incense in Manny's apartment might be just what the doctor ordered.

$$\Omega$$

Grace wasn't surprised when she slipped into saying the blessing along with Manny. It felt right, especially when he added a special prayer for her mom. What surprised her was how easily a litany of prayers flowed through her mind, beseeching a God she wasn't sure she could trust.

"Pizza was a great idea for lunch," Manny said, as he bit into the last piece of pepperoni and sausage.

"It was." Grace dabbed a napkin to her lips. She felt better and wanted to stay that way a little longer. "Tell me about your Shroud theory."

Manny dropped the half-eaten pizza slice and looked up. "Now?"

"It'll take my mind off all this nonsense." Grace ran her fingers through her hair. "Impress me, Lusum." She plopped her elbows on her knees and leaned forward. "I'm *waiting*."

"You sure?"

Grace nodded. She was absolutely sure.

"Be careful what you ask for, Gracie."

"No pain, no gain."

He grinned and disappeared around the corner, wiping his hands on his shirt as he went. Seconds later, he returned with the draft copy of his thesis and placed it carefully on the kitchen table. "My hypothesis proposes a new type of experiment," he said as he sat down. "An experiment that will not only prove the source of the image as the crucified Christ but also the age of the Shroud *and* the specific location of the event."

"No way."

"Way." Manny extended a curled-up pinky finger. "Wanna bet?"

Grace laughed and, for the first time in days, it felt deep and genuine. She folded her arms across her chest. "Go on."

"My tests should prove *conclusively* that the image on the cloth is the byproduct of energy released from the body of the man in the Shroud, something akin to laser light. This light affected only the first layer of fibrils on the cloth, in other words, the primary cell walls. All with the same chromaticity and each with a coloration depth of less than 0.2 micrometers. In other words, the Resurrection's event horizon was recorded onto the linen cloth covering Jesus in a process something similar to the Big Bang. The information was right there in front of me the whole time but, for a while, it felt like I was chasing a ghost."

"Whoa, whoa." Grace reached across the tiny kitchen table and grabbed Manny's hand. "Pretend for a second I'm not a theoretical physicist like you. You need to pick words from the bottom shelf."

"Sorry." He grinned sheepishly. "I can get a little carried away.

Are you *sure* you want to hear this. It can be a little dry."

"You've been talking about it non-stop the whole four years I've known you, Lusum. I think it's high time I know more about this theory of yours. Just do me a favor and stick with English, okay?"

"I'll do my best." Manny opened the document and brought his hands together as if in prayer. For the next ten minutes, Grace watched the handsome young man in front of her, fascinated by the way his brain worked, by his ability to penetrate the fog surrounding complex concepts.

"Truly impressive," she said when he finished.

Manny twirled a pencil between his fingers. "The part about the particle radiation?"

"No, the fact you didn't take a single breath."

"That's just the Reader's Digest version." He poked her in the arm with his pencil. "Seriously, what do you think?"

"I try not to, but I'd sure hate to hear the *un*abridged version. You came up with all of this on your own?"

"Pretty much. A lot of the base research and some of the preliminary testing were on the web, but to my knowledge, no one has put forth this consolidated theory for serious consideration. I guess I'll find out if I'm right about that when this paper gets published."

"You are very impressive, Soon-to-be-Doctor Lusum." Grace got up and kissed Manny on the forehead. There was no denying his intelligence and passion. Her wall of denial continued to crumble and crack. How long before it disintegrated completely and exposed the longings she'd kept barricaded for so long?

Chapter 15

Manny clasped his hands beneath his chin as Grace quietly rearranged the food on her plate. The pleasant afternoon they had spent together was now just a distant memory. Five minutes had passed since the archbishop's call, five minutes since he'd given Grace the news. The silence seemed to scream.

A siren rose and slowly fell on the street while he waited. He tried to pick the right words. "It's only for one year."

She didn't speak.

During their entire four-year friendship, he'd never put physical distance between them. He knew how hard it was—for both of them. "I can't afford to pass up an opportunity like this, Grace. It's quite an honor to be selected."

She set down her fork and slowly dabbed the corner of her mouth with a paper napkin. "What exactly is the Pontifical Academy of Theology?"

Dropping his hands to his lap, he smiled at her question. Of course she wouldn't know. "It's an elite seminary run by the Vatican to reinforce the Catholic faith. I was extremely lucky to be asked."

She met his unsteady gaze with the same brooding eyes he had seen before.

"Archbishop Baggio has connections in the Vatican and got me the gig. But I swear, Gracie, I didn't even know he was working on it, or I would have told you. All I have left for my PhD is the thesis, and NYU doesn't care where I'm living when I submit it."

"Even in Rome?"

"Even in Rome."

"And they have to have you right now? You can't even finish this semester here in New York?"

Manny shrugged. "Seems so."

Grace lifted her glass and slowly sipped her wine. "The whole thing is ridiculous."

Ridiculous to you maybe, he wanted to say, but didn't. Instead, he tried to lighten the moment. "I figured since Peter passed away, they probably want me to be the next Pope."

"That's kind of above your pay grade, isn't it? Don't you have to at least be a priest first?"

"A mere technicality."

She pushed back her chair, got up, and walked to the window. "Are you sure the holy academy is ready for your version of Catholicism? You're pretty liberal for New York City, much less Vatican City."

He spoke to her back. "The Archbishop believes the Church needs young priests like me." And then he picked up both wine glasses and carried them to Grace. She took one, and he leaned back against the window frame, watching her sip slowly. "He believes we need to become more relevant in a time when humankind is splitting the atom and traveling to other planets. He also believes a spiritual leader will come along some day and bring the world religions together into one."

She looked at him, making no attempt to hide her displeasure.

"I don't agree with his theology, Grace. I'd say he's more of a religious philosopher than a priest."

Another silence fell between them. He hated this. He hated leaving her. And he hated his own conflicting feelings.

Surely, the feelings would pass. He wanted them to, didn't he?

"I'm not sure how well-received you're going to be in Rome," she said quietly. "I think they tend to frown on religious philosophers masquerading as priests."

He ran his tongue nervously over his upper lip.

"I don't think they would agree with a lot of the things I've heard you say over the years, Mr. Lusum. In fact, I'm surprised you're even in the seminary in the first place." She turned her gaze out the window. Leaning forward, she squinted.

"What?" Manny said.

"Look over there. At that roof across the street."

Manny followed the direction of her pointing finger. It looked like a figure, dark-clad. He grabbed his camera with the telephoto lens, but by the time he got it focused the apparition was gone.

"We get Peeping Toms every now and then. Just keep the shades drawn while you're in the bedroom."

Grace wrapped her sweater more tightly around her shoulders and pulled down the tattered blind. "Perverts."

"Let's finish our dinner."

"Then a shower?" Grace asked.

"Anything you want, but you need food first."

$$\Omega$$

Manny woke slowly to see Grace standing silently at the window again, staring out at a leaden sky. He slid his baseball bat under the futon and mumbled, "Morning."

"Good morning, sleepy head. I made coffee. Would you like some?"

"My kingdom for a cup." He rubbed the sleep from his eyes. "Have you been up long?"

"Long enough to know you keep strange bedfellows." She nodded at the bat's hiding place.

"Oh, that." He sat upright, fingers combing his unruly hair. "I'm probably the millionth person to live in this apartment over the years. No telling how many people still have keys, and you've seen the neighborhood."

Grace smiled and headed to the kitchen. "You were on a mission, Lusum. I would've needed the jaws-of-life to get that bat out of your arms."

"I suppose I just—"

"Wanted to protect me?" She set a steaming coffee on the low table and plopped down next to him. "You're *too* sweet."

He cradled his mug, breathing in the scent before his sipped. "Good coffee. Thanks." Another sip, and he asked, "How did you sleep?"

"Great. I think I probably felt safer last night than I have in a while. I owe you one."

He shook his head. "I'm glad you got some rest. You looked pretty beat last night."

"Well, it isn't often you find out that," she held up her index finger, "the dad you never knew is actually a priest and didn't run out on you like you'd thought." Another finger, "your mom's a fugitive." A third, "you were apparently attacked by a demon as a child, and—" She paused as she raised the fourth finger and leveled a hard stare at him. "Your best friend is moving to Rome."

"It's not as bad as it sounds," he said. "I think this will all sort itself out in the next few days. Then we can—"

"You seem to forget *we* won't be here in a few days, *Mr. Seminarian*. I'm going to be stuck here while *you* go gallivanting off to Rome, searching for your own personal Holy Grail."

"Grace, I . . ."

She shook her shoulders, waved away his words. "Sorry," she said. "I'm just being melodramatic. I'm sure you're right, this will sort itself out in a few days, and everything will be fine."

A ring tone floated in from the bedroom. "It's my mom," she said, leaping up to find the phone and returning with it pressed to her ear. "Mom?"

Chapter 16

Grace clicked off the phone. She was having another Oz moment, complete with wicked witches and flying monkeys. She wanted to click her heels three times and return to her life—the one she'd enjoyed before the emotional tornado had swept her away.

"I only picked up bits and pieces of the conversation," Manny said. "What's up?"

"I'm scared." She turned to face him, swiping at the tears that wouldn't stop leaking from the corner of her eyes. "Someone broke into Mom's room."

"Room? What are you talking about?"

"Her hotel room. In Rome. She got back from Father Ceste's funeral this morning to find her room had been ransacked."

"What did they steal?"

"That's the scary part. All of her stuff was thrown around but nothing was missing. She said some of her best jewelry was on the bathroom counter. Untouched. It wasn't a simple robbery. They were looking for something specific."

Manny leaned forward, a thin sheen of sweat on his forehead. "The package?"

"She thinks whoever killed Ceste might know about it after all. She wants me to check her house."

"Get your coat." He stood quickly. "I'm going with you."

$$\Omega$$

Grace's hands shook as she punched in numbers for her mother's cell phone. Manny had gone to check the back rooms of the modest Long Island bungalow where shattered glass lay strewn along with overturned furniture.

"It's been broken into too," Grace said in halting gasps. "Manny's looking around, but I think they went through the entire house."

"The mail, Gracie." Her mom spoke over a staticy connection. "Did they go through the mail?"

"I'm not sure, we came in through the garage." Grace looked up at Manny, now standing in the archway leading to the bedrooms. "Can you check the mail?" she said. "There's a box inside the entry foyer mounted on the wall next to the front door."

Manny nodded and hurried through the living room, disappeared through a double French door. Grace could hear papers being shuffled in one ear and her mother's heavy breathing in the other.

"It looks like they went through it all," Manny yelled. A second later, he came back through the door with an assortment of envelopes and flyers in his hands. "Nothing in the box. It's all over the floor."

"Is that Manny?" Kellen said.

"Yeah, he came with me."

"Ask him to look for anything with an Italian postmark."

"Manny, look for an Italian—"

"Way ahead of you, Grace." He'd disappeared again and was yelling from the entry foyer. A few seconds later, he said, "Nothing here from outside the U.S."

"Get out of the house, Grace. *Now*."

"But we haven't checked the—"

"Now. I mean it." Her mother sounded frantic. "They may still be there or nearby. Go."

As Grace hurried toward the kitchen, she called to Manny. "We need to go."

He reemerged from the foyer and didn't hesitate. He raced to the door leading back to the garage and held it open for Grace as she grabbed her purse.

"Grace." Her mother's voice sounded urgent. "On the way out, grab my set of keys in the drawer by the back door."

"Mom, I already have your keys. Why do I—"

"Just do it."

Manny slammed the door behind them and used the remote keypad to close the garage door before they dashed to the sidewalk. Grace cradled the cell phone under her chin as she placed the keys together in a side pocket inside her purse. "We're out. Do you want me to call the police?"

"Not yet. Father Ceste told me to be careful what I said and to whom I said it. He didn't know how wide their reach is. For now, just get yourself away from the house."

"We're already past the Fitter's place." Grace huffed as she half-ran down the sidewalk. "Why do I need these other keys?"

"The key to my Post Office box is on that ring," her mother said. "Father Ceste's package may have been too big for my mail slot. I use the Aquebogue branch on Linda Avenue. Can you go there now and check it?"

"I guess so, but I don't—"

"Hold on." Her mother called to someone in the background, "Just a minute," before coming back to Grace with, "Hotel security's at the door. I'll call you when I finish up here. Are you okay for now?"

"Sure. I'll talk to you later." Grace dropped the phone into her purse, shivering in the cold wind.

"What was that all about?" Manny checked over his shoulder.

After she filled him in, she asked, "Can I keep you out a little longer?"

"I'm not going to bail on you now, Barden. I think it's the only way we're going to get any answers."

She slid her hand into the crook of his arm and leaned into him, hiding from the wind. Up ahead, a large man in a black overcoat turned his back to them, trying to light a cigarette. They crossed the street, and when she looked back a second later, he was gone.

Chapter 17

Comandante Generale Michael Lombardi tried not to be awed by the Vatican's Palace of the Concatinate as a secretary ushered him into the office of Cardinal-Carmerlengo Tarcisio Marini. Approaching the ornate desk, Michael bowed his head. "Thank you for agreeing to meet with me, Your Excellency."

Clad in a simple black robe with red sash and a white Roman collar, Cardinal Marini narrowed his eyes. "Eminence."

"Excuse me?"

Marini waved Michael to one of the two chairs facing his desk and waited before saying, "The official address is Your *Eminence*. *Excellency* is used for a Bishop or Archbishop."

Michael shifted in his seat to keep from rolling his eyes. "Your Eminence, my condolences on the death of His Holiness."

"Thank you. Peter will be greatly missed around the world."

"I trust His Holiness passed peacefully."

"He struggled in his final days," Marini said, "but his pain and fears were not in the death itself."

"Fears?"

"Whatever these were, I am afraid they accompanied him to his grave, may his soul rest in peace."

Michael Lombardi lowered his head and made the sign of the cross. He'd return to the subject later. "I know this is a busy time for you."

"*Si*, Comandante. It is." Marini leaned back and steepled his fingers as if in prayer. "However, the security of Church leadership is of utmost importance. Your brother's included."

Ah, yes, his brother the cardinal. The brother who *perhaps* harbored secrets. "How is Anthony?"

"He is well, although we are all saddened by Peter's death and the horrible crimes."

"Which brings me to the purpose of my call."

"Ah."

"Security, of course. But first," Michael said, trying not to be annoyed by the cleric's tone, "we must consider the bigger picture."

"My time is limited." Marini's eyes grew darker, colder. "From what I have been told, Comandante, you have a tendency to *draw* the big picture rather than merely to observe it. Please be so kind as to get to the point."

"*Certamente*." He leaned forward, focused on Marini. The Carmerlengo would not be easy to intimidate. "The string of unusual events in recent days strikes me as quite odd."

"The murders?"

"They were not simply murders, Your Eminence. They were assassinations. Although we have yet to find a direct connection between the woman slaughtered in the church and the two men at the Colosseum, the brutality of the deaths appears to be intended to convey a message, in my professional opinion. We have not ruled out serial murders, perhaps by someone with a personal grudge against the Church."

Marini's fingers, still steepled, tapped against each other.

Michael watched for a moment before continuing. "Also, we have the College of Cardinals coming into Rome for conclave much sooner than normal. And, of course, the highly unusual proclamation scheduled for tomorrow night."

"Save Peter's death and conclave, I fail to see any connections."

"The fact that these events all happened within forty-eight hours would probably strike the average person as nothing more than coincidence, but I do not believe in coincidence."

Marini raised an eyebrow. "I am not good at riddles."

"Then let me be more explicit. I believe a connection exists between the Vatican's Pontifical Academy of Science and these murders."

As the interim leader of the largest church on earth, the Carmerlengo stood in the eye of a religious and political hurricane. And yet Marini recovered quickly from what appeared to be an involuntary flinch. "What you suggest is ridiculous," he said. "Academy scientists are not murderers."

"I make no official statements at this point, Your Eminence. However, the facts speak for themselves. The dead woman was a nun who had served at the Academy. She mysteriously disappeared for years before showing up brutally murdered in a confessional booth at Santa Maria della Concezione."

Michael paused, waiting for some reaction. When the other man remained stoic, he continued. "The Vatican's science academy and Cardinal Lombardi are the only known connections between the Colosseum victims." Still nothing, not even a raised brow. "A day later, you have the untimely death of a Pope who has been known to be at odds with the scientific community. And then comes the announcement of an immediate call for conclave and of the televised reading of a posthumous declaration from His

Holiness. To take place in seventy-two hours."

"There will be no—" Marini raised his fist above the desk, but before he completed the movement, he paused and folded his arms across his chest. In a calm voice, he said, "I would prefer you not make assumptions, Comandante Lombardi."

Alarm bells went off in Michael's head. He'd seen that angry reaction. Eyes did not lie. But they could pretend, and the Carmerlengo assiduously avoided looking into his. "False assumptions often litter the road as we try to solve a crime. It is part of my job to make connections and decide which are true and which are false."

"The absence of facts can often lead to fiction, can it not, Comandante?"

Michael suppressed a smile. The man was intelligent, certainly. One couldn't rise to his rank without being smart—and probably clever. Or did he mean *crafty*? "We have many concerns with the events of this week," he said. "Not the least of which is the content of the Papal proclamation."

"As I told your office several times already, no one knows the specifics of the proclamation. I was Peter's confidant, and I have no knowledge as to its exact contents."

Michael paused and waited, hoping silence would elicit more information. Marini again seemed unmoved. "This is highly unusual, Your Eminence. And therefore unacceptable, because I cannot rid myself of the idea that all of these issues are related."

"Do you assume that from a point of logic, Comandante?"

"At the moment, let us call it an educated guess." Michael kept his tone level. "I am paid to make suppositions based on evidence and fact, suppositions that will either be confirmed or not as we follow leads. My job is to solve these murders and to provide stringent security for the conclave."

"You must be careful with your suppositions. Careful that they do not lead you to a conspiracy theory that has no basis. Conspiracies can be contagious."

"True. But conspiracies themselves may also run many layers deep."

"I am not sure I follow you. How deep?"

"All the way to hell." Michael's words seemed to echo around the large office.

The Carmerlengo wheeled his chair to the window that overlooked the courtyard. With his back to the room, he said, "Have you uncovered any information that could substantiate your *professional* insights? Any physical evidence?"

Michael did not care for the cleric's tone, but he kept his voice calm. "Some. We have discovered the existence of a woman who may have information. We will question her shortly." He glanced down at his wristwatch. "Ah, she awaits me even now. We believe she may be able to shed some light on recent events."

"A woman?"

"A member of the American media. She is in Rome to attend Father Ceste's funeral."

"They were friends?"

Standing, Michael slid his notebook into the breast pocket of his overcoat. "It appears so. Now, if you will excuse me, Your Eminence."

The words seemed to hang in the air. Marini pressed a button on his armrest and maneuvered his wheelchair to his office door. "It was a pleasure to see you again, Comandante Lombardi. I, too, have other demands on my time. I trust you will keep me posted on any further developments."

At the door, Michael reached out and kissed the ring on

Marini's extended hand. "Of course."

The edge in Marini's voice seemed to soften. "You must have more faith, Michael. Seek, and ye shall find."

"You are welcome to seek via faith, Your Eminence. I shall search using more conventional methods. However, do not be surprised if we wind up at the same place."

Chapter 18

Grace considered the events of the past few days as late afternoon shadows lengthened on the narrow city streets outside of Manny's apartment. Connections formed, broke apart, and formed again, circling around theories that made sense one minute and seemed ludicrous the next. The truth was, nothing made sense.

She eyed the mysterious package out of the corner of her eye. About the size of a shirt box, it was wrapped in plain brown paper and had her mother's name and address in black print in the center. She hit redial on her phone and waited. Voice mail again. She disconnected.

Manny called from the kitchen. "Still no answer?"

"I've tried four times. It goes immediately to voice mail."

"Four times?"

"The last two were just to hear her voice." She sighed. "I miss her, Manny."

"It's probably just a dead battery. I'll bet she doesn't have a converter for her charger. You can't plug American electronics into most European plugs without one."

Her neck muscles relaxed. It could be that simple. "She did leave in a hurry."

"Here." He pushed the innocuous package to the other side of the coffee table and perched on the futon, setting a thick glass mug down in front of her. "Camomile with honey, your favorite."

"You're too good to me, Lusum." She wrapped her hands around the mug and took a sip of the hot tea, inhaled deeply, and released a slow breath. "Perfect," she said, distracted by Manny's intense focus, the depth in his eyes, the warm smile on his face. "I don't know what I'm going to do without you."

"I'll be back." He said. It sounded like a promise. "It's only a year commitment."

"What if they ask you to stay? You'll have to if you're going to be the next Pope. I doubt they'll move the Vatican to New York City."

His eyebrows danced over laughing eyes. "Good point."

"Are you sure this is right for you? Your dad could use a smart physicist like you. Who will run the company for him when he retires? How will he even stay in business unless people like you stay around and invent things?"

"I can't turn my back on my calling, Gracie, even for someone I..."

She caught her breath. Even for someone he *loves*? The simple word spun around in her head, bumping into others like *passion* and *commitment*. Clearing her throat, she tried to keep her tone casual. "What?"

"You're my best friend, Gracie. You know I'll always be there for you."

Best friend? *Always?* Sure. From four thousand miles away. Would he ever realize that God also valued other vocations, ones that included marriage and children? "Sounds great, except you're going to be in Rome."

131

"A plane ride away. And you can call me any time."

"You'll be busy with priestly stuff."

"You could visit me over the holidays."

"Whatever." Enough of that. "I think we need to open the package."

Manny exhaled loudly. He looked cautious as he picked up the package and examined it carefully. "I'd love to, Grace, but I'm not so sure we should. People have died, and it has something to do with what's in this box."

"Everything my mom told us yesterday was true. I don't think there's any reason why we should question her today. If this box contains information worth killing for, she's going to want to know what's in it, sooner rather than later."

"That's the exact reason she probably *doesn't* want you to read it."

"Nobody knows about you or your apartment. They searched the mail and the house and came up with nothing. For all they know, it could be anywhere. I think we're safe here." Grace paused. "I have to wonder if Mom would be better off if I opened it or not. Since she won't be back in the States for a few days, I think she'd want me to."

He stared at the box and over at her. "Good point."

She reached for it, but something stopped her. "You open it."

He took a deep breath, tore the brown paper, pried open one end of the box, and peered inside. "There are three or four things in here."

"Pick one."

He pulled out a large manila envelope with *Kellen* handwritten on the front. He fondled it for a few seconds, peered back inside the box, and slid the envelope across the table toward her. "This is probably the best place to start."

Picking it up, she flipped it around in her hands. No clues on the outside. "I'm having second thoughts."

"You were right, Grace," he said. "You *need* to know."

She sighed as she carefully peeled back the adhesive flap and slid the pages onto her lap. "The letter's addressed to *Padre Genovese Ceste*, but it looks like it's in Italian."

Manny examined the first page and turned it over. "Here. It's translated on the back." He began flipping through the pages, handing them to her one by one.

"He must have done it for my mom. Boy, his handwriting stinks." She began reading but stopped when Manny interrupted her.

"Listen to this. He ends with, 'In case we do not meet again this side of heaven, Genovese, may God's blessings be with you always. In Christ, Francis.'"

"Francis. He was the other murdered guy, wasn't he? Doctor Adakem."

"Think of what this means, Grace."

"I am. Now, let me finish this," she said, picking up where she'd stopped. Random words leapt off the pages, words like "discovery," "unprecedented," and "astonishing." Reaching the end, she leaned back and sighed. "Oh, my."

He waited.

"You've got to read this. You've been right all along."

"Talk to me," he said, grasping her hands in his.

"Your thesis . . . this letter. They know the Shroud is real."

Chapter 19

Father Genovese Ceste
Congregation for the Doctrine of the Faith
Piazza del S. Uffizio, 11
00193 Roma, Italy

Dear Genovese:

As I write this letter to you, my heart is heavy. It bears a profound burden of guilt, a guilt I find very difficult to relate to you, my old friend. I should not have turned away from you and your testimony to me so many years ago, as you were right in confronting me. I was wrong in so many ways.

This letter contains much of what I hope to share with you in person just a few hours from now. The rest, which I struggle to put into words, you will find in the Academy White Paper I am including in this package.

When I first joined the Academy, I considered it a great honor. I *viewed our work as many do within these hallowed halls, a means for God to reveal His creation to mankind. I was too quick to view any science as good science and, if the truth be told, it was science itself that eventually became my god.*

As a result of the fervor of my youth, I joined the covert organization I once tried to recruit you into, the Evangelists. We sought out miracles from science and turned our back on those from our Creator.

I have a story to tell you, Genovese, one that you will find very difficult to believe. One that needs to see the light of day, a day I pray I live to see. In addition to official Academy documents that will substantiate my claims, I have also included a secret and holy relic whose value is beyond measure. They sit before me now as I write this letter with a shaky hand.

Manny looked up to see Grace staring at him, her knees huddled under her chin. "What is this? Pray I live to see?"

"It gets worse," Grace said.

Cold penetrated Manny's thick sweater as roiling black clouds darkened the sky outside his apartment window. He began to read again.

I have chosen to reveal these truths to you for two reasons, Genovese. One is that I trust you. I know your faith is undeniable, and I know your love for Christ and His Church is beyond reproach. The second reason is integrity. As a fellow scientist and respected priest, your reputation and credibility will be critical to putting an end to the evil that has infiltrated the Holy Mother Church.

The Evangelists are not just a group of rogue scientists within the

Academy. Their members also include a select group of high-ranking Catholic and Protestant clergy, businessmen, and politicians. They trace their origins back to the seventeenth century. To a time when Galileo attempted to convince the Church that the Earth revolved around the Sun, not vice versa, and was labeled a heretic. To a time when religion and science were at great odds with each other. To a time when their members were held in greater contempt than Galileo himself and, when discovered, were often burned at the stake.

I was recruited not just because of my passion for all things scientific, but also for my extensive training in molecular genetics. At first, I was indoctrinated by performing minor tasks involving the carbon dating of various religious artifacts. Eventually, however, I was exposed to the true purpose of the organization--to establish undeniable scientific proof that Jesus was God. I was provided with the most sacred of all test samples, the actual burial cloth of Our Lord.

Manny whispered, "The Shroud."

"Yes."

He finished reading just as a distant church bell chimed the hour. Rain slapped the window panes. Adakem had mentioned the Edessa Cloth and more. Much more.

Too restless to sit, he wandered over to stare at the bleak prospect below. "I can't believe it."

"He said there's proof of everything in the package," Grace said. "You need to help me understand all this. I'm so confused."

She sounded more scared than confused. He plopped down beside her, moving the box from the coffee table to his lap. "I'm not sure I get it all either," he said. "Dr. Adakem says he was given the actual Shroud of Turin for experimentation, right after the Savoys deeded it to the Church. I'm guessing the Evangelists created a duplicate of the Shroud in anticipation of the transfer and swapped it for the real one during the carbon dating tests."

Grace stared at him.

"The Evangelists confirmed the linen's origin as first century, not the Middle Ages as had been revealed by previous carbon dating. But they kept the findings to themselves instead of releasing the information to the public. What bothers me is the fact that he referred to the White Paper four times in the letter, but never said what was actually in it."

"Maybe they went beyond carbon dating? Maybe they actually performed experiments like the one you outlined in your dissertation?"

The thought had been dancing around in his head. "Maybe," Manny said. "But why didn't he just state that? The cat was already partially out of the bag with the carbon dating. Plus, that's no reason to kill people."

"And why would they want to keep it a secret if they could actually prove it was real?"

"That's the part that doesn't make any sense," Manny said. No, it was just one of the parts that made no sense. Had the Evangelists proved the Shroud's authenticity? Was his soon-to-be-published doctoral thesis, his life's work, already old news?

Grace shifted so that she was sitting cross-legged next to him on the couch. "Why don't we start with what we do know?"

"Good idea."

Categorization was a critical step to the scientific method and had often helped him organize his thoughts. He pulled a mechanical pencil from his shirt pocket, flipped the opened envelope over to its blank side, and wrote the words *First Century Carbon Dating Proof* to the right of the number one. Next to the number two, he wrote *Real Shroud replaced by Fake*.

137

"We pretty much figured that out yesterday."

"Could the actual Shroud be one of the stolen relics Ceste told Mom about?"

"I don't think so," Manny said. "It was too long ago. The Academy was given the task of confirming the Shroud's authenticity when the Church first got it way back in eighty-three."

"Oh. Right."

"Plus, they didn't need to smuggle the Shroud out of the Vatican Archives. The Evangelists had it from day one and simply placed the phony Shroud in the archives when they completed testing. What amazes me is that the Church never realized it."

"So, whatever experiments they performed were on the actual Shroud." He wrote the number three and *Experiments = Actual Shroud* on the back of the envelope. "The White Paper might explain—"

"Hold up. Before we go on, clear something up for me." She'd reached out to touch his arm. "*The Edessa Cloth* mentioned in Adakem's letter. What does that have to do with the Shroud of Turin?"

"He's claiming they're one and the same." He jotted down *Edessa Cloth = Shroud* next to the number four. "If that's true, and he claims there's proof in the box, we can also historically trace the Shroud all the way back to Jesus, not just rely on the carbon dating."

"You're getting ahead of me here."

He shoved the pencil above his ear. "Sorry. Edessa was the capital of the Assyrian kingdom of Osroene in what is now Turkey. King Abgar V of Edessa was converted to Christianity by Addai, one of the seventy-two disciples Jesus sent out after His resurrection. According to legend, Abgar wrote to Jesus, asking if He would cure him of leprosy. Jesus had already ascended by the time the letter arrived. However, as the story goes, the apostle Thaddeus brought Jesus' burial cloth to Abgar, and he was healed immediately."

"Manny Lusum, scientist and historian?"

Grinning, he bowed his head to acknowledge the tribute. "Well rounded, my dear," he said and flipped back into tutorial mode. "The story isn't well known outside of the Eastern Orthodox Church. Abgar's successor was a pagan, so the Archbishop of Edessa hid the cloth in the wall above the city's gate. In 944 A.D., the Byzantine Emperor Romanus sent an army to Edessa to remove the cloth and transfer it to the capitol. We know the Archbishop of Constantinople gave a speech about the cloth when it arrived, because the original transcript of that sermon was uncovered in the Vatican Archives, of all places. It was translated in 2004. It verified that the cloth contained a full-length image of the body and face of a man who had apparently been crucified. It also mentions bloodstains from a wound in the side."

"Amazing," she said. "But can you hold that thought for just a minute?"

"Sure," he said.

As Grace headed to the bathroom, he poured another cup of coffee and nuked it, calling to the closed door, "You want more joe?"

He heard a muffled 'No' and water splashing in the sink followed by the bathroom door creaking open.

"Thanks anyway," she said.

He lifted the heated cup. "You sure?"

"Yeah. My stomach's acting up from all this tension." Curling back on the futon, she waved him over and said, "Continue, please."

His set the cup on the table in front of his knees and began again. "Constantinople was sacked in 1204 during the Fourth Crusade, and many believe the cloth was stolen by a French knight.

The first historical reference to the Shroud of Turin was in 1390 when it showed up in Lirey, France. France, of course, was under the control of the Roman Church."

"Why did they change its name?"

"The linen cloth was moved to a chapel in Turin, Italy, in 1578, and gradually became known as The Shroud of Turin over the next few decades. No one on the Roman Catholic side has admitted the connection, so they would claim they're two different relics. Bottom line, it's a political thing."

"Political?"

"It all has to do with the separation of the Eastern Orthodox and Catholic churches," he said, running his fingers through his hair and dislodging the pencil. He retrieved it from the floor and set it on the envelope before taking a sip of his coffee. "In 330 AD, Emperor Constantine moved the capital of the Roman Empire from Rome to Constantinople. He was the empire's first Christian Emperor, and the move essentially established the Greek Church, or Eastern Orthodoxy, as it's known today."

"I had no idea the Roman Empire's capital wasn't in Rome," Grace said.

"It was for hundreds of years, in one form or another, but was moved to Constantinople in the fourth century. Then the Goths overran what was left of Rome in 410 BC. The Eastern Church survived and became known as the Byzantine Empire.

"A fount of knowledge, aren't you?"

"It's what we do."

"We who?"

"Eternal students. History buffs. You know."

She patted him on the knee, and he felt her touch reverberate through his body.

Okay, focus.

"The rivalry between the two branches developed. Which one would control Christendom? After years of charges of heresy and ex-communications on both sides, the two churches finally separated in 1054."

"I still don't get why that has anything to do with the Shroud."

"Well, think about it. If anyone can prove that the Shroud of Turin is actually the Edessa Cloth, the Roman Church would have no moral right to it and would have to return the Shroud to the Ecumenical Patriarch or some other Eastern Orthodox body. It would get even stickier because many Russian Orthodox believe the Eastern See moved to Russia after the fall of Byzantium, so they would have sole rights to the Shroud over all the other Orthodox. Bottom line, it's a political football the Roman Church wants no part of."

"All right, all right." She waved a little *get on with it*. "Why does Adakem even mention all this?"

"To establish historical credibility. He refers to a logbook in the package that details the history of the Shroud. It dates all the way back to the first century, to the death and burial of Jesus. Here's the really interesting part—according to Adakem, the beginning of that logbook contains the writings of St. Peter."

A frown settled on Grace's face. "Okay . . ."

A familiar ring tone sounded from her purse.

"Who's that," Manny asked.

"Becka. She's been like a mother hen since—"

"Don't answer it."

"Okay," she said, but she didn't look happy.

"This is too important. We've got to figure it out."

"I know. Go ahead."

"Okay. Adakem says Peter sent the Shroud and his personal letter with Thaddeus to Abgar, and the letter became the first entry in the logbook. There are also several lines in Adakem's letter, but they were scratched out in a different color ink. Like there was something in the Adakem letter Ceste didn't want anyone to see. My guess is, he originally intended to send your mother just the letter and hold onto the rest . . . but things must have heated up fast."

"Weird," Grace said.

"Do you realize what all this means?"

"More proof it's the real deal?"

"A lot more than that." Manny tried to loosen his grip on the cardboard box. "If what he says is true, there's something in here that will rock the Christian Church around the world."

"Come again?"

"Most of the books in the New Testament are actually letters written by an apostle to a person or a church, much like Peter's letter to Abgar. They were called epistles, and Peter wrote two of them. The First Epistle of Peter, which is usually just referred to as First Peter, was a letter he wrote to the churches in five provinces of Asia Minor. Second Peter was written just prior to his death at the hands of Nero and . . ."

His stomach muscles suddenly contracted, and he fought to keep the bile in his throat. Another coincidence? No. There had been too many already.

"What?" She reached toward him again. "What's the matter?"

"Nero crucified Peter not long after he wrote his second epistle." He damped down the lump in his throat and quietly added, "Upside down."

Chapter 20

Grace recoiled, searching for something, anything, to replace the vivid images of the Colosseum murders. Her words tumbled out in a breathless rush. "I'd forgotten Peter was crucified. How could I have forgotten? And upside down?"

Manny's raised brows were her only answer.

She took a deep breath. "You don't think it's a coincidence." She didn't make it a question. "So, you're telling me that box contains a third letter from Peter? A missing part of the Bible?"

His fingers slid over the box's cardboard surface as if he were reading Braille. "No, I'm not saying that," he mumbled. "Some letters written by the apostles never made it into Scripture. This letter may have only been read by Abgar and perhaps a few others, so that alone could have kept it out."

Grace hoped she looked more relaxed than she felt. "But it doesn't matter, does it? I mean, even if he actually wrote it. Because it only went to that guy, Abgar."

"Right." He stared at the box and whispered. "You do know that we're on the verge of a major discovery here. Much bigger than the Dead Sea scrolls."

"I get it. You look. I'm going to go try to reach my mom again."

This was making her crazy, worrying about her mother, thinking about the contents of that box. Her legs felt stiff and crampy. She walked into the bathroom, dialing her mother's cell. As it rang, she stared unseeing at her reflection.

The odd ring tone of a European connection sounded in her ear. Her call again went to voice mail.

Where was her mom?

Grace's stomach rumbled and she thought for a second she might lose her lunch. She set the phone on the sink and sat on the toilet, because it would be better to be right here if she did.

Manny might be discovering something important. Something else important. She ought to go back out there and help.

Finally, she relieved her overactive bladder, settled her stomach with some pink tablets Manny had in the medicine cabinet, and returned to the living room.

"You've been gone a while," he said, barely looking up. "You okay?"

"Yeah. I still can't reach Mom." She stared hard at him. "You look awful."

His face appeared ashen. "You won't believe."

She eased down next to him on the futon. "It's in there, isn't it? Peter's letter to Abgar."

He nodded.

"That's unbelievable!" She threw her hands over her mouth to muffle a scream. "Handwritten?"

Another nod. His lips trembled slightly as he spoke. "I scanned the logbook, and it definitely chronicles the Shroud's history over the years. This is a photocopy of the original entries. The first page has Peter's original letter to Abgar, written on parchment."

"That's incredible."

"The rest is here. Seventeen additional pages. I've been trying to count the number of people who made entries. I'm up to thirty. And so far, I've recognized eight different languages. Look here," he said, flipping through the pages. "That's Arabic. Of course, there's Greek and Hebrew and everything in between."

"What about Peter's letter?"

He flipped back to the first page. "It specifically refers to Jesus' image on the cloth and asks Abgar to make sure it is protected for future generations."

"I can't believe what you're saying."

"Grace, I . . . There's more, something I can't seem to wrap my brain around."

A familiar unease returned. She was almost afraid to ask what he meant. "Tell me."

He took both of her hands in his. "Listen to me carefully."

"You're scaring me."

"Please, Grace, listen."

He closed his eyes as he inhaled deeply again. When he exhaled, his eyelids lifted, and she saw something in his familiar, dark eyes that had not been there before. Something that made her bite her lip.

"Peter . . ." He looked everywhere but at her. "Peter's isn't the only handwriting on the first page."

She tightened her grip on his hands and waited, her feeling of dread intensifying.

"Look at this." He pointed to the photocopy of the first page. "I've read the translation, but look at those nineteen words written above Peter's letter. Different handwriting." He flipped to the next two letters. "These are also in Hebrew, but in a completely different handwriting."

"What do they say?"

"What matters was *who* may have written the words."

His grip had tightened so much that her fingertips were numbing. She wiggled her hands free, fisting them a few times to revive the feeling in them. What he was suggesting seemed so impossible that she could barely wrap her mind around it.

"You're not saying . . . ? Are you sure?"

He shook his head.

"Jesus?"

Silence.

"The actual handwriting of Jesus of Nazareth?"

He coughed as if to release his words, and when he spoke, his voice had a new edge to it. "There's no record of Jesus ever writing anything Himself, except the time He wrote something in the dirt in John's gospel."

She knew the story. "When the crowd wanted to stone the prostitute?"

He nodded. "Scribes were responsible for physically recording much of the Old and New Testaments. So, although the words may be Jesus', there's no way to know if He actually wrote it Himself. But if it could be His handwriting . . . I mean, can you imagine? The whole idea has me a little freaked out." He slid out a bundle wrapped in thick gray plastic and slid it toward her. "Be careful."

She hefted it cautiously and rotated it around in her hands. Although definitely inert, it was as though her fingers could sense something alive inside. Manny leaned forward as color slowly returned to his face.

"The plastic is designed to keep out harmful moisture and UV rays, not eyes," he said. "It looks like the original is typical of important documents from the first century, parchment pages sewn together with wool thread."

"What does it say?"

He cleared his throat, but he didn't pick up the translation. It was obvious he had it memorized. "'Abgar, son of Mannos,'" he began slowly. "'Blessed are those who have not seen, yet still believe. Your faith has healed you.' The Vatican document did not translate the two characters at the end, but the words are either Jesus' or someone quoting His words to the Apostle Thomas."

She replaced the package to its place on the table. "Was Abgar healed?"

"The historical record seems to indicate that."

"Incredible. How could any document last two thousand years?"

"Most didn't," Manny said. "Most were written on papyrus and didn't last very long. Parchment, on the other hand, is made from animal skins and was very durable. Before it was sealed in this plastic, I'm sure it was well protected in a dry climate somewhere, probably sealed in clay jars."

"Did you read it all?"

"I did. I just can't believe what I read. After Jesus' words, the second entry in the book is exactly what we thought, Peter's letter to Abgar." His dark eyes now sparkled like a black diamond. "Peter actually says in the letter that he removed the burial shroud from Jesus' tomb late on the third day."

"Easter."

She could imagine him rubbing his hands together with all the excitement that seemed ready to burst. None did, except through his eyes.

"What's really interesting is the fact that Peter didn't even notice the image at the time. He told Abgar about the women who were confronted by angels outside the empty tomb. He didn't see the image on the Shroud until days later."

"Amazing."

"It is, isn't it?" Manny's right knee started to jump.

She watched it. He was going to need a good run after all this.

"Peter added his words to the ones on the parchment," he said, "then gave the Shroud and the letter to Thaddeus, who took it to Edessa."

"I don't know what to say." Grace's own energy level began to rise. Maybe they'd run together. *Breathe*, she reminded herself. "This is so huge."

"Way beyond huge. This whole thing will rock the world if it goes public." He slid the Vatican document toward her. "The rest of it is essentially the log." Although just a copy, the yellowed paper looked like ancient papyrus, dried and splintered along brown edges. "The entries trace the history of the Shroud from the day Peter removed it from the empty tomb until the Savoy family deeded it over to the Roman Catholic Church. A span covering over nineteen hundred years."

Grace touched it, trying to imagine that length of time, that many years of history. "I can't believe it's here. That we're touching it."

"I know."

"Look," she said, standing up, because sitting no longer felt comfortable. "I need to move. You want something? Tea? More coffee?"

Manny seemed surprised by her question. "Water?" he said.

"Water coming up."

She filled a mug and put it in the microwave for a cup of tea and got a glass down for Manny's water. During the two minutes it took for the water to boil, her thoughts returned to her mother in Rome, dead bodies, hidden documents, a bloody Shroud . . . and a cover-up.

She carried both her green tea and the glass back into the living room, setting Manny's in front of him and holding the mug between her hands to warm them. Manny upended the glass and finished half before he set it down far from the fragile documents.

"Okay," she said between sips. "Where were we?"

"I keep thinking that what we have here confirms some of the legends I had heard over the years. Not to mention what Adakem said in his letter."

"I got the bit about him saying the Shroud and the Edessa Cloth are the same thing, but what legends?"

"There are many. Did you know that the Germans tried to steal the Shroud in World War II?"

She hadn't. "You mean, like they stole all that art?"

"That was mostly to fund the war effort. It seems that Hitler was a big-time occultist and thought the Shroud was some sort of talisman with secret powers he could use. The Savoy family worked with the Roman Church to hide it in a Benedictine monastery in southern Italy during World War II."

"This is beginning to sound like Indiana Jones," she said and grinned when Manny responded with a momentary twinkle.

"There's a ton more, which makes me think the logbook must have actually traveled with the Shroud the entire time." His expression sobered as he lifted a document from the box. "There's more."

More? How much more could there be? She started to groan, but covered it with a cough.

"Ceste also included some information on the Evangelists." He held up two pieces of Vatican stationary stapled in the corner. "It's in his handwriting, so my guess is Adakem dictated it to him at some point. It provides an overview of the organization—people, places, goals."

"Names?" she asked.

He nodded. "There are only twelve official members in the

Order. Each one is referred to as an apostle."

"Did you recognize anyone?"

"Several names sounded familiar, but Capello wasn't one of them."

"Capello?"

"The guy we came across the other day when we were doing research. The Papal advisor who's connected to the Academy."

"So, he's not involved?"

"I wouldn't assume that," Manny said. "He could still be pulling strings in the background. Listen to what Ceste wrote under the heading, *The Truth*." He spread the document open on the coffee table. "They seek to establish a new covenant between God and science, an unholy alliance based on human pride and arrogance."

"His *truth* is starting to sound a lot stranger than fiction."

"You don't have to be a Catholic historian to know the Church has guarded many secrets over the years," Manny said, his tone disgusted. "However, I doubt many could stack up to this. There are tons of catacombs that run beneath Vatican City, most of them not used for centuries. Apparently, in the mid-seventies, the Evangelists sealed off a large section under the Academy building, anticipating that they'd eventually get their hands on the Shroud. When they made the switch with the fake after the carbon dating tests, they began their experiments and operated covertly until 1990. Then they abandoned it."

He paused, and Grace could sense an emotion rising up in him she rarely saw. Anger. The fingers of one hand drummed against his thigh. She waited for the leg to start jumping again.

Instead, he said, "I'm trying to imagine men of God doing all this. Picture it—non-Academy scientists used to parade around in black cassocks so they'd blend in."

"Like I said, Indiana Jones. Or maybe James Bond."

"Sounds like it. What I want to know is what kind of experiments they conducted." He reached around the document toward a stack of bound paper and slid it in front of her. "It seems the details are recorded in the White Paper." His fingers plowed through his hair. "It's Greek. I don't read Greek."

She opened the thick document and scanned the first page. Strange curves and lines seemed to merge together, forming one giant question mark. "The lettering across the title page is different. '*Lasciate ogni speranza voi ch'entrate.*'"

"That's Italian. The handwriting also looks like Ceste's. Abandon all hope ye who enter here."

"I didn't know you could speak Italian."

"A little." His eyes had darkened again. "It's a quote from Dante's Inferno, required reading in my first year of seminary."

"Oh, yeah," Grace said. "I remember that from Language Arts in high school, the infamous words inscribed on the gates of hell. Any idea what *Superficies Secretum* or *Deus Duo* mean?" Grace asked, reading the only typed words on the cover page.

"Those are Latin. *Superficies Secretum* means Top Secret. *Deus Duo* means God Two."

She frowned up at him. "Sounds to me like they're trying to make science their true god. Putting God number two, behind science?"

"That's the way I interpret it."

"We need to find someone who can translate the White Paper," she said. "Somebody we can trust."

His hesitation caused her to raise her brows in question. "I know the perfect person, but you're not going to like it."

"I don't care who it is," she said. "This may have something to do with my mom's safety and I . . ."

Then she grasped his inference.

"He studied Palaeography in seminary, Gracie, and continued to study ancient languages during his priesthood. He's one of the best linguists in the state, and you know he can be trusted."

"I don't care if he can speak Swahili. I'd rather not see that man again."

"You don't have to. I'll handle it. I can be back at St. Williams in twenty minutes if I take the Lexington Express. He's our best option. Really."

A tense silence hung for several seconds, finally broken by the sound of Grace's cell phone. She reached into her purse and felt her first real smile of the afternoon crease her face.

"I've been trying to reach you, Mom. Where've you been?"

Barely intelligible words emerged, but what Grace could make out caused her to whisper under her breath.

"One Mississippi . . ."

Chapter 21

Manny's eyes blinked at the bright sunlight. For a moment, he resisted waking at all, trying to remain in the cocoon of a dreamless sleep. He lifted his head off Grace's shoulder to mumble, "Where are we?"

"About a thousand dollars farther than I can afford." Grace closed the airline magazine and shoved it back in the seat pocket in front of her. "I am *so* glad you finally woke up."

"Was I snoring?"

"You tried a few times. I need to go to the Ladies Room." Grace handed over the black nylon briefcase and unbuckled her seatbelt. "Your turn."

As she worked her way down the narrow aisle, he slid open the zipper. Adakem's letter, check. Hand-written Evangelists summary, check. Logbook copy and translation, check. White Paper, check. One of the most valuable religious relics in the history of mankind, check. All here. He zipped the case shut and placed his arms across it and focused his gaze on white puffy clouds drifting by thousands of feet below the Boeing 767.

"Hey." Grace interrupted his trance, slumping down in the aisle seat next to him. "I want to thank you again for coming to Rome with me," she said. "I'm not sure what I would have done without you."

"No big deal," Manny said. It *was* a big deal, but he wasn't letting himself go there. "I was flying out today anyway. I'm just glad I was able to change my flight and get on the red-eye with you."

"I just appreciate you being here for me." She leaned over and kissed him gently.

The touch of her lips on his cheek sent his heart into overdrive, matching the rhythmic pulse of the jet's engines. "We were in such a hurry to get to the airport last night that I still don't know why your mom was arrested."

"I don't think she was officially arrested," Grace said, worry lines puckering her brow. "She said she was just brought in for questioning. It turns out she was the last person Ceste called the night of his murder."

"How did they even know she was in Rome?"

"She thinks the hotel reported the break-in to the Italian police—the Cara-something—who had her name on some watch list."

"Carabinieri," he said. "The national gendarmerie of Italy."

"The who?"

"They're a branch of the armed forces that polices both the civilian and military populations. They have a tight relationship with the Vatican's Gendarme and the Swiss Guard, their elite military unit."

"I've heard of them. Don't they wear the colorful uniforms with the baggy pants?"

He grinned at her. "They secure entrances to the Palace and protect the Pope when he's in public. I wonder if your mom told Father Dan about the package."

Grace looked out the window for a few seconds in silence before saying, "That might explain why we couldn't reach him."

"Plus, Cardinal Lombardi knows Father Dan from . . ." He stopped abruptly. *Klutz.*

She squeezed his arm. "Not a problem. Ancient history."

He hoped so. He'd hate to add that worry to the burdens she carried. "He may have come over here for the funeral too."

Grace sighed. "The more I think about it, he *is* the only person we can really trust with this. I just hope we can track him down."

"Your mom will know how."

"Probably." A wistful look crossed her face. "I don't think she ever stopped loving him."

"I don't think Father Dan stopped loving your mom either, Gracie. They're both good people, good people who tried to do the right thing in their own way."

"I suppose so." She leaned her head on his shoulder. "This whole thing is just *so* weird."

"I know. Maybe not quite a movie, but still very unreal."

"My turn for some shuteye, boyfriend," she said, her voice drifting off on those words. Her eyelids drooped as she nuzzled deeper into his shoulder.

"Okay, sleep tight," he whispered, taking one hand off the nylon case and picking up hers. "Sweat dreams."

$$\Omega$$

Kellen Barden worked her way through the hordes headed in every direction. She ran her fingers through long red curls, hoping she looked better than she felt.

"Mom!"

The disembodied voice cut through the thick din of the Leonardo

DaVinci-Fiumicino Airport, as if on its own unique wavelength. Kellen stopped abruptly and spun around, searching for its source. Suddenly, a familiar face emerged from the crowd, lips peeled in a wide smile.

"Gracie!" Kellen screamed as she hurried toward her daughter. She wrapped her arms around Grace and squeezed hard, hoping to absorb at least some of the anxiety she had inflicted over the past few days. "It's so good to see you, sweetheart."

"You too, Mom."

Her daughter didn't look well—with a new tick accompanying dark circles under her eyes.

Manny approached, extending his hand, which Kellen took. "Manny Lusum! I can't tell you how much it means to me to know Grace has you as a friend, especially now."

Manny smiled and shrugged his shoulders. "It's been my pleasure, Mrs. Barden." He looked at Grace, and Kellen noticed something unexpected. The eyes of her daughter's best friend revealed a spark she'd never seen before. Something beyond friendship, *something* clearly reflected in her daughter's wide smile.

Grace leaned into Manny and kissed him on the cheek. "He's been wonderful."

"And to come all this way."

"No problem, Mrs. Barden," Manny said. "I was already scheduled to come here for seminary anyway."

"Here? In Rome?"

He nodded.

"I just found out about it yesterday," Grace said. "I can't believe we were able to get on the same flight. And a nice gentlemen changed seats with me so we could sit together."

Something didn't connect, but it would have to wait until another time. Kellen gestured toward the black nylon case slung over Manny's shoulder. "Is that it?"

He patted the case gingerly. "Everything Grace described to you on the phone . . . and more."

She shuddered at his ominous tone and the thoughts it conjured. Turning toward the baggage claim area, she spotted a large man in a black trench coat watching them. As soon as he noticed her attention, he changed direction and left.

"Get your bags," she said, keeping watch as they waited for the suitcases to slide out of the shoot.

Manny grabbed his first, then Grace's. Rolling the bags behind, they followed Kellen outside.

The man seemed to have vanished, and Kellen felt the tightness in her chest ease. Moments later they were in a taxi, headed east toward the city, Grace seated between the two of them.

"Where are we going?" Grace asked.

"Your father got me the appointment with Cardinal Lombardi," Kellen said, watching for some reaction from the driver. Seeing none, she lowered her voice and continued. "He knows most of what's going on and is anxious to meet with all of us."

Grace whispered back. "What exactly did you tell him?"

Kellen glanced again at the front seat. The driver seemed to know only a few words of broken English and had just begun a heated exchange with dispatch. A low-voiced exchange seemed safe enough.

"I told Daniel what you told me, and he shared everything with Cardinal Lombardi." With another quick glance forward, she said, "He left me a message saying Cardinal Lombardi summoned him to Rome and he would be at the meeting. I was surprised, to say the least."

Manny cast an apprehensive look at them both.

"What?" Grace asked.

"Lombardi seems to be connected to everyone," Manny said carefully. "Are you sure we can trust him, Mrs. Barden?"

"I'm not *sure* of anything," Kellen said. "But I put my daughter's life in the man's hands twenty-three years ago, and I have no reason not to trust him still. I know Grace's father feels the same way."

Grace frowned. "Manny says the White Paper's written in Greek, Mom, and it contains all the detail behind the experiments. He thought—he thinks Father Neumann might be able to do the translation."

Kellen could see the hurt in her daughter's eyes and felt a lump form in her throat. "He's probably right," Kellen said softly. "Daniel studied linguistics over the years, and I know we can trust him. Let's hope he's at the meeting, because it'll be next to impossible to see the cardinal again."

"I understand the Italian police called you in for questioning," Manny said. "Did you tell them anything?"

"They could have put a gun to my head, and I wouldn't have been able to tell them much. Not then. I said I was here to attend Father Ceste's funeral and left it at that."

Kellen sneaked a quick peak out the taxi's back window as they headed north on Viale Guglielmo Marconi toward Vatican City. As far as she could tell, no cars followed them. She breathed a sigh of relief and another when the rain began, shielding them from the view of others.

"I need to hear the whole story. It's not far to the Vatican entrance, so make it quick."

Chapter 22

Manny stared intently through the taxi's dirty window as worn wiper blades sluiced away heavy rain. Cars sloshed streams in every direction, obscuring the view of the city streets.

As quickly as it had begun, the deluge slackened, and the Holy City rose before them. The window of the vintage Fiat taxi framed the scene, stirring familiar images that felt like dusty memories. Memories of a place he had never before visited, giving the surreal scene the quality of a dream.

He shoved the door open before the taxi came to a complete stop and hopped out. A fog that drifted across the sidewalk and over the high stone walls had replaced the rain. A steeple seemed to disappear into the low-lying clouds, and he could almost imagine the granite finger of the holy place somehow touching heaven.

Kellen followed Grace out of the taxi and handed the elderly driver a folded stack of euros. "*Grazie.*"

"You're practically a native."

"It just means *thanks*," Kellen said and looked sheepish. "But you knew that."

Grace nodded, her own grin spreading. "I've got the 'thanks' down in several languages. It's useful."

Taking his time, Manny ushered them toward the security station. A young man, dressed in a simple blue tunic, brown belt, flat white collar, white gloves, and a black beret, appeared from out of the shadows as they were being processed by Vatican security.

Manny nudged Grace and whispered, "Swiss Guard."

"Where are the puffy pants?"

"Saved for public events. That's their regular duty uniform."

The officer approached, nodded respectfully, and said he'd been sent by *il Cardinale* Lombardi to help with the security process. He led them inside and down two flights of stairs and then through a maze of underground passages. Manny lagged behind, focusing on his breathing and trying to fill his mind with images of the incredible architecture that was directly over his head.

After a series of long hallways and serpentine turns, they passed through another security checkpoint that guarded another entrance. The Swiss guardsman satisfied the Vatican gendarme and led them to an elevator that required special keycard access. He swiped the reader with his card, reached in, and pushed a button on the elevator's control panel before stepping out and snapping to attention.

"I wait here," he said. "You go up to ground, then right. You see Abissini."

Manny reluctantly followed Grace and Kellen into the small elevator. As the doors closed and the small car began its slow ascent, he tried counting. He thanked God when the creaking and groaning stopped and the door opened into a vestibule that faced a courtyard. He hurried to open the glass door and hold it for the women to exit into the beautiful open space.

"Thank you, Manny," Kellen said, before starting down the walk toward a small stone building. "That's it, the Church of Santo

Stefano degli Abissini. Cardinal Lombardi said the hedges in front are designed to form the coat-of-arms of the reigning Pope, and there's a statue of the Virgin Mary on top."

Finally, his heart began to find its normal rhythm. The fog had lifted, and they made their way across the meticulously manicured lawn and past the flower garden toward the ancient church. The front door was unlocked, and the interior lit only by dim light filtering in through leaded windows and several banks of candles along the side walls.

He dipped his fingers in the holy water font and bowed his head, making the sign of the cross. Grace and Kellen repeated the ritual.

Kellen whispered, "He said we should meet him behind the altar."

The air felt colder within the stone walls, and gooseflesh flared across Manny's skin. A fresco decorating the nave's ceiling came alive in the flickering candles, but dark shadows dominated the front of the church, covering the altar like melting tallow. An elderly man, dressed casually in dark blue slacks and a black sweater, stepped from the shadows into dim candlelight.

He spoke softly. "Mrs. Barden."

"Father Lom—" Kellen halted, bowing her head. "I'm so sorry, *Your Eminence*."

Manny glanced at Grace. There was no indication that she recognized the man. *Thank God.*

Cardinal Lombardi brought two fingers up to his lips and whispered, "Follow me, please." After genuflecting before the altar, he guided them through the darkness to a recessed area behind it. There, he opened a massive wooden door and flipped on a single incandescent bulb, exposing the top of a circular stairway.

Manny stared down the stairwell. The Evangelists had set up shop in catacombs beneath Vatican City, and Lombardi was apparently leading them into one. The familiar panic began tightening its grip as his arms tightened around the nylon case. He felt like a fish drowning in air. His eyes clouded at the thought of *more* dark and tight spaces.

Again, he counted.

Grace must have noticed, because she laid a hand on his arm. "You okay?" she whispered.

Nodding, he eased one hand from the case to the railing, sliding it along as he followed Lombardi down the creaky iron stairs in silence, concentrating on the feel of the metal under his palm.

They emerged into a small candle-lit space that looked as though it had been hewn out of solid stone. The walls were a greasy brown, almost black, and pitted. They smelled of mold laced with decay. In the center of the small chamber stood a wooden table with several candles and five chairs, as well as another familiar face. Daniel's.

His mentor and friend smiled at them, giving Manny a slight comfort. But tension still pressed against his chest, and his hands still felt clammy, his throat bone dry. He closed his eyes and struggled to slow down his racing heart. And then Grace was standing next to him, gently rubbing the base of his neck, softly counting in his ear. "One . . . two . . ."

He opened his eyes as Kellen shot Grace a quick look of reassurance and exchanged a hug with the smiling priest before turning toward Cardinal Lombardi. "It's good to see you again, Your Eminence."

Lombardi wrapped his arms around her. "It has been a long time," he said. As he turned toward Grace, his face seemed to brighten. "You have grown into a beautiful young woman indeed."

"Thank you," Grace said, sounding stiff and cautious.

Lombardi looked toward Kellen and Daniel. "You both must be very proud."

Kellen smiled, nodded, and reached out to take Daniel's hand in hers.

"Father Neumann told me what you did for me," Grace said, again in a careful tone. "I don't remember any of it, but if what he said is true, I guess I owe you one."

Lombard smiled warmly. "You owe me nothing, child," he said. "It is our Lord and Savior Jesus Christ to whom you should direct your gratitude."

"Well, sure, but thanks anyway. This is my friend Manny." She leaned into him and whispered, "You're doing great."

"Short for Immanuel?" Lombardi asked.

Manny stopped counting and said, "Yes. Yes, Your Eminence."

Lombardi's face brightened. "God with us."

"Excuse me?" Grace said.

"The name Immanuel in Hebrew means, *God with us*. A very special name indeed." Lombardi turned. "I believe you all know Father Neumann?"

"Of course," Manny replied smiling.

"We've met," Grace said coolly.

Cardinal Lombardi gestured to seats in front of the desk and retreated to the lone chair behind it.

Manny had too much nervous energy to sit. His heartbeat slowed, but the need to flee—and quickly—felt overwhelming. Breathing as deeply as possible, he surveyed the tunnels heading off in different directions. "Your Eminence," he said, drawing the other man's attention. "Is this part of the network of catacombs running beneath the Holy City?"

"It is. You entered through Santo Stefano degli Abissini, the national church of Ethiopia." Lombardi paused as if waiting for a response. When no one spoke, he continued. "It was built by Pope Leo III at the beginning of the ninth century and originally named Santo Stefano Maggiore. The place we are in now is indeed part of the catacombs, but it is also the ruins of a temple dedicated to the pagan god Vesta."

"It's creepy down here," Grace said.

Manny's shudder felt audible. He wanted out.

Let's get this show on the road. Instead of speaking the words, he forced himself to pull out a chair and sit.

"My apologies," Lombardi said. "With the sensitive nature of our dealings, I wanted to meet outside the watchful eyes of Vatican security cameras. The Palace is closely monitored, but very few know of this place." Lombardi turned his gaze toward the black nylon case Manny held in his lap. "The items Mrs. Barden spoke of. Do you have them in your satchel?"

Manny tapped the case gently. "Is it safe here?"

"You did not see them, but the Swiss Guard have been monitoring you since you arrived at the Holy City in your taxi. The young man who left you at the elevator remained to make sure no one followed. Several more of my most trusted men are stationed inside and outside the church, out of sight. I can assure you, we are very safe here."

Manny unzipped the case, looked over its contents once more, and glanced up at Kellen. At her nod, he set it on the desk, sat back, and exhaled. It felt as though a heavy burden had been removed from his shoulders.

Lombardi lifted up the flaps of the case and peered in. "Tell me everything," he said. "Omit nothing."

Ω

Less than ten minutes had passed, yet Manny felt the change in the dark and dank catacomb. Kellen had given the bizarre story life again, making no mention of his beliefs about the first entry in the logbook. The air held a tingle, and the atmosphere felt thick with tension.

Lombardi's hands and voice trembled as he delicately pushed the gray plastic bundle to the side of the table. "May I see the logbook copy?"

Manny removed the bound photocopy of the logbook from the nylon case, set it on the desk, and pointed to the *Vatican Secret Archives* crest on the cover page. Opening the document to the first page, he spun it around so it faced the cardinal.

"The translation is on the page opposite the photocopy of the original parchment," Manny said, pointing at the right side of the opened document. "It says—"

Cardinal Lombardi held up his hand and opened his mouth to speak, but nothing came out. He slumped in the chair, dark lines now etched deeply across his forehead. When he finally spoke, his voice was thin and sharp. "I know what it says." The old man's fingers caressed two characters just below the first entry on the page.

"Those characters weren't translated, Your Eminence," Manny said. "My theory suggests they could be—"

"Aleph Tav," Lombardi said, his voice now barely above a whisper.

Manny glanced from Grace to Kellen. Both seemed confused, and Kellen's knuckles had whitened from gripping the arms of her chair. At least he wasn't the only one freaked out. "Excuse me?" he said.

Lombardi's eyes glowed. "The characters are Hebrew," he said. "Some Biblical scholars believe *Aleph Tav* to be the signature of

God in Scripture. They are the first and last letters in the Hebrew language."

Manny made the connection instantly. He should have done so when he first saw the two characters. He put his hand up to his mouth and muttered, "Whoa . . ."

"The two characters were inserted at numerous places within the Old Testament," Lombardi continued. "For centuries, scholars were confused by their presence and omitted them from most translations since they made no sense in context. It has only been in recent years that the significance of their presence has been understood."

"The Alpha and the Omega," Manny said.

Lombardi nodded his head. "In Revelation 22:13, Our Lord says, '*I am the Alpha and the Omega, the beginning and the end. I am the one who is, who always was, and who is still to come, the Almighty One.*'"

Father Daniel cleared his throat and leaned into the candle's light. "Does this mean what I think it means?"

Lombardi nodded. "The words are definitely Jesus'."

Daniel released a deep breath. "Does the fact the two letters weren't translated like the rest of the text have *anything* to do with the ancient Jew's unwillingness to speak the true name of God?"

"No," Lombardi replied. "Aleph Tav is God's unique mark on Scripture, His signature, for lack of a better term. The true *name* of God is something else altogether. His Holy Name was reduced to the letters YHWH many thousands of years ago by the Jewish High Priests, but its true spelling and pronunciation are long lost to antiquity."

"Yahweh," Manny said.

"Yahweh, Hayah, Jehovah . . . there are many names given to

God. But no one today knows how to actually *pronounce* the name of God."

Lombardi stood, circled the table slowly, and sat on the corner of the desk. He rubbed his face with both hands. "I do not fully comprehend what is happening, but I feel compelled to bring the discussion back to the potential dangers you feel threaten you."

"I'm worried, Your Eminence," Kellen said. "Worried for my daughter, Manny, and myself. Father Ceste was murdered, and it has something to do with the items in the case. Since both my home in the States and my hotel room here in Rome have been broken into, someone must think I have it all. Plus, I'm pretty sure I'm being followed."

Lombardi's eyes seemed to glaze over for a moment and quickly regained their clarity. "I realize stealing these priceless relics and creating a forgery of the Shroud would forever stain the Academy, but is keeping the secret worth the lives of two men?"

"They didn't just steal it, they performed experiments on it," Manny said.

"Could these tests harm the Shroud, Immanuel?" Lombardi asked.

Manny shook his head. "Not if they followed the process I outlined."

"Would they confirm the Shroud's authenticity, above and beyond the historical evidence we apparently now possess?"

"I believe so," Manny said. "I'm convinced that what happened to create the image on the Shroud is consistent with a nuclear event, an event which would have left physical evidence like we see on the Shroud."

"Particle radiation," Grace said.

"Exactly." She *had* paid attention to his ramblings. He suppressed a smile. "I believe the image on the Shroud was caused by a burst of what physicists refer to as *particle radiation*, Your Eminence. In other words, the physical form of Jesus of Nazareth became something else altogether at the moment of the Resurrection and left behind a physical signature on the linen cloth."

Manny slid the White Paper out of the nylon case. "In my opinion, this document most likely outlines experiments that could prove my hypothesis—or may already have."

"How can this be?" Lombardi asked. "How can you be so sure when it is two thousand years later?"

"My hypothesis is based on the *Scorch Theory*," Manny said. "Otherwise known as thermonuclear radiation. It suggests the intense light and heat generated by Christ's body at the moment of Resurrection burned his image into the cloth. Like the permanent shadows of people in Hiroshima were burned into walls and other surfaces by the atomic explosion in 1945."

"The experiments will . . . *would* have verified this?" Lombardi asked.

"If that is, in fact, what the Evangelists were up to, then yes. The White Paper appears to be written in Greek, so I was unable to confirm my beliefs." Manny held the document out. "We were hoping Father Neumann could help."

"I believe that is a prudent request," Lombardi said. "Daniel?"

Father Daniel Neumann exchanged nods with Lombardi and took the paper. He opened the first page, studied it for a few seconds, and fanned through the document slowly. "The text is definitely Greek," he said. "However, the formulaic syntax appears Western."

"You can translate it, Daniel?" Lombardi asked.

"Yes." Father Neumann set the White Paper on the table and crossed his legs. "I could do it manually, but it would take me longer. I have translation software on my laptop which will allow

the linen god

me to turn it around much more quickly."

Lombardi nodded and folded his hands in front of his face. "Many secrets lie behind the walls of the Holy City," he said solemnly. "Some hidden so deep in shadows, they are likely to never see the light of day. However, what we have before us is a fuse." He paused. His voice took on a more grave tone. "To a bomb that could explode across all of Christendom."

For a few moments, no one made a sound in the ancient pagan temple. Manny felt yet another tendril of cold air wrap around him, and a familiar shiver worked its way from his spine out to his arms and legs.

Kellen pointed at the gray plastic bundle. "Should we at least open it to make sure it's the real deal?"

"Two men have died, Mrs. Barden," Lombardi said. "I have little doubt what we have in our midst is the genuine artifact."

"Not to mention, breaking the seal in an environment like this could do irreparable damage," Manny said. "Too much moisture and dust. I agree with Cardinal Lombardi. I don't think there's any doubt."

Lombardi stood and leaned on the table with both hands. "We are at a tipping point in history, my friends, when faith may give way to fact, hope to certainty. The Church has waited two thousand years for proof of the Resurrection event. It can wait a few more days until we better understand what exactly we are dealing with."

"You'll take this?" Kellen asked.

"I must," Lombardi replied. "They are the property of the Roman Church and must be returned to the Archives. However, I will wait to do so. We still do not know if the current prefect can be trusted."

"Are you sure you don't want us to hold onto them for now?" Manny asked.

"No, that would be putting your lives in further danger," Lombardi said. "I will keep them on my person and have the Guard to accompany me to my meeting with the Carmerlengo. Which, by the way, I am late for."

"The who?" Grace asked.

"Carmerlengo," Lombardi said. "It is simply an Italian word for chamberlain. Cardinal Tariscio Marini was one of His Holiness' personal assistants and senior advisors, but he was by far the closest to Peter."

"Can he be trusted?" Kellen asked.

"I believe so," Lombardi said. "However, I will not share any of what I learned today. It is of such magnitude, I must consider all potential implications before I act."

"Is the meeting about conclave?" Manny asked.

"Many issues," Lombardi said. "The Church is issuing a statement from the Basilica tonight."

"I've heard," Kellen said. "It's across *all* the television networks."

"They said it would be read from the Papal Balcony over St. Peter's Square," Manny said. "That's a bit unusual isn't it?"

"It is." Lombardi said. "However, it was Peter's last wish, posthumously."

Manny lowered his head.

"I am sorry, but I must leave you," Lombardi said. "There are many demands on my time now. In order to minimize suspicion, I have asked the Swiss Guard to escort you to a different exit from which you entered. Mrs. Barden, Grace, Immanuel, you will be taken to the north gate where you can hire a car. This will keep you away from the press and tourists gathering in St. Peter's Square. I would ask you each to go back to your hotel rooms to rest."

Lombardi placed all but one of the documents and the gray plastic bundle carefully in the nylon case and zipped it shut. He turned toward Father Neumann and gestured to the document in his lap. "Please make this a priority, Daniel. It is imperative we confirm the facts. Do you know how long it will take?"

Daniel tucked the document under his arm. "I will do my best to get it back to you as soon as I can, Your Eminence. Two hours, perhaps three."

"Time is of the essence," Lombardi said.

Daniel nodded.

Lombardi walked to the bottom of the spiral staircase and turned. "Please wait here for a few moments before you leave," he said. "My meeting with Cardinal Marini and the Papal advisors should take less than two hours. I would like to ask each of you to convene with me in my office in the Palace of the Concatinate in three hours. Daniel, I will have a courier assigned to you in the event you are not finished. Make sure we have something by then."

Daniel nodded again.

"Return here through the East Gate again," Lombardi said. "I will have security escort you to my office."

"We'll be there," Kellen said.

"Can we do anything in the meantime?" Grace asked.

Lombardi paused halfway up the staircase and looked back, a fearful countenance across his face. "The fire we are about to ignite will show no favoritism," he said solemnly. "It will consume both the weak of faith and those strong in scientific conviction as it devours the world we know today. Pray, my child. Pray."

Chapter 23

Father Daniel Neumann poured himself another cup of hot coffee, looked at his computer's clock, and frowned. Connecting the scanner and establishing conversion parameters with his laptop's translation software had taken over an hour, but doing so insured the rest of the conversion from the hard copy version of the White Paper to Microsoft Word would go quickly and provide a high level of accuracy. He had already scanned the first page, and the translation looked pretty good.

The body of the White Paper turned out to be relatively short, just thirteen pages. But the Reference section was extensive, forty-plus pages, providing supporting formulas and data. Time was running out. Even using the conversion software, the Reference material would have to wait until later.

Daniel made a couple of minor formatting corrections to page one on his computer screen, entitled *Table of Contents*. He wasn't a scientist, but this seemed typical of most technical White Papers.

I. Participating Personnel
II. Project Background
III. Hypothesis
IV. Experiment
V. Conclusion
VI. Reference Material

He resisted the temptation to skip immediately to page thirteen and set the second page of the document on the glass surface of the optical scanner. He pressed the Start button, and listened to the scanner's hum.

$$\Omega$$

Thirty minutes had passed. Daniel sipped his now-lukewarm coffee and finished editing the last paragraph of page six, correcting minor grammatical, conversion, and formatting errors. He shook his head, unable or perhaps unwilling to fathom what he'd read.

On the one hand, the research team was exactly what Manny had presumed. Doctor Francis Adakem had been the leader of a small yet elite group of chemists, molecular biologists, and geneticists—all affiliates of the mysterious Evangelist organization. The project had indeed been secret, operating within the Creationist Science discipline in the Academy's molecular biology group.

On the other hand, the project itself appeared inconsistent with Manny's theory. Although the White Paper confirmed that they'd used the genuine Shroud as their primary test subject, it contained little information on its physical, chemical, and biological makeup, or references to physical evidence traceable to first century Palestine.

Instead, the paper focused on an amazing discovery, the astonishing detection of human DNA embedded in certain traces of blood found on the Turin Shroud. DNA featuring approximately seven hundred base pairs, consistent with the theoretical makeup of blood—ancient blood, in this case. DNA containing both X and Y chromosomes, which established the subject as both human and male. AB blood type, common among Jewish people.

The White Paper used the Greek word ανέλπιστος to describe the find. The conversion software translated this to mean *unexpected*. Daniel would choose *incredible*, *unbelievable*, and *unfathomable* to describe the almost impossible presence of intact human genetic material, pristine DNA gleaned from blood fragments left over from a brutal crucifixion.

An extraordinary hypothesis began to take root as he read each page. His thoughts coalesced with every word, every data point he reviewed. It drove him with greater fervor into the depths of the experiment itself.

He poured a fresh cup of coffee and placed the first of seven remaining pages on the scanner's glass surface. The machine hummed, and the green light began its slow crawl across the page. As the translated version of page seven painted his computer screen, Daniel's stomach began to churn.

Ω

Daniel pushed himself up from the toilet bowl, wiped hot sweat off his forehead with the back of his hand, and gripped the sink to steady himself. A stabbing pain pierced his chest.

As much as the first six pages of the White Paper had gripped him, the next five had defied logic and stretched his imagination as they challenged long-held concepts of good and evil.

the linen god

The bizarre sequence of words and numbers had appeared incomprehensible at first. But, gradually, the pages seemed to turn themselves, like time-lapse photography that exposed the incredible facts. The laws of physics, laws suited in a world where logic and reason were paramount, no longer sufficed to explain the stark reality in these pages.

Daniel staggered back to the computer and slumped in his chair, staring again at the last words he had read before losing his lunch. Words that spoke of prophecy and faith and science seemed so incredible, so inconceivable.

He hadn't yet read the conclusion, but time was up, and he needed to get the translated pages to Cardinal Lombardi's office. Summoning Lombardi's hand-picked Swiss Guardsman from the lobby, he settled shaky fingers on the keyboard, finished making a few minor edits to the remaining translated text, and hit *Print*.

"It can't be," he told the room, his voice quivering slightly. *It can't be.*

Behind him, the printer spat out the last of the eleven translated pages on stock white paper in twelve-point Courier font. A knock on the door caused him to whip around and grab a large envelope into which he slid the stack of paper.

He gave the young guard detailed instructions for the delivery and was about to send him on his way when he grabbed the man's sleeve, pulled him into a hug, and blessed him. The guard barely hid his surprise and left with a quick, *"Grazie."*

Daniel reengaged the deadbolt before pouring the last of the coffee into his mug and settling down to scan the two remaining pages of the White Paper.

They turned out to be simply a brief synopsis of the complicated experiment. But at the bottom were two familiar handwritten names, as well as a reference to specific verses in Scripture. He spun back to his computer and keyed in *Exodus*, the second chapter, verses one through eight, and the familiar narrative appeared on the screen.

Moses. Pharoah's daughter.

Daniel's stomach was already empty, but bile again rose in his throat.

Chapter 24

As they waited in Cardinal Lombardi's office for additional word from Father Neumann, Grace studied the elegant space with its massive fireplace and bookshelves crammed with beautiful leather-bound volumes. The cardinal leaned back in his chair behind a huge mahogany desk. Files rested on a matching credenza.

She definitely preferred her tiny, windowless office in the basement of Wiggs Elementary School in Brooklyn. She would never accomplish anything if she spent her working hours in a room crammed with so much artwork by the Renaissance masters. As now, she'd find her attention darting to them or out the tall windows that overlooked the beautiful manicured gardens.

"Still no answer," Kellen said, closing her cell phone and dropping it into her purse.

Cardinal Lombardi cleared his throat and said softly, "I am sure he is on his way here, Signora Barden. You must not worry."

In his Yankee's T-shirt, Manny appeared incongruous among the antique elegance as he sat hunched over the translation Father Neumann had sent. The cardinal had asked Manny to interpret the

English translation of the complicated experiments into words the rest of the group could understand.

When he'd first held the pages, Manny's eyes had lit. Grace smiled. She knew that look, as if he imagined he was about to unveil a great mystery or perhaps the latest wonder from the world of science. Soon, however, his eyebrows knit into a thoughtful frown.

The gray plastic bundle drew her attention. What secrets lay hidden within it? Her imagination conjured up the cries of those who had protected it over the centuries, trying to guard its secrets. And now it lay here. And Manny was reading something that just may hold the key.

She turned to him again. The frown had morphed. His eyes seemed crazed, more white than iris.

"Manny?"

"What's wrong?" Kellen asked, moving to his side.

Cardinal Lombardi stood and grabbed a glass of water from the credenza behind his desk. He crossed the room quickly. "Drink this."

Manny ignored the cardinal. He continued to stare, seemingly at nothing.

"What's wrong?" Grace said, kneeling beside him. "Talk to me, Manny."

His mouth opened, but no words came out. He pushed the document toward Grace and slumped back in the chair.

$$\Omega$$

The mantel clock's off-key chimes broke an eerie silence. Manny lay on the sofa, the back of one arm resting on his forehead, the other dragging on the floor. He had managed to collect himself enough to provide a summary of the White Paper's text, and now all eyes stared silently at the crumpled pages sitting on Lombardi's desk.

Grace again crouched next to him and stroked his face. "Manny," she said softly. "We need to talk about this."

"It just can't be true," Kellen muttered.

He sat up slowly. Some color had returned to his face, and the flames from the fireplace danced in his eyes. "The processes described in the experiment were flawless, the test sample pure. In my opinion, the results are undeniable."

"We—" Lombardi cleared his throat. "The implications to the Church could be staggering if this is not contained."

"Contained?" Manny stared at the old man, sounding impatient. "Do you understand what has happened, Your Eminence?"

Lombardi walked to the window overlooking the courtyard and looked out without saying a word.

"How can this *possibly* be contained?" Manny said. "More importantly, why would you want to contain it?"

Lombardi braced himself on the window frame. "If we could somehow . . ."

Grace longed to wipe away the words she'd heard. She moved over to the cardinal and placed a hand on his shoulder. "Cardinal Lombardi," she began softly, "they confirmed the Shroud of Turin was authentic, that it's the *actual* burial cloth they wrapped around the body of Jesus. The DNA they discovered in the blood must be His."

Manny leaned forward and clasped his hands together. "The *true* Holy Grail," he said. "The actual DNA of God," he said, as if stunned by the thought. "Your Eminence, they cloned Jesus Christ."

"How's this possible, Manny?" Grace asked. "How could

they have cloned a human being way back in the eighties? The technology didn't even exist back then, did it?"

Manny folded his arms across his chest. "Scientists realized a single human cell contained the entirety of human definition in the early twentieth century," he began. "The double-helix deoxyribonucleic acid cell was officially identified way back in 1953."

"DNA?" Kellen said.

Manny nodded.

"But there's a huge gap between knowing about DNA and actually *cloning* someone," Grace said.

"True, but some of the most talented scientific minds in the world work at the Pontifical Academy," Manny said. "They always have. Plus, they had access to incredibly advanced technology from an *outside source*, according to the White Paper."

"A major American biosciences company," Grace said carefully. "Could that be—"

"Nothing my dad does would surprise me," Manny said. "He's an amazing man, and his company has been a leader in that field for many decades, but we can't assume that yet. What's *most* amazing to me is how they found it. Those scientists literally went on a fishing expedition in a sea of molecules and somehow managed to find the impossible. Not to mention the fact the DNA survived as long as it did."

Manny wrung his hands as if kneading thoughts, and Grace could see a familiar intensity in his eyes.

"They extracted the DNA using a process called *somatic cell transfer*," he began. "Primitive by today's standards, but very advanced for the eighties and very effective. The team recruited a woman to participate in the project. Her donated egg cell was stripped of its nucleus and inserted with the somatic cell. The two were then fused with electricity causing the resulting egg to absorb the genetic donor DNA. The group then stimulated the fused egg, which activated the egg and caused it to divide just as one would if it had been fertilized by a sperm cell in conventional reproduction. The activated egg was then placed in a culture medium."

Manny stood and began pacing the office. "Then they transferred the blastocyst into the donor's uterus where it continued to develop. In the final weeks of her full-term pregnancy, she was transferred to a private facility in Bethlehem, Israel, where she gave birth to the baby, code-named *J2*."

"Remarkable," Lombardi muttered, not happily. Grace was right there with him.

"The infant was brought back to the Vatican and raised initially in the catacombs under the Academy, but there's no mention of what happened to the surrogate mother."

"Or to the clone," Kellen said.

Manny pursed his lips.

"I can state without any reservation that the leadership of the Church was unaware of its existence," Lombardi said.

"That doesn't surprise me," Manny said. "The whole thing sounds like a skunkworks project similar to the ones the military had going during the Cold War. The U.S. President often didn't know what was going on."

"Immanuel." Lombardi crossed his arms over his chest, an intense look in his eyes. "Am I to believe we have had a part-man, part-god, part-ghost wandering the catacombs, or perhaps the very halls of the Vatican now for thirty years?"

"I don't think we should assume *J2* is still somewhere here in the Vatican, Your Eminence," Manny replied. "Or in Italy for that matter. Who's to say he hasn't been wandering around Europe or America—living as a normal man, learning, teaching, reaching out? Or perhaps in the Middle East like Jesus?"

"Fascinating." Lombardi brought both index fingers to point in front of his face. "It has been a long time. Perhaps he will remain in hiding?"

"Keep in mind the *real* Jesus kept out of the public eye for the most part until he was thirty," Manny said. "Based on the dates in the White Paper, he should be around that age now. If there *is* a grand plan in mind, my guess is his public debut isn't far off. Just don't expect him to simply step into the Jordan River to be baptized."

"He must be found," Lombardi declared suddenly. "Before he does incalculable damage to the Church."

Manny offered Lombardi a curious look.

"How can we find him?" Lombardi said.

"He may find us." Manny resumed his pace around the room. "My main concern is over several published articles I've read in recent years by Doctor Adakem. He was well known in the physics world and wrote extensively in the journals I read. I'm just now understanding what he might have been alluding to."

"Articles?" Kellen asked.

Manny raised his right hand and extended his index finger upward. "A fundamental rule of particle physics is that for every *positive* sub-atomic particle," he said, extending his left index finger opposite the first, "there's a negative."

"Got that," Grace said.

"Good. Adakem referred to processes that seemed contrary to the laws of physics, which to him were the laws of God."

"He equated the two laws?"

"Exactly. And he said that these processes could result in a separation of positive energy, or God, and negative energy, or evil. He said this would be opening Pandora's Box."

Lombardi stepped into Manny's path and grabbed him by the upper arms, bringing him up short. "Are you saying Adakem believed they released a horror upon the Church? That an evil has been encoded in the cells of this . . . *being*?"

Manny touched the older man's hands. The cardinal continued to stare at Manny.

"He's not a *being*, Your Eminence. He's a man. And Adakem was a theoretical physicist." He sighed as Cardinal Lombardi released him. "His article didn't refer to anything particular, but considering these circumstances, I consider his wording particularly odd."

"You're not saying something, Manny," Grace said. "I can hear it in your voice."

Manny turned and reached for her hand. "I believe they set something incredible in motion. Consider the possibility of a spiritual event of Biblical proportions happening in a time when only science is known to have the power to work miracles." Manny's eyes scanned the room. "What is beyond the reach of science?"

"That which is un-measurable," Anthony said.

"Precisely," Manny said. "Simply put, *God*. I would love to find J2, Your Eminence, but I'm not sure where to start."

The room fell silent. "If he's a *clone*," Grace said cautiously, "wouldn't he look just like the man in the cloth?"

Manny slapped his forehead. "Of course. How could I have been so blind? It won't be an exact match, because they had different mothers. But, considering all the protocols they followed, J2 should look *very* much like the image in the Shroud. It would be a great place to start, especially if you can enlist the Gendarme to assist in the search, Your Eminence. All we need is someone to—" He spun to look at Grace. "You're an artist."

She nodded. "I could draw a likeness without the long hair and beard."

"I appreciate your offer, Grace, but that will not be necessary." Lombardi punched a button on his desk phone. "Maria."

An older woman's voice replied over the phone's loudspeaker. "Yes, Your Eminence."

"Have a taxi meet us outside of the St. Anne Gate in five minutes."

"A *taxi*, Your Eminence? I could have a car—"

"A taxi will suffice, Maria, but do not use my name. Also, get my brother on the phone, immediately."

"The comandante?"

"Yes. Tell him we will be at his office in twenty minutes."

Chapter 25

Grace stared out the taxi's foggy window, trying to make sense of her thoughts. The sky had cleared of rain clouds, but the day rapidly surrendered to dusk, and a nearly full moon had appeared on the eastern horizon. What little sunlight remained seemed cast at the wrong angle, stretching shadows to impossible lengths.

The trip across Rome took more time than she had expected, with traffic around St. Peter's Square already heavy in anticipation of the Papal decree and conclave. The group had left the Vatican grounds over thirty minutes ago, and the only words spoken had been Cardinal Lombardi's to his brother.

The beep of a text message alert sounded from Manny's phone. Grace asked, "Father Neumann?"

Manny stared at his phone, the light of his screen casting a strange glow across his face. "Archbishop Baggio."

"Baggio?" Cardinal Lombardi said. "What does he know of this?"

"Nothing," Manny said. "He was a little freaked out yesterday when I told him I was coming over here early. I think he can wait until tomorrow."

"Manny was asked to finish seminary in Rome, Your Eminence," Kellen said. "The Pontifical Academy of Theology."

"An outstanding bastion of Catholicism, my son." Lombardi spoke slowly, his lips defined only by a thin line. "As evidenced today, there is a need for more faith in our world in the face of the ruthless attack by science. Let us pray the Academy exists long enough for you to graduate."

"With all due respect, Your Eminence," Manny said. "I believe science is nothing more than a vehicle to expose the truth about God's creation."

"I could not agree more, Immanuel, but that same science threatens to overwhelm the weak of faith." Lombardi turned and rested his arm on the back of the car seat. "As a result, we have 'guided missiles and misguided men.'"

"Einstein?" Manny asked.

"Doctor Martin Luther King," Lombardi replied. "He, too, felt that we need more faith in these challenging times."

Manny turned to the window and sighed. Grace wished she had words of comfort.

The taxi came to a stop at the back of a large brick and stone building. A black metal door nudged open slightly, and Cardinal Lombardi signaled the group to follow. He eased out of the car with his head lowered and a black overcoat pulled tightly around his chest.

A large man with a cigarette dangling between his lips emerged from the shadows and bolted the door as the last of their group entered.

"The back, Michael?" Cardinal Lombardi said in the dim light of the stairwell. "We are not criminals."

The resemblance between the two immediately identified this man as the cardinal's brother, Michael Lombardi. "Entering through the front would have required identification and property checks," he said. "If *any* of what you tell me is true, I could not allow that to happen."

"They would check even if you escorted us?"

"In this building we have faith in God only. Everyone and everything else is processed through security." The policeman turned toward Grace's mother. *"Signora."*

She nodded, acknowledging him. Cardinal Lombardi waved toward Grace. "This is *la signora's* daughter, Grace Barden. And Immanuel Lusum. My brother, Comandante Michael Lombardi."

"Piacere," the comandante said, stubbing out his cigarette. "Please now, follow me."

Grace focused on Manny as she trailed the group up three flights of stairs. His steps and breathing seemed labored.

The comandante leaned toward his brother and said something she didn't understand. At least the cardinal's answer was in English. "Everything I told you is true. I assure you, I have not overstated the gravity of the situation."

His words renewed the chill Grace felt.

After several pauses for hallways to clear and one for a bathroom break for Grace, they wound up in a small, nondescript room not unlike her classroom in Brooklyn, which seemed much farther than a continent away.

A single desk supporting a large computer workstation, printer, and monitor occupied the center of the room. Metal folding chairs surrounded it. A ceiling-mounted projector hung above the workstation, and the front of the room contained a large screen and several large pads of paper mounted on easels, each with crude drawings of faces and unfamiliar words scratched in multiple colors. Comandante Lombardi closed and locked the door behind them.

Grace moved to one of three large windows and glanced at the busy street below, crossing her arms to warm herself. Behind her, she heard a forceful tread and buttons depressed on what sounded like an intercom. She turned.

A woman's voice answered. *"Pronto."*

"*Agente* Rugerri?" the commandant said.

His next words and the woman's were in Italian and unintelligible to Grace. But the conversation ended with a, "*Si, Comandante.*"

To the room in general, he said, "Our profiling expert will be here shortly." And then to Manny, "So you are the physicist. I am anxious to hear more about this incredible fairy tale Anthony related to me."

"I'm afraid all I know is what we all learned less than an hour ago."

"From the document?"

"Yes." Manny pulled Daniel's typed pages out of the nylon bag and set it on the desk. "This is a translation of the White Paper provided to us by Father Ceste and authored by none other than Doctor Francis Adakem of the Pontifical Academy of Science."

"Translated by whom?" Comandante Lombardi looked at it suspiciously.

"Father Daniel Neumann," his brother answered. "A trusted associate, Michael. I left a message for him to meet us here. I was hoping he would have already arrived."

"Adakem is a name I know. Academy member, senior advisor to Peter the Second. And murder victim." The comandante slid into a chair behind the desk, waving them to seats around it.

The cardinal sat, leaning forward and bracing his hands on the metal surface. "We have every reason to believe that what is written in this report is true, Michael. Despite how absurd it may sound, we believe a rogue group within the Academy extracted DNA from blood fragments on the Turin Shroud and created what is, in essence, an offspring of the Christ."

Michael Lombardi let the words hang in the air for a few seconds. When he smiled, it was without humor. "Apparently, they left their moral compasses at home that day?"

"We are afraid this anomaly may have been walking the streets of Vatican City and Rome for almost thirty years now."

"Or his evil twin," Manny said.

The comandante turned his gaze from his brother to Manny. Before he could speak, a knock on the door roused him.

"Please, will you unlock it for her?" the comandante asked Manny, who sat closest to the door.

He did. A no-nonsense woman with jet-black hair and emerald eyes entered.

"*Inglese, per piacere,*" Michael Lombardi said, rising from his chair.

"*Certamente,*" she replied and switched languages. "Certainly."

"Time is of the essence. I suggest that we begin."

He focused on his subordinate while the group around them remained silently watching. Grace noted the tense lines around her mother's mouth. Hers probably reflected the same.

"As you wish, Comandante." Rugeri slid into the chair in front of the computer screen. "When creating physical profiles of a suspect, we normally begin with the shape of the face."

The group turned in unison to Manny, who pulled a piece of paper from his pocket and handed it to the comandante.

"We have an image with which to begin," he said, unfolding the paper and placing the facial image of the man in the Shroud on the desk in front of her.

"*Bene.*" Rugeri hit various keys that brought up the proper program, not looking at the photocopy as she focused on the computer screen.

Grace watched intently—they all did—to see what the woman's reaction would be when she finally looked at the photo. One quick glance before hitting more keys, and then the officer stilled before lowering her gaze again to the photo. When she looked up, her eyes narrowed to pinpoints. "I do not understand."

Comandante Lombardi's breath whistled through his teeth as he released it. He pulled up a chair and sat down next to the young policewoman. "The suspect resembles the man in the photo."

"I see," she said. "Is the—"

He waved away her question. "Can you use this image as a point of beginning?" The inflection in his voice made his words sound more a command than a request.

"Of course," she said. "I will establish a base model with the photo. It should only take a few moments."

"Excellent."

Officer Rugeri lifted the lid to the scanner and placed the photo image face down on the glass. She pressed a green button on the console and a sliver of light emerged from the sides of the lid.

"Please think about the changes you want to make after the initial image is processed," she said, as the system began to paint the face of the man in the Shroud across the screen, line-by-line, pixel-by-pixel.

"Changes?" Grace asked.

A nervous smile tweaked the corners of the other woman's mouth. "I am fairly certain this is *not* the man you are pursuing."

Manny scooted his chair closer to the screen. "At a minimum, we will need to make certain adjustments due to the environmental and social differences between today and—" Manny coughed. "He will probably look younger than the photo, Officer Rugeri."

She nodded.

"Not to mention how he . . ." Cardinal Lombardi swallowed

and held his hand up to his lips. His face paled.

Grace felt the force of the image the old man must have seen. Her mother, too, must have pictured the death wounds from that brutal crucifixion if her widened eyes were any indication.

Manny didn't seem to notice. Instead, he said, "The person in the image would've appeared much older than he actually was by today's standards. Can your software make him look younger?"

"Of course," Rugeri said. "Simple age regression. I shall enter the actual age of the subject as perhaps forty and tell the software to adjust him to age…" She paused, cleared her throat, and suggested, "Early thirties?"

Manny nodded.

"What color should I make the eyebrows and hair?"

"Dark brown,"

"Can you open the eyes?" Kellen asked, leaning forward.

"Yes," Rugeri repositioned the cursor and performed a series of clicks and drags.

"They should be brown too," Manny added.

"What about the beard and long hair?" Grace said. "Can we adjust that?"

Rugeri nodded.

"Good point," Manny said. "How about shorten the hair a little bit, but take away the beard. Maybe leave a heavy five-o'clock shadow?"

As Rugeri executed a series of mouse clicks and keyboard entries, Manny spoke over her shoulder. "The man in the photo was somewhat malnourished by today's standards. Can you add twenty or thirty pounds to his total body weight?"

"Easily." The woman's fingers danced across the keyboard before she hit the *Enter* key. "What else?"

"I'd lighten up the skin tone a bit," Manny said. "Can you clean it up?"

She entered data via the keyboard and used the mouse to manipulate specific areas on the computer model. "More?"

"That should provide us with an excellent start." Comandante Lombardi sounded pleased.

"We can make further changes if this is not what you are looking for." Rugeri used the keyboard's mouse to press buttons labeled *Save*, then *Render*. She spun to face the group. "This will take a minute or so to process, but I should warn you. With all the changes we made, the face on the printout may not look like what you expect."

"Explain please," her boss said.

"It will be the same basic person with the same basic facial features, but the changes we made were substantial. He'll probably wind up looking like a younger, healthier relative of the person in the photo. A *very* close relative."

"Makes sense to me," Manny said.

A worried frown appeared on the young officer's face. "May I ask a question?" She addressed the comandante, her voice soft.

Everyone turned to him, but he nodded toward his brother. "Anthony?"

"Of course," Cardinal Lombardi replied.

"What did this man do?" she asked.

Grace couldn't breathe while she waited for his answer.

Cardinal Lombardi closed his eyes for a moment and looked up slowly at the young woman dressed in a crisp dark blue Carabinieri uniform. "Nothing, my dear," he said, his voice full of pain. "The man did nothing at all."

The minute hand on an old analog clock advanced as the software chugged through the process until the computer finally beeped. The screen refreshed itself and a single prompt appeared on the screen.

"It asks if you would like to print." Officer Rugeri looked up at her superior officer, and at his nod, she clicked the box and wheeled her chair in front of the printer. Tiny colored dots slowly began to form an image. Within a few seconds, the tip of the subject's hair appeared.

Suddenly, a bolt of lightning seemed to strike the building itself, causing the walls to tremble and shudder, and the machine to hesitate briefly.

"What was that?" Grace asked, but no one answered. The printer had resumed its march.

All too-familiar brown eyes emerged below a thick, dark hairline. A familiar nose followed and an upper lip no longer hidden by a beard. Then a mouth.

It couldn't be. Grace bit her lip until she could taste blood.

This must be the technician's idea of a sick joke. Or perhaps a cruel trick of the mind. It had to be the lightning bolt.

She slammed her eyes shut against the emerging reality. It was as if a magician were slowly pulling back a veil, one that had thinly disguised what lay beneath.

She looked again. Shook her head. Glanced at the horrified faces of the others. No one spoke. And Manny merely stared at the screen.

They were like actors playing out a scene too bizarre to comprehend. It felt surreal.

But there it was, Manny's face mirroring the expression and every detail of the suspect's image on paper.

Chapter 26

How could Manny be the clone? Grace could neither accept that revelation—nor deny it.

Comandante Lombardi quickly dismissed the young profiling expert. He told her in English that she was not to speak a word of what she had witnessed. He must have repeated it in Italian. She nodded at the English. Responded to the Italian.

The comandante then ushered the stunned group back down the empty stairwell into the cellar beneath the building, his hand on Manny's arm as they went.

The dank space looked as though it had not been used in years except as a home to some dusty office furniture, metal filing cabinets, and puddles of water from a leaky pipe. Michael used a flashlight to locate pull-chain lights around the cellar and lit every one he could find, as if trying to drive away an invasive darkness.

Grace slumped on the cold floor in the corner of the cellar next to Manny. As unruly streaks of matted blonde hair fell across her eyes, a convulsive tremor coursed through her body. She peered at him suspiciously from the corner of her eye as images of the linen shroud bounced around in her head.

Manny sat silently, staring at the computer printout in his hands. When he looked up at Grace, his tender brown eyes seemed to plead for help.

Grace wrapped her arm around him and squeezed. "There's got to be another explanation."

"What, honey?" Her mother spoke for the first time since the printer had spit out the picture. "What explanation?"

"I don't know, but there has to be."

"If history has taught us anything . . ." Cardinal Lombardi hesitated as Manny tore the rubber band that held back his long dark hair and held up the likeness.

"What can history possibly teach us about *this*, Reverend?" Manny said, pointing from the image on the paper to the one that stared back at them from his face. "Nothing like this has ever happened. *Ever.* There is no precedence, no track record, nothing to learn from. *I'm* your abomination."

He crumbled the printout into a ball and tossed it into a dark corner and stared at a shallow puddle of water between his feet. Grace nuzzled against his shoulder.

"Immanuel." Cardinal Lombardi crouched in front of Manny. "You see evil as a mad scientist in a Vatican lab, as corrupt priests who decided to play God. In many ways, you are right, but those who perpetrated this sinful act lack power."

"I don't need your platitudes."

The priest stood slowly and spoke with conviction. "The most powerful force in the universe is not science—not gravity or fusion or molecular genetics. The most powerful force in the universe is faith. In its purest form, faith can help a child jump into a swimming pool for the first time. It has built and destroyed civilizations and is responsible for miracles beyond human comprehension."

The cold, empty look on Manny's face terrified Grace.

"What has happened to you does not define you," the cardinal continued. "Despite what you might think, your life—"

"I don't fear for my life," Manny said, pressing his hand from his forehead back over his scalp. "I fear for my soul, or what's left of it. Assuming I even *have* a soul."

"We are all created in God's image. The—"

Manny held up his hand. When he spoke, his voice no longer quivered. "You're right, Cardinal Lombardi, we *are* all created in God's image. But I believe I'm the only one who can claim to be His grandson."

Chapter 27

Manny brought his knees up and rested his forehead on them with his arms crossed, shielding his face from the room. He tried to recall his life, the things that had brought him to this place, but memories had grown fuzzy.

He was no longer the man he'd been an hour ago. But that, too, had been a pretense, hadn't it?

He wasn't Immanuel Lusum of New York, New York. Oh, no. He was some synthetic *god* extracted from a linen cloth—forever trapped in this unspeakable nightmare, forever consigned to a darkness, a virtual hell from which there was no escape.

The comandante's cell phone interrupted the eerie quiet that had fallen over the cellar. Manny heard him answer. He didn't bother to look up.

"Stay here," the policeman said sharply before hurrying back to the stairwell. A minute later he returned with someone else.

Manny raised his head. It was Father Neumann. The priest's face was pale, his eyes hollow.

"I trust you know everyone," the comandante said as he closed the door behind them.

"I do." Father Daniel Neumann scanned the group and hurried across the room to kneel in front of Manny.

"Are you okay?" he asked, running his fingers through Manny's tangled hair.

Grace picked up the computer printout, un-crumpled it, and held it out for Father Neumann to see. He merely sighed. "This doesn't change anything."

Manny struggled to focus on Daniel's familiar face.

"Where *were* you?" Kellen said.

Daniel stood and turned to her. "The translation took longer than I expected, which meant I had to send over what I'd already completed before I could work on the summary." His shoulders slumped. "And then I was so upset that I accidentally left my cell phone behind when I ran over to Cardinal Lombardi's office. You had already left by the time I got there. I went back and got the phone, and when I heard your message, I grabbed a cab immediately."

"Did you learn anything else?" Cardinal Lombardi asked.

"Nothing in the actual summary itself," Father Neumann said.

Something in the man's familiar voice warned Manny that he wouldn't like what else had been uncovered. The cold sank deeper.

"At the end of the summary were hand-written names in English, as well as a Bible reference. Exodus chapter two, verses one through eight. When I realized what it meant, I . . ." Daniel stopped and took a deep breath, releasing it as he looked around the room until his gaze rested on Manny once again.

"That's okay." Grace's mom drew close and wrapped her arm around Daniel.

"It's *not* okay. You remember that the second chapter of Exodus tells of Moses' birth and his mother's attempt to hide the baby from death and persecution by floating him down the

Nile River in a papyrus basket."

Manny's body stiffened as the story continued to Moses' rescue and subsequent rearing by Pharaoh's daughter as an Egyptian child. As Daniel finished the story, everyone was watching Manny.

"So, now I'm J2 *and* Moses?" Manny said.

Daniel didn't answer.

Manny exhaled loudly. "And I suppose Adakem was Miriam?"

Daniel shook his head. "According to the handwriting, Cardinal Capello was Miriam. He was the one who put you in the Nile River, Manny. He sent you to America."

Lombardi's mouth gaped open. "Lucius?"

Daniel nodded soberly.

"And Pharoah's daughter?" the comandante asked.

Manny knew. It had been Philip Lusum. His father.

Chapter 28

Cardinal Anthony Lombardi drummed his fingers on the armrest as the police van wove back and forth across lanes. He kept a careful watch on Manny, seated on the back bench between Kellen and Grace. The young American was breathing hard, and his head had slumped onto Grace's shoulder.

He tried to steady his own breathing. There were so many questions, so few answers. Should he expose this atrocity to Church leadership or protect Manny's identity? Was it right merely to sit in the van and observe Manny, or should he be kneeling at his feet?

Anthony's brother Michael closed the bulletproof security panel between them and the driver just as the van's siren began to wail. "Traffic on Via Flaminia is lighter than I would have expected," the comandante said. "We should be at the Vatican in fifteen minutes."

Cars cleared a path for the police van, whose flashing red and blue lights bounced off metal, glass, and damp pavement. "The College of Cardinals has been summoned to the Sistine Chapel, and it would have taken far too long in a taxi," Anthony said. "Thank you, Michael."

"To prepare for the proclamation, I assume?"

the linen god

Anthony could feel his brother's steely gaze. "Yes," he said. "Peter's decree is scheduled to be read from the Papal Balcony in St. Peter's Square in less than three hours."

"When we all learn His Holiness' wishes simultaneously?" his brother said, a brow raised.

Anthony decided not to respond.

"Do you intend to reveal to your colleagues what we have discovered?"

"I believe I must." Anthony tried to suppress a shudder. "I realize some within Church leadership may already be aware of what has happened, perhaps even be involved, but I believe full exposure is our best chance of ridding the Church of this curse."

Comandante Lombardi held an unlit cigarette up to his lips, hesitated, and dropped it into his shirt pocket. He tapped on the glass next to him with his knuckle, gesturing to the traffic outside the van's window. "I would have taken the A1."

His brother's comment seemed out of context. Anthony just stared at him.

"It is normally a much faster route into the city," the comandante added. "However, Via Flaminia appears to have been the correct choice."

"What are you talking about, Michael?"

Comandante Lombardi pulled a small notebook and pen from his breast pocket and turned toward Manny. "May I ask you a few questions, Mr. Lusum."

Manny lifted his head slowly. His voice sounded distant and hollow. "Questions?"

"This Baggio, he is your mentor?"

Manny cleared his throat. "He was my pastor when I was young, Comandante. He's also the one who arranged my final semester of seminary in Rome."

"He must have powerful connections for such an appointment, yes?"

"I suppose. I don't really know."

"How did he know where you were today?"

Manny looked down into his lap and lifted his head slowly. "He didn't. I haven't talked to him today."

"Interesting," he said, turning. "Father Neumann?"

Daniel looked up pensively. "I didn't know Baggio was in Rome."

"Anthony?"

Anthony shook his head. "Where is this going, Michael?"

"Baggio's ability to assist us in navigating into the city is quite impressive."

"Come again?" Kellen said.

"That text Manny got from Archbishop Baggio. It suggested we take Via Flaminia into the city in order to avoid traffic."

"What difference does that—" Anthony's confusion dissipated in an instant. Baggio knew Manny was at the Carabinieri station. Manny must not have made the connection yet.

"His knowledge of Roman traffic patterns aside for now," the comandante said, "how did he know where you were in the first place, Mr. Lusum?"

Manny turned toward Grace for a moment and then back. "I have no idea."

"May I see your phone?"

Manny handed it over without hesitation.

Comandante Lombardi glanced at the screen. "Who is this *Becks?*"

"A mutual friend, Comandante," Grace said. "She's been checking in with both of us a lot lately."

Comandante Lombardi tilted his head at an angle and began manipulating the smart phone's screen. Seconds later, his voice again broke the silence inside the van. "As I expected."

"Excuse me?" Manny said.

"There is a GPS tracking application running on this phone, Mr. Lusum. A rather sophisticated one, I might add. It runs in the background, even when the phone is off." He popped open the back and removed the battery.

Manny looked even more confused. "I'm being tracked?"

"That appears to be the case," the comandante replied. "Where did you get this phone?"

"My dad..." Manny put his hand up to his mouth and coughed. "It was a birthday gift last year. He wanted to make sure we could keep in touch."

"Philip Lusum?"

Manny nodded.

"It appears your father got his wish," the comandante said. "It also appears Archbishop Baggio has been aware of your whereabouts for quite some time."

Manny shook his head and muttered something Anthony couldn't hear.

"In light of everything we now know, I believe the archbishop, and perhaps your father, know much more than they have let on." Michael turned to Anthony and asked, "Who is his superior?"

Anthony uncurled his fingers from their grip on the seat's armrests. "Capello," he said softly. "Cardinal Lucius Capello."

Michael frowned and scratched in his notebook. Anthony's thoughts spun as the van turned off its flashing lights and exited Via Flaminia.

The Carabinieri driver leveraged an occasional bleat of the siren to navigate a river of red brake lights onto Viale Vaticano and alongside thirty-foot high walls and police barricades flanking the northern boundary of Vatican City. They drove past the entrance to the Vatican Museum and pulled to a stop in front of the little-used Porta Santa Rosa Gate on the city's northeast corner.

Anthony peered out the van's window for familiar faces. None. At least that much was in their favor. As he climbed out of the van, he said, "Thank you again, Michael. For the escort and for Manny's disguise. We would not have gotten here this quickly without your assistance."

"Or the archbishop's," his brother said with arched eyebrows. "The items I provided Mr. Lusum should help you navigate the grounds a little easier, in case there are those looking for the young man."

"Agreed," Anthony said, as he assisted Kellen out of the van. "You are very wise."

"The previous owner will have no further use of those clothes or that wig for the next twenty years." Comandante Lombardi closed the van's side door closed and stepped up into the front passenger seat. "Now, I have security issues to deal with. My prayers are with you all."

Anthony stopped abruptly and slowly turned back to his brother. "When did you take up prayer, Michael?"

"Today," the comandante replied. "I learned to pray today."

Chapter 29

Grace followed Cardinal Lombardi and the others through Vatican security and across the Pigna Courtyard to the new wing of the Chiaramonti Museum, where the cardinal finally released his hold on Manny and nodded him toward a nearby restroom.

When Manny emerged in black cassock and white Roman collar, he looked much more his familiar self—except for the blond wig. If she ignored that, Grace could almost imagine they were at the Met—a lifetime ago it seemed.

As the setting sun set fire to the western sky, the cardinal guided the group through the Apostolic Library and across the Belvedere Courtyard, stopping between two minivans parked alongside the long, thin shadow of the Borgia Tower. "Immanuel and I must leave you here," he said to the three others.

Her mother and Father Neumann nodded, but Grace felt a sudden panic. She didn't want to let Manny go anywhere without her, not now. Not like this.

"We will go to the Sistine Chapel, where we will wait for the others to gather," Cardinal Lombardi continued. "When my colleagues are assembled, I will remove Immanuel's disguise and reveal him and our story to Church leadership." He patted the black nylon bag hanging from his shoulder. "They must be apprised of the evil perpetrated within these walls."

"What do *we* do?" Kellen asked.

Grace interrupted his reply by saying, "May I have a minute with Manny?"

The cardinal hesitated. "You must be brief, my child."

Manny leaned against one of the vans, right foot on the ground and the left propped up behind him. Grace tucked a loose strand of long, dark hair back up under the wig. He didn't flinch. Instead, his gaze seemed to prowl the packed parking lot as if searching for unseen ghosts.

She studied him closely, searching for something out of place, something that didn't belong, that she might have missed in the past. There was nothing but the familiar friend.

He suddenly stood straight, throwing back his shoulders as if shaking off the remnants of a bad dream. As he turned to face her, she thought she saw an expression of wistful longing, but his voice held a new strength. "Thanks for sticking with me today, Grace." He held her motionless with his eyes and a slight smile tweaked the edges of his mouth.

"Listen to me." She squeezed his hands as she spoke. "There are people in this place who killed to protect the truth about you. I'm afraid for you."

He gripped her hands tightly and smiled down at her.

Grace felt his strong pulse. "Sometimes it's smart to be afraid."

"There's nothing they can do to my physical body that's of any consequence, Grace," he said. "I only fear for my soul, if I even have one."

"Don't say that," she said, fighting back the tears. "You have more soul in your little finger than most people have in their whole body."

Manny moved his hands to her shoulders. When he stepped toward her, she was close enough to see her reflection in his dark brown eyes. "I've never told *anyone* this, Grace," he said. "But I've always felt as if something were missing in my life. I just assumed it because I never knew my biological parents, but now I know it was more."

"Manny—"

"I know I'm not a ghost," he said, his smile slightly twisted. "I cast a shadow, I can see myself in a mirror. And I know I'm not a monster. But, I think I'm about to learn what real monsters never do."

"What?" A shiver snaked through her, but she focused on his brilliant eyes.

"I think I may discover whether man chooses evil, or if evil can choose a man. Whether something besides free will is involved here."

Grace flashed back to her own childhood experience and shuddered. "I only want to know one thing," she said softly. "What you tried to tell me at the café in Manhattan the day I met my father. I just . . ." Grace swallowed the lump in her throat.

Manny looked down at his feet for a moment. When he gazed into her eyes, his face seemed to change, his smile transforming him back to the man she had fallen for so many years ago. "You've always known I loved you . . . right?"

Grace nodded as a single tear rolled down her cheek unchecked.

He kissed her gently on the lips and said, "I just wanted you to know I was also *in love* with you."

That quickly, the invisible line separating friend and lover evaporated, and his eyes felt like hands reaching out to her. Grace tried to speak and failed. She placed her palms to his cheeks and focused on the lips that had just touched hers.

A tap on her shoulder interrupted them. Father Neumann and Cardinal Lombardi stood behind her. She turned, and the cardinal touched her cheek, gently wiping at her tears. "Fear not, Grace. The world will look *into* him, not just *at* him."

She did her best to smile.

"Where should we go, Your Eminence?" Daniel asked as the cardinal took Manny's arm.

"To St. Peter's Square. Go through that door." Cardinal Lombardi pointed toward the east side of the courtyard and gave them detailed directions. "That will take you directly out to the Square without having to battle the crowds. Wait by the tall, granite obelisk in the center. If I can not reach you via your cell phone, I will look for you there when I am able."

Grace didn't want this. She didn't want to be separated from Manny. "I'm afraid," she said.

The cardinal rested his hand on her shoulder. "Faith will overcome your fear."

What faith? She felt as if hers barely functioned. Her chest hurt from the pounding of her heart as she watched Cardinal Lombardi lead Manny between rows of cars across the paved courtyard.

Her mother's arm drew her close. "What happened?" Kellen asked, whispering in her ear. "Did he tell you he loved you?"

Grace stiffened. How had her mother known?

Kellen smiled and kissed her gently on the cheek. "I knew the minute I picked you up from the airport, Gracie. You both had it written all over your faces."

"I—"

"It's okay, sweetheart." Her mother's fingers stroked Grace's face. "Despite everything that's happened to him, Manny's a good man.

God does not forsake those who love him."

Her mother's soothing words didn't change the fact that Grace's world had grown inexplicably evil in the past few days. It was so easy to blame everything on the devil and those who consorted with him, but her questions remained. She found herself trying to make deals with a God she wasn't sure she even believed in—or could trust.

Chapter 30

On the ground floor of the Borgia Tower, Anthony Lombardi stopped to catch his breath and peer out across the small parking lot at the Sistine Chapel. Manny leaned against an inner wall, his arms folded across his chest, his lips a thin line.

It would not be long before his colleagues began to arrive. He was grateful for the light that still streamed from the six arched windows high on the chapel's north face, revealing a clear passage. "Come," he said to Manny.

His cell phone vibrated in his coat pocket. The display showed Withheld, but he decided to answer it.

"*Pronto.*" Anthony heard breathing on the line before it went dead and a rustling sound behind him.

"*Buonasera, Eminenza.*"

He turned at the voice.

A young Swiss Guardsman with a pale complexion and steely gray eyes sneered as he snapped shut his cell phone and dropped it into a pocket in his uniform. Another man circled behind Anthony, his gun drawn and pointing. Two additional Swiss Guardsmen flanked a now-wigless Manny.

"We have been looking for you, Cardinal Lombardi," the first guard said, making no attempt to hide the contempt in his voice. "As well as your friend."

Anthony studied the young man's face. It looked familiar, but there were so many. "And you are?"

A darkness enveloped the young officer—one that didn't come because of shadows in the hall. He stepped forward and placed a powerful hand on Anthony's shoulder, squeezing hard enough to inflict pain. "I am a shepherd. Sent to gather the lost sheep."

Chapter 31

Anthony woke suddenly to the reek of blood and fear. At first he thought he was back in the dark catacomb beneath the ancient Abissini church, but there was no iron staircase or wooden table. Only this dark cave.

He scanned the room by the light of a single candle set in a small niche in the rock to his left. The only opening seemed to be through a stout wooden door mounted on iron hinges, under which thick tendrils of fog crept. Next to the door, ensconced in the gray vapor, lay the black nylon case, his cell phone, and the crucifix that had been around his neck.

Anthony tried to move, but shackles held his hands and feet to what looked like an old medical examination chair. The cold metal was painful and unforgiving. He gritted his teeth against another pain slicing through his head as warm blood dribbled down the side of his face.

He didn't know how long he had been unconscious, but it couldn't have been too long since the blood had not yet coagulated. Still, he had to free himself before the College of Cardinals proceeded without him.

A cold draft filtered through the dank space, and Anthony sensed something taking form in the blackness. He lowered his head in prayer, but a voice emerged from the shadows to interrupt him.

"A miracle took place here three decades ago, Anthony."

He knew the voice. He knew the face that stepped into the dim light. Cardinal Lucius Capello. His friend and colleague.

"This cannot be." Anthony's own voice sounded strange to his ears.

"Fortunately, old friend," Capello said with obvious relish, "disbelief does not protect you from me or from anyone else, for that matter. It never has."

Anthony struggled against his restraints. "Where are we?"

Capello walked slowly behind Anthony, out of his line of sight. "As you know, there are many places like this within the walls of our *Holy* City," he whispered in a tone that seemed to echo in the small space. "But this one holds special memories for me. From here we set forth a series of events that will ensure the genie is never returned to its bottle.

"Immanuel was here?"

"Indeed. From this very place, the God-child stepped out of the pages of your *so-called* holy book and into history, from the finite to the infinite."

"You won't get away with this," Anthony said, shaking his head. "Immanuel will not cooperate."

"Ah, but he will, Anthony."

Capello suddenly stood directly in front of Anthony, but no light flickered in his eyes. Anthony stared into the deep pools of darkness. How many souls had drowned in their depths?

"We have invested much in young Mr. Lusum over the past thirty years," Capello continued. "I can assure you he will be everything we expect from him. And more."

"*We*, meaning the Evangelists?"

"Ah, yes, the Order. They proved to be a very useful ensemble over the years but hardly realized their true purpose. Innocent lambs, you might say, who will all be led to slaughter in due time."

"I know this young man. He did not know the truth about his origins until this very day. He will have no part of this ruse."

Capello stooped at the waist and placed incredibly strong hands on both of Anthony's forearms, pinning them to the chair painfully. "When the time comes, he will say and do what he has been programmed to say and do."

"He is not a machine."

"You are correct, he is not a machine." Capello straightened, smoothed out his crimson robe, and adjusted the white Roman collar around his neck. "He is flesh and blood and consciousness. A consciousness that was planted and has been nurtured for many years. Now, the time for harvest is upon us."

Anthony pulled on the restraints. His head throbbed. "I do not understand."

"Then I will assist you. It is the least I can do."

As Anthony watched, a wooden chair slid silently from the dark corner, untouched, and stopped directly behind Capello. Without looking over his shoulder, Capello sat down and leaned forward, steepling his hands as if in prayer.

"As you may have already guessed," Capello said. "Immanuel's adoptive father is a member of the Order. I personally recruited him many years ago. What you may *not* know, however, is that Philip's company did extensive scientific research for the American military. Specifically in the areas of genetic engineering and biological warfare."

Capello chuckled and rubbed his hands together vigorously.

"I'm sorry," he said. "I often find myself giddy with the thought of war."

"Science once again overstepping its bounds. Stepping on the toes of theology."

"Consider the Big Bang," Capello said, his voice calm and sure. "Or string theory, multiple dimensions, evolution, $E=MC^2$. Even with no clue as to what preceded these grand theories, man now naively believes he understands the universe. Face it, Anthony, science is the new belief system, the new God. Is it *that* much of a stretch to envision God and science coming together in perfect unity?"

"God created science," Anthony said. "Of course they can coexist. But what you have done cannot exist in *my* God's world."

"Then perhaps we are not in *your* God's world." Capello leaned back and exhaled. "In any case, once the DNA of the Jewish carpenter was discovered intact on the Shroud, Immanuel's father was more than willing to provide the zealots within the Academy with the necessary equipment and technology to make my vision a reality."

Anthony's head fell forward. "The duplication of Our Lord's physical body," he mumbled.

"*The cloning of the carpenter*," Capello replied. "While Immanuel was still an infant, Mr. Lusum was gracious enough to agree to marry the boy's earthly vessel, making them ideal candidates as adoptive parents."

"Vessel? What are you talking about?"

"The young nun who agreed to provide her womb for the greater good. The surrogate mother, if you will."

"Immanuel's adoptive mother was his actual birth mother?"

"*Was* being the operative word, my old friend. Ana's faith in my vision faltered a few years ago, and she returned to her religious order here in Rome, leaving poor Philip a single father. Shortly thereafter, she began to challenge the wisdom of my plan."

"The murder at Santa Maria della Concezione." This was too much. The horror of it made bile rise in Anthony's throat. *Please, God.*

"Ah, you remember Sister Anastasia's untimely end," Capello said grinning. "A bit dramatic I'm afraid, but I had no choice."

"Ceste and Adakem," Anthony said. "They too questioned your wisdom?"

"Unfortunately, they went well beyond that. Father Ceste and Doctor Adakem threatened to expose my plans and corrupt others within the Order. Therefore, I was forced to deal with them in a manner that would prevent others from questioning me. Great accomplishments often come at great sacrifice. Nevertheless, back to my story. I think you will agree it is a wonderful story, quite like a fairy tale."

Capello described Manny's upbringing in Manhattan, the counseling sessions orchestrated by Baggio at St. Williams, the subliminal messages he received via post-hypnotic suggestion.

"Oh, yes, knowledge of a previous life was implanted into Immanuel's young brain." Capello rubbed his palms together, saying with a smile, "Soon, Immanuel will not be able to forget that which he does not yet know."

Anthony shook his head. "What are you talking about?"

"It is a tale you are very familiar with, Anthony. The scourging, the crown of thorns, nails hammered through his hands and feet, the Roman sword piercing his side…blah, blah, blah. Very soon, clear memories of his torture and death at the hands of mankind will resurface in young Immanuel's awareness. Along with his true purpose and his role in this new world. All this has been safely tucked deep inside Immanuel's subconscious, all waiting to manifest itself upon command."

A key piece to a complex puzzle slid into place, and a nightmare scenario emerged. "You're going to stage the Second Coming," Anthony stammered. "The greatest deception in human history."

"Not that I don't appreciate the compliment, Anthony, but I would say it will be the *second* greatest deception. Convincing most of humankind I don't exist would be my greatest work."

"You said *command*. What command?"

"A keyword, you might say," Capello replied. "A *single* word which, when spoken, will trigger in Immanuel all that has been taught to him over the years. He will be a simple physics student and seminarian one moment, a god the next."

"That is impossible. How can a single word do that? And how could you have possibly prevented that word from being said in his presence during his lifetime?"

"The specific word I chose is very unique. Mankind has not spoken it since long before your *Christ* was born. For centuries, speaking it was forbidden by the Jews, its true form only known by the Chief Priest of the Tabernacle."

Another harsh awareness swept over Anthony as he slumped further down in the chair. "Yahweh," he mumbled.

"Excellent, Anthony! You know your Scripture. And, since you know your Scripture, you also know that is not how the four consonants, YHWH, are actually pronounced. Tonight, the true name of your *God* will be spoken again for the first time in over three thousand years. When it is, your young friend will take his rightful place."

"And you?"

"Every messiah needs a Baptist," Capello smirked. "Think of me as a voice crying in the wilderness."

"How can this be?"

"Patience and teamwork, my old friend. Since young Immanuel left St. Williams, he has never been out of sight of our many loyalists. Parents, teachers, nuns, priests."

Anthony felt the shudder rise at the thought. "Daniel?"

"I am afraid not," Capello replied with a grin. "Father Neumann, however, came about most fortuitously. It was actually when you and I made each other's acquaintance for the first time."

Anthony gasped out loud this time. "Grace? Why??"

"I decided to spend some time inside the young Miss Barden for reasons of my own. As it turned out, I was fortunate enough to meet you and Genovese. It was a lovely time. I almost regretted it when I decided to leave."

"Decided to leave?" Anthony felt a surge of adrenalin-laced anger. "You did not *decide* anything, demon. You were exorcised from that young child, by Christ!"

"Believe as you wish. However, your precious *Christ* accorded certain powers on Earth to me."

Anthony felt the scream rise, heard himself cry, "Liar! He will not permit this abomination to stand." He tried to squeeze his hand out of the manacle and felt the cold iron cut into his skin.

"Apparently, you are not as well versed in Scripture as I had thought." Capello frowned as he wiped off the sleeves of his robe where Anthony's spittle had landed. "I, on the other hand, can quote your holy book word for word. And do you know one of my greatest delights?" His small laugh resembled a cackle. "It is so easy to twist those words ever so slightly in the ears of those who lack knowledge or conviction. However, there is no need to manipulate when it comes to my dominion on Earth and among humans. Your own Bible says as much."

"You will fail, even if God has to come here Himself to thwart you."

the linen god

"His time has not yet come, Anthony. *This* time belongs to me."

Capello stood at the sound of movement outside the door. "Your, or should I say, *our* Scripture, will say much more on this subject once young Immanuel has the chance to add his own words and deeds to it. The *Holy Bible* will become much more relevant in a society seeking religious tolerance. Only a miracle can save your dying church, and I intend to give it one."

"Your power is like your time—limited." Anthony's voice rose as he said, "He shall come in power and—"

"Silence!" Capello's voice exploded, and several small rocks fell from the wall, rolling onto the stone floor "Your *religion* and those held captive by it have become nothing more than a giant mural across the human landscape, *Your Eminence*. All bearing pious faces, bent knees, and hands in prayer. However, this mural is two-dimensional—lacking depth, completely devoid of substance. Little is required to shake the faith of most of its adherents. Their true colors will run—right into the ground like the blood of sacrifice."

"They will see through you."

"Ha!" Capello's laugh echoed. "They cannot recognize the evil in their *own* souls, you old fool. Do you expect humankind to see through the perfect disguise of a being who is capable of god-like powers?"

Anthony stared at the ground between his feet. His head throbbed and heart pounded. "You argue semantics," he said. "Religion. Faith. A thin line separates the two."

"I would argue it is not a thin line at all. I would say it is not even a thick line. It is a chasm to the extent that one has often prevented the other from flourishing. I intend to pull back the veil. Prove to humankind you are *not* the indigenous species of this tiny planet. We existed long before you and will exist long after you."

"When?" Anthony asked.

"During the Papal declaration tonight."

"His Holiness? Are you saying Peter also conspired with you?"

Capello folded his arms across his chest. "I would have loved to have worked with the man. But I am afraid he was a bit beyond my reach. However, his aid was not."

"Marini?"

Capello grinned. "Tarcisio proved to be in invaluable resource in guiding the late Pontiff. Whispering the prophecies of Malachy into an old man's ear was enough to prime a dying pump. When Tarcisio suggested Peter delve into the matter more, Peter discovered the truth that he would be the final Pope. That the time had come for the end of the Church era. That a new day would soon dawn."

"Mary's prophecies to the children of Fatima?"

"You could say that."

Vivid memories of the night of the Pope's death flashed in Anthony's mind. "This is nonsense," he said. "Regardless how long the Church delayed releasing its contents, the third prophecy speaks only to the assassination attempt on John Paul II in 1980."

"Or so the faithful have been led to believe." Capello snickered. "The children were told of this day and wrote what they heard, but the actual text of the third prophecy was suppressed by your Church."

"How could you know this?" Anthony said.

Capello smiled a knowing smile. "Suffice it to say, I have appeared in many forms over many years, Anthony, and whispered in many ears. Once Malachy sparked Peter's curiosity, Marini had little difficulty in getting him to reopen the third secret. The rest, as they say, shall be history tonight with the reading of the proclamation when Immanuel makes his triumphant appearance. Would you like me to read it to you, Anthony?" Capello laughed. "Would you like to be the first person to hear words that will rock the shallow roots of your faith?"

"Your deception and false miracles are of no interest to me, Capello. You are the Prince of Lies."

"I'm flattered." Capello grinned and bowed at the waist.

A knock sounded, accompanied by a low, powerful voice from the other side of the door. "It is time, Your Lordship."

"*Lordship?* Time for what?"

"I like the title, Anthony. I think it befits me, considering my impressive resume." Capello moved toward the door and looked over his shoulder. "It will soon be time to read the proclamation to the world. I must prepare."

"The *world* will not be watching," Anthony said. "I will admit the rumors circling the proclamation have generated some interest among Catholics, but the rest of the world will be watching their favorite reality TV show."

"Then I shall give them the *ultimate* reality," Capello said. "Events are unfolding as we speak, Anthony. Events that will draw the entire world to tonight's broadcast. Those unable to see the miracles on live TV, which should be few, will undoubtedly see them within hours across every medium on your planet."

"Miracles?"

"*So* many questions, old friend. Who, what, when, where, how. However, you have not asked the most important question of all."

"I know *why*, demon. The appearance of the Antichrist was foretold thousands of years ago."

"Ah, yes, again your precious *prophecies*. I often forget how pathetically bound you beings are to time and space. But, alas, your thinking is too narrow. It is so much more than just old stories of beasts and plagues. It is also about fulfilling the greatest of your prophecies, the return of your Lord and Savior."

"Regardless of how it happened," Anthony said. "Manny was

born a human boy and chose a godly path to manhood. What you say he will become is nothing but a creation of your perverted science. He is not my savior."

"Let's just keep that little secret between you and me, shall we?" Capello offered a sly grin. "He will be much more than you realize. Your church is all about seeking, Anthony. Helping the lost find their way. Finding truth in a complex world and all that nonsense. I intend to provide absolute proof of at least one thing you and your kind have preached for eons. That there *was* a Jesus of Nazareth, and he's back, down to the last molecule, I might add. He has returned to clarify all that has been written and preached about him."

Anthony's persistent pull on his restraints abruptly went slack as the implications washed over him like a tsunami.

"His message will not be as *conservative* as your writings claim," Capello added. "He will preach much more religious tolerance, about the many ways to find God or nirvana or Mother Earth or whatever humankind wants to call it. All from the most visible pulpit on the face of the planet, and all thanks to a little *deception*. My specialty."

As the room around Anthony began to spin slowly, all he could do was pray. "Though I walk through the valley of the shadow of death, I shall fear no evil. For—"

Capello's voice slashed through the cold air like a sickle "You should *run* through the valley, Anthony," he said. "It is far more *evil* than you can possibly imagine."

Capello crouched down and placed his hands on Anthony's. "I am like an owl. I not only see very well in the dark, but also *into* the dark. So well, in fact, that I can see the darkness in your own soul. Your proud and very arrogant soul."

"I am like any other man," Anthony said softly. "I have sinned and fallen short. But my Savior died for my sins on Calvary and—"

"Yes, yes. I was there." Capello stood suddenly, and his eyes flared to a dull red glow. "Spare me the gory details. What is important today is this—your *savior* will be on stage with me this evening. In fact, at one point in tonight's festivities, I will be closer to him than his next breath. I'll be sure to put in a good word for you."

Anthony recoiled with a jolt of nausea. Breathing shallowly, he said, "The man you tried to resurrect via your corrupt science cannot be brought *back* to life, demon. You cannot bring to life the One who still lives. Alive, yet He still died for my sins."

"I tire of this." Capello pulled open the heavy oak door open and spoke to a large shadow of a man lurking just outside. "Make sure the distinguished Cardinal is alive only until the proclamation is read and I have no further use for him. I have found the dead keep much better secrets than the living, so bury him and his belongings where we've put the others. Burn the contents of the bag."

A burly man stepped forward and bowed. "As you wish, Your Lordship," he said, his hand resting on a four-foot steel sword hanging from his waist.

"You shall pay," Anthony called after Capello. "Hell is your destiny."

"Hell?" Capello stopped short and turned. His grin had disappeared. "What do you know of hell, Anthony? Trust me, Dante did not do it justice."

He stepped out the door and without turning said, "Perhaps today is your judgment day. Perhaps today your well of grace has run dry."

"To hell with *you*."

"No need, Anthony." Capello glanced over his shoulder and smiled. "I brought it with me."

The door slammed behind him, and the lone candle went out. In the silence, a cacophony of voices rose up as if from the very stones, and Anthony heard cries of despair, anguished groans, and pleas for death.

O, Lord my God, have mercy.

The voices faded suddenly, and a strange peace found him in the darkness. He was going to die. He deserved to die. And so he prayed for the fate of mankind, for Immanuel, and for his eternal soul.

Anthony Lombardi wasn't sure how long his eyes remained closed and his head bent in supplication when he became aware of another soul in the darkness. At first, he assumed it was the guard who had returned to mete out his earthly judgment, until without warning, his shackles fell to the floor, and he felt something like the palm of a hand on the top of his head, a gentle touch coalescing from pure nothingness. A warm light suddenly flooded the room.

A soothing yet powerful voice spoke. "Peace be with you, Anthony."

Anthony tried to control his trembling body. "Who are you? Where are you?"

"By your side."

"*Who* are you?"

"I am the one sent by Him."

Anthony couldn't speak.

"The God of Abraham, Isaac, and Jacob has sent me. The great *I AM*."

He froze, his entire being consumed by the magnitude of what was happening. "What name . . ." But his words were reduced to a nearly incoherent babble. He could not force his mouth to speak.

There was a brief pause before the calm voice again seemed to coalesce from the air around him. "You may call me *Michael.*" Michael the Archangel, the Prince of the Seraphim, the General of the Armies of God, did not wait for Anthony to answer. "You have His work to do, Anthony. Godspeed."

Chapter 32

Outside the cave and in the dark catacomb, a guard's body lay impaled on his own sword. Anthony hurried past, swallowing the rising bile, navigating the space by the light from his cell phone's screen. The angelic presence still clung to him, and although his lungs rebelled and his legs ached, his head no longer pounded.

He exited through a door marked *Hazardous Materials* into a storage facility he recognized as the Pontifical Academy of Science. He hitched the black nylon case up on his shoulder and worked his way out through the building's small receiving dock. The area was unattended, which was odd, and the back door of the highly secure facility swung open on its hinges.

Peering out the door, he noticed three men and a woman in white lab coats in a close huddle. They stood in silence, heads cocked up to a single focal point in the sky. He followed their gaze and almost dropped the nylon case. A bright white light pierced the early evening sky and seemed to pulsate in a flucuating patter, the stars shrunken and pale in comparison.

"What is it?" Anthony said, startling the scientists.

The woman replied without taking her eyes off the anomaly. "We are not sure. It appeared just a short time ago."

The strange object, about half the size of the full moon, shone much brighter and seemed much closer. "Have you consulted the third floor?" he asked.

"We *are* the third floor," the woman said flatly, still not looking at him. "We have no idea."

"Do you not have equipment?"

"We don't have telescopes here at Casina Pio," she said, turning toward him, but not reacting to his disheveled state. "Data from our observatory at Castel Gandolfo as well as the European Space Agency are inconclusive."

And suddenly, Anthony got it. In his gospel, the Apostle Matthew had made specific reference to a star that signaled the birth of Jesus. Hadn't Capello spoken of a miracle that would draw the world's attention to his abomination? As he stared at the architecture of the heavens, the implications of a non-celestial source for the anomaly were clear. Capello's *miracle* loomed overhead.

Anthony cleared his throat and said, "Is it moving?"

This time, the youngest of the three men looked down at Anthony with deep-set eyes. If he recognized the distinguished Cardinal, neither his attitude nor voice revealed it. "If it is, then the object is violating all known laws of gravity and orbits."

"Excuse me?"

The man returned his eyes to the sky as he spoke. "If it is moving, it is not following an elliptical trajectory." Before Anthony could question this, the man said, "If it is moving, it is heading right at us."

$$\Omega$$

Anthony checked his wristwatch and released a deep breath. Excellent. He had some time before the meeting was scheduled to begin at the Sistine Chapel, so he stopped at his quarters in the Apostolic Palace to gather his wits and change from street clothes. He tuned the television in his room to *CNN Italia* as he slipped into a red cassock with matching biretta and black cincture around his waist.

As expected, normal programming had been interrupted with live coverage of the bizarre astronomical event taking place in the night sky over Rome. He nudged up the volume, focusing his attention on the young reporter and a flickering image of the dome of the Basilica in her background.

"This is Gabriella Luchesi," the woman said, "CNN correspondent in Rome. I stand just outside Vatican City, spiritual home to over one billion Catholics around the world. CNN cameras are present here in St. Peter's Square to cover the highly unusual, posthumous proclamation by the late Peter the Second, as well as the election of his successor. These events, which had once again placed Vatican City on the center of the world stage, now seem to pale in comparison to the phenomenon occurring above us at this very moment."

Anthony sat on the edge of his bed as the camera angled upward to capture the bright object. Brilliant white and pulsing, it seemed to be alive. The reporter spoke over the live video feed.

"The entire world is captivated by the atmospheric phenomenon taking place over the city of Rome. According to reports from the European Space Agency, NASA, and the Italian Air Force, the object you now see on your television screens apparently did not pass through Earth's outer atmosphere.

"Scientists are at a loss to explain the phenomenon, but facts seem to eliminate some of the more exotic theories such as extraterrestrial intelligence. Many faithful here outside St. Peter's Square see it as a sign and are tying it to the late Pope's posthumous declaration, scheduled to be aired in little over an hour.

"We switch now to CNN's Chief Science Correspondent, Doctor Henry Osbourne in London, for his take on this extraordinary event taking place in the skies over Rome."

Various talking heads took turns providing theories to explain the bizarre phenomenon. He switched off the set.

Little did they know.

With the black nylon bag once again draped over his shoulder, he covered the short distance to the Sistine Chapel in minutes. The massive wooden doors were flanked by huge marble columns and two Swiss Guards in full regalia.

He tried to slow his breathing. Something wasn't right. He had the strangest feeling that when the door opened, he wouldn't see the familiar chapel, but rather a gaping abyss belching out fire and brimstone.

A guard pulled open the door. No fire, no abyss. He entered the familiar chapel as the heavy doors closed behind him.

His colleagues weren't engaged in vigorous discussion over the Papal decree as he had expected but instead stood transfixed, gazing upon the incredible celestial phenomenon occurring outside the high arched windows.

The glass' bevels in the windows fractured the mysterious glow into a broad spectrum, splashing the interior walls of the chapel with a range of color that did not seem random to Anthony. His hands clenched into fists as he called out loudly, "Where is Cardinal Capello?"

Holy Law ordained the Bishop of Ostia to preside over conclave, and his was one of only a few heads that turned. "We are behind schedule," he said. "Where have you been, Cardinal Lombardi?"

Anthony ignored the question and repeated his. "Where is Capello?"

"He has been chosen to assist Marini in the reading of the proclamation."

"Who decided this, Gregorio?" Anthony said.

"The Carmerlengo."

"Tarcisio?" Anthony felt his heart leap in his chest. "Where *is* Cardinal Marini?"

An unfamiliar voice rose from the gathering as more heads turned. "He and Capello are in the Palace, preparing for the proclamation as we speak. It is in mere minutes."

A third voice rose. "You have been outside, Anthony. The light . . . what is its source?"

Then another. "It is like the Star of David. Is it a sign?"

Now, everyone faced him. Anthony stepped on a small raised platform built for conclave. He took note of the apprehension in the eyes focused on him and used carefully measured words. "My brothers in Christ," he began, his voice strong and vibrant, "I believe what is happening today is indeed a sign, a harbinger for an event which could change the world."

In confusion, they looked at one another and back at him. Patrick Dougherty stepped out from the crowd and approached.

"Anthony," he said, a look of compassion on his face. "Something unique is taking place in the heavens above us, something which is truly miraculous. We are all gathered here in Rome to hear a posthumous declaration by our brother Peter, an Ex Cathedra pronouncement that could forever change the Church. To which world-changing event are you referring?"

Dougherty's questions opened the floodgate. As dozens of new voices rose from the crimson sea, Anthony felt a familiar warmth rush over him again. He instinctively dropped to his knees and lowered his head. From the crash of voices, a tense silence ensued, one that seemed to extend beyond the chapel and into the night.

A litany of prayer flowed over his lips, beseeching a God Whose presence now felt closer than his next breath. He looked up into the focused stare of almost two hundred old men, knowing his next words could change the course of human history.

Chapter 33

Grace leaned up against the cold stone wall inside the Apostolic Palace and took a deep breath. It had taken them much longer than expected to find their way to the Bronze Doors, and a growing apprehension had turned her knees to mush.

The crowd's voices resonated against the walls. Next to her, Kellen and Daniel reassured each other—and her—that Manny would be fine. But she had quit listening. She felt his danger.

A cell phone buzzed from her mother's purse. Kellen pulled it out, glanced at the screen, and handed it quickly to Grace.

Grace fumbled with the phone. "Hello."

"Signora Barden?"

"This is her daughter Grace. Who's this?"

"Comandante-Generale Michael Lombardi. I have called to tell you that Signor Lusum and my brother Anthony have been arrested."

"Arrested?" Her voice squeaked the word as she exchanged nervous glances with her mother and Daniel. As they began to speak, she held up her hand to shush them. "Please explain."

"I fear it was more of an abduction than an arrest. Friendly sources within the Vatican Gendarme tell me a rogue element within the Swiss Guard has done this."

"Why? I don't understand."

"I am at a loss, but in light of recent events, I feel certain senior church officials with ties to the Academy are responsible."

"Where did they take them? What are you doing to get them free?"

"Security footage may reveal this, but I think it is possible that my brother is no longer imprisoned." There was a pause on the line. "He left me a very peculiar voicemail."

"Voice—mail?"

"I am not sure what to make of it." The comandante seemed to struggle with the words. "My brother seemed very upset, and his words were absurd. Perhaps it was merely the fault of the connection, which was weak, and his phone actually died in the middle of the message, but he spoke of . . . "

Grace wanted to scream. *Get on with it.* "What? What did he say?"

"He spoke of angelic beings. And demons."

Grace almost dropped the phone as a chill filled her. She grabbed her mother's hand, pulling her toward the Bronze Doors. "I'm very worried, Comandante."

"These men are very powerful," the comandante said. "However, they have much invested in Signor Lusum." He paused before continuing in a softer tone. "I believe he is safe, at least for now."

"What can we do?" Grace said, as two members of the Swiss Guard opened the doors for them.

"I am en route as we speak. I am not sure how long it will take me to get there, considering the traffic. It is more than I've ever seen in my lifetime, so I am not sure if I can get there before the proclamation. What is the tone of the crowd in St. Peter's Square?"

"We're just now exiting through the Bronze Doors," Grace said. "But there's a ton of people out here."

"Then you cannot see the entity from your position?"

Grace stopped short and her parents ran into her back. "Entity?"

"In the sky above Vatican City," the comandante said. "An entity for which I have no name."

"What *entity* are you . . ." And then her gaze became fixed on a bright object in the night sky, a bizarre pulsating light that seemed to cast the entire square in an unnatural light.

"What . . . is . . . that . . . ?" It mesmerized her, as it seemed to do to everyone around her. She peeked over her shoulder and saw her mother and Daniel standing with gaping mouths.

"No one seems to know," the comandante said. "It appeared less than an hour ago in the skies over Rome and eventually settled over the Holy City. The television stations have suggested theories ranging from extraterrestrial life to atmospheric anomalies, but no one knows for sure. Our Air Force has flown several sorties past the object but learned nothing. It does not appear to be a military threat."

"Do you think it has anything to do with Manny?"

"I am not as familiar with Scripture as my brother. However, was it not a star that signaled Christ's first coming?"

Chapter 34

Cardinal Anthony Lombardi felt like his head was in the lion's jaw. For three decades, the church he devoted his life to had fought an external enemy, unaware of the nefarious presence in their own midst. An aberration of evil for which there was no frame of reference, no designated patron saint to pray to for relief.

Now he stared out at the gnarled faces of the men who stared back at him, talking among themselves, their voices rising and falling. The reading of the Papal proclamation was in less than an hour, and the tension in the Sistine Chapel was like a thick cloud.

"Hear me!" he bellowed over the cacophony, his arms thrown wide. He had to swallow twice before the words could escape, but when they did, they tumbled out in a breathless rush.

He told the amazing story of demonic possession and ancient catacombs. Of scientific realities that defied logic and challenged traditional concepts of good and evil. He trembled as he spoke. His audience gaped. "Everything I have told you is true," he added, struggling to regain control over his ragged breathing.

The awkward silence was broken by a weak voice emerging from the middle of the crowd. The cardinals parted, and Cardinal

Dingxiang Wu of China stood alone and motionless, his face bleached to the color of bone.

He bowed. "You say Capello devil," he said, his words heavily accented. "You say he bring back Jesus?" Wu looked from his colleagues to Anthony. "I find very hard to believe."

From among the frail bodies draped in blood-red cassocks, some faces showed confusion, most revealed concern. A few displayed cautious disbelief, as if his story were part of an elaborate practical joke. Anthony gripped the lectern.

"I have proof, my brothers." He measured his words as their attention again turned to him. "Satan has long sought out the weak within the walls of this Church, some of whom may be among us at this *very* moment."

Anthony hesitated as a low rumble of murmurs moved through the gathering. "Yes, he has found some among us over the years, and like a cancer, they have metastasized throughout our Church, cell by cell. The evil ones among us use traditional, sometimes even pious language, in an effort to inoculate themselves from any suspicion. But you must hear me, my brothers! Our beloved Church housed an incubator of evil, a literal birthplace for hell on Earth."

Anthony's words echoed in the silence of the dimly lit chapel, creating an almost hypnotic effect. Cardinal Vladimir Svabotka stepped forward and removed a crimson biretta from atop smoky gray hair. Anthony knew him from their time together on the Pontifical Council for the Family. A survivor of Soviet gulags and the infamous Siberian labor camps, the elderly cleric was both well-respected and not easily intimidated.

"Please indulge me, my old friend," Svabotka said in his familiar, heavy Russian accent. "As you know, my Italian is not as fluent as it should be."

Anthony nodded. The whispers swelled and quieted as Svabotka continued. "If I understood you correctly," Svabotka spoke slowly, precisely. "You were in the actual presence of Lucifer? Within the very *walls* of our Holy City? In the form of our colleague Cardinal Capello? And . . ." There was a hush across the chapel as Svabotka paused and took a deep breath. "You would not be here at this very moment, had it not been for the direct intervention of Michael the Archangel?"

Anthony looked into Svabotka's aging eyes and sensed the old man wanted to offer him a way out. A final opportunity to say it had all been a joke or to claim some form of temporary insanity. A chance to smile awkwardly and tuck his tail between his legs before he got on with the business of stewarding over a billion Catholics around the world.

Under any other circumstances, it would have been an attractive offer, this opportunity to pretend his words were nothing more than the product of stress or a warped sense of humor. But that was not an option.

"Very well." Svabotka breathed a heavy sigh and began rubbing his temples with bony fingers. "You also claim that a group, operating within these very these walls, used some form of biological sorcery and alchemy forbidden by the Church and created an offspring of Jesus Christ?"

All Anthony could do was nod. He too had once shared those doubts.

"You also claim to be in possession of, what *could* be, the actual writings of our Lord and Savior. As well as those of the Rock upon which He built this very church? Writings that you say would help to substantiate your claims?"

Anthony's eyes dropped from Svabotka to the case hanging from his shoulder. He rubbed his hands across the black nylon and felt the reassuring outline of solid, rectangular objects. His voice held conviction when he said, "Yes. Yes, I do."

"Finally, you claim to have actually met this young man . . . this *Immanuel*," Svabotka said. "You say not only is he the mirror image of the man in the Shroud of Turin, but he is even now being held somewhere here within the walls of the Vatican." Svabotka paused, closed his eyes momentarily, and then looked back at Anthony. "My words, would you say they are accurate?"

"I would."

An invisible breeze brushed through the room, causing the candles to flicker. Shadows gathered in the far corner of the chapel, and something snarled. Anthony struggled to see what he hoped wasn't there.

A new and familiar voice rose. "These are grave accusations you make, Anthony." Cardinal Patrick Dougherty's normally blue eyes had darkened, and his anger-laced words hung in the dimly lit chapel. "All based on a story that is—and I believe my colleagues will concur—exceedingly difficult to believe." This last he said with a sweep of his hand to include the rest of the gathering.

Was Dougherty one of *them?* "You know me, Patrick. You were there with Peter the night of his death."

Dougherty took several steps forward, his hands piously clenched at his waist. "I can also vouch for the fact that His Holiness re-opened the Fatima prophecies and spoke of the future of the Church. Both are true. However, to claim Mary's prophecy to the Church was altered or perhaps *demonic in origin* is simply preposterous. As laughable as the Catholic Church being taunted by the business end of a pitchfork." Dougherty's tone morphed from concern to a mocking compassion. "No doubt, I am sure, the product of stress."

"Truth is the one thing man has always wanted to invent and yet could not," Anthony said. "I have proof of my claims."

"Proof of what, Anthony? Proof of the existence of a cloven-hoofed demon? Do you know how well that will fly in the media? We would be a laughing stock!"

"You cannot believe in here," Anthony said before pointing to the chapel's doors, "and not believe out there. Too many *enlightened* priests have dismissed, with a sneer, the idea of evil in the form of an actual being. Perhaps it is *we* who lack faith, Patrick? Faith in an evil so profound it has infiltrated the very bastion of Christianity. I intend to shine a light into the darkness that has—"

"Enough!" Dougherty ripped open his robe from the front, and the dark red buttons scattered across the floor. "This is blasphemy! Show us all this *proof* you claim to have."

Dougherty's actions jolted Anthony. Hadn't the High Priest of the Sanhedrin behaved just so at the cross examination of Jesus? Anthony lifted the nylon bag for all to see. His lungs burned. "In this bag is the proof, in the very words of those who worked for the Academy. As well as a two-thousand-year-old artifact of immeasurable value. The very words of Jesus, *perhaps* written by His very hand."

A collective gasp echoed in the chapel. Rather than inching forward to see the incredible relic, the crowd slunk back, perhaps out of reverence for what could possibly be in their presence. All except Dougherty, who stepped forward with his arms across his chest.

"Ah yes," Dougherty said. "I am anxious to see Peter's third epistle . . . as well as *First Jesus*."

Anthony placed the nylon bag on the slanted top of the lectern. He pulled the zipper open and made the sign of the cross on his head and torso. Reaching in gently, his fingers were met by an unexpected sensation. He stood rooted in fear and disbelief, his eyes now transfixed on the contents of the bag.

"This cannot be," Anthony said, reaching in to touch the gray ash and melted plastic.

"Let me guess." Dougherty stepped up onto the raised platform. "Your *evidence* has been tampered with?"

"It is destroyed. Ashes." He could barely speak. "How? It was just here, seconds ago."

"Was this bag ever out of your grasp, Anthony?" Dougherty asked, leaning forward to examine the contents.

"No, I've had it with me since I left the catacombs. It is not possible."

"No one has entered this place since you arrived. You are welcome to watch security footage, but I'm afraid we do not have any popcorn or any more time for this nonsense."

"I don't know how . . ."

"Are we to believe that what was inside this case—which as I observe, shows no sign of damage—incinerated spontaneously?"

"I have no explanation." He couldn't believe it. Shutting his eyes, Anthony prayed. Surely, if God had sent the Archangel Michael to encourage him, there would be a way out of this. There would be some explanation. There must be.

And then it came to him. "The face!"

"What face?" came a voice from the crowd.

"The face in the Shroud, a face everyone in this room has seen. The young man I told you all about. He is among us!"

Heads pivoted as chatter arose in the chapel, dozens of voices speaking at the same time. Dougherty's voice again rose above the clamor. "No offense to those present, but I see no one here who could qualify as a young man. Not to mention, a mirror image of the man in the Shroud."

"Not in the chapel," Anthony said. "Here, in the Holy City. As

I told you, the Swiss Guard arrested us both when we entered the city. He is somewhere—"

"Enough of this nonsense," Dougherty bellowed. "If this young man exists, I am sure he will make his presence known in due time. The Holy Father's declaration will be read in minutes, and it is important we are present in the Square. The world awaits."

Anthony watched as the College of Cardinals shuffled out of the chapel.

Yes, the world awaited. As did heaven and hell.

Chapter 35

One minute, Manny was in the Borgia Tower, two Swiss Guardsmen holding him as another struck Cardinal Lombardi with the butt end of a handgun. The next, he floated in a silent void, surrounded by perplexing images. One would dominate, and then another, eventually merging into a discordant patchwork of dull colors before fading to pitch black.

Was this death?

Bit by bit, he became aware of his various body parts. First, his hands and feet, followed by his arms and legs. He placed a hand on his chest and could feel the beat of his heart.

If he wasn't dead, where was he? Certainly no place he had been before. Instead of being earthbound, he was weightless, floating in a blackness that was much more than a visual thing. He could taste and feel, even *smell* the darkness. He had the strangest feeling that it had been waiting for him. Not just now, but for a long time.

A wave of rising sound interrupted the silence. Voices below him. Thousands of voices, maybe millions. They ceased suddenly as a more familiar voice replaced them—this one in his head. But his thoughts weren't in English anymore. Were they in Hebrew, perhaps Aramaic?

Without warning, a shaft of sunlight, or something like sunlight, cut through the blackness. A brilliant luminescence embraced him, almost as if he were an organic extension of it. The light revealed a multitude below him in a place he knew. A place the whole world knew. St. Peter's Square.

Tiny snippets of disparate memories followed. Not just those from a past he was *sure* he had lived but also blurred recollections of places and times that seemed to flow from a book. Something deep inside him longed to fill in the missing pieces.

Then a single, raw sensation rose above the rest. He was falling.

Chapter 36

St. Peter's Square barely resembled the pictures Grace had seen over the years. Instead of pious worshipers with their heads bowed in prayer, reporters and camera crews jammed in among them, and mobile broadcasting vans and their satellite dishes made the grounds look more like a NASA launch site than one of the holiest places on earth.

Eight massive video cameras were tuned to an empty balcony attached to the Apostolic Palace as a queer light emanated from the mysterious pulsing star that hovered a few hundred yards above the obelisk. As the star closed on the square, its light painted the travertine walls and the cupola of the Basilica.

Grace switched her cell phone from one ear to the other and tried to stay close to her parents. She had to scream into her cell phone as she struggled against the crush of humanity. "We're almost to the obelisk."

"The star." Cardinal Lombardi's voice came in a rush, as if he too were hurrying. "Have there been any changes?"

"There's a light coming from it now."

"A light?"

"A shaft of light pointing down on the obelisk. It's very bright. Also, the star's moving."

"Excuse me?"

"It's coming down. Slowly, but it's still—hold on. Some guys just came out on the balcony."

Grace slid between her parents for protection. Daniel wrapped his arms around her and continued to push through the throng. "I'm afraid, Cardinal Lombardi."

"Immanuel is under the protection of Our Lord," he said. "I don't believe his abductors will harm him."

"That's not all I'm afraid of."

The cardinal paused. When he continued, he spoke with authority. "You and your parents must know we are dealing with the same evil that attacked you as a child, Grace. I am certain of that."

"*Please* don't tell me it's in Manny."

"No. The Abomination now resides in the body of a fellow cardinal. I faced him again this day."

"Why here? Why now?"

Disconnected syllables came through the phone as background noises absorbed the cardinal's words. "Cardinal Lombardi?" Her voice cracked.

"I believe Immanuel is his ultimate target," Cardinal Lombardi said. "We must pray for his deliverance."

As Grace fought back tears, her cell phone echoed the din around her.

"I have arrived with my colleagues in the Square," he said. "Can you see us?"

"Yes."

A swarm of crimson-robed men flowed through the Bronze Doors. She redirected her focus to the Papal Balcony where a man clad in a white robe and red skullcap guided himself onto the balcony in a wheelchair. When the man raised his right hand, the star emitted an odd humming noise, causing the vast crowd to immediately fall silent. She felt her father's arms tighten around her.

"What was that?" Grace could hear Cardinal Lombardi's heavy breathing. "I think they're going to start reading the declaration" she said. "Who's the guy in the wheelchair?"

"Cardinal Tarcisio Marini," the cardinal replied. "He was Peter's personal assistant and was chosen to read his posthumous declaration. I must warn you, the words you are about to hear are not inspired by God. They are to be feared. Pray, Grace. Get your parents to pray."

The connection ended. She turned to her parents and had only time to say, "He wants us to pray. It's bad," before everyone began pointing toward the Papal Balcony.

Marini reached down and raised an object in the air. Through the closest video camera they could see that he held a leather portfolio with some type of insignia on its face. Dim outlines of other robed clerics showed from the shadows of the Apostolic Palace. Marini was not a big man, especially confined to a wheelchair, but he towered like a giant on the video screens around the Square.

He pulled the microphone from its mount and gestured with his other hand toward the College of Cardinals huddled outside the Bronze Doors. "Your Eminences." His voice echoed across the vast space. "Venerable Brothers in the Episcopate and the Priesthood, dear Brothers and Sisters, welcome. I am Cardinal Tarcisio Marini, Carmerlengo to the late Holy Father, Pope Peter the Second."

As Marini spoke, Grace drew her parents close enough to tell them the rest of what the cardinal had said. Her mother's eyes rounded, but Daniel merely closed his eyes, obviously praying.

"Don't worry, Mom," Grace said, as much to soothe herself as her mother.

Marini's voice boomed again over the loudspeakers. "It is my distinct privilege to be here today," he said. "To have been given the honor of reading the posthumous declaration of my dear friend and our late brother."

Grace turned her attention back to the monitor as Marini placed the leather portfolio on the balcony's railing and brought his hands together in front of his face as if in prayer. Looking up to the sky with pious eyes, he said, "I believe the phenomenon taking place above us is not merely a bizarre coincidence. As the Star of Bethlehem signaled the birth of Christ over two thousand years ago, I am led by faith to believe that we are once again witnessing a true miracle of God."

As his words thundered out toward the stunned multitude, the other clerics stepped out on the balcony, bowed their heads, and raised their eyes to the sky as though the entire scene had been carefully choreographed.

"The one on the left is Capello," Daniel said of the distinguished looking man standing behind Marini. The unease in her father's eyes chilled Grace to the bone.

Marini picked up the leather portfolio and, with great reverence, broke what looked like a wax seal, as the video monitors followed his every movement. Folding open the front of the portfolio, he said, "The words I now read are the words of our late Pontiff, Pope Peter the Second. This declaration was written by his own hand before several witnesses and sealed just prior to his death. His Holiness spoke from the Chair of Peter, which means the Roman Catholic Church is bound to the following words as holy law."

The scene appeared surreal. The strange glowing orb had detached itself from the night sky and settled directly above the pointed top of the obelisk. It bathed everything in an eerie glow, and Grace felt a strange, cold air settle around her. She turned back to the monitor.

Marini slid glasses up his nose. As speakers around the Square amplified his voice, network and cable television stations broadcast his words to the entire planet.

"Brothers and Sisters in Christ, my time is short, yet I am compelled to address the Church in a manner not invoked by my predecessors for over sixty years. I speak the following words Ex Cathedra."

Marini paused, removed his glasses, and wiped his brow with a handkerchief. Almost in unison, the other clerics on the balcony made the sign of the cross. Marini exhaled loudly enough for it to be captured by the microphone and replaced his glasses.

"I, Peter the Second, the former Lorenzo Agostini of Naples, former Bishop of Bologna and Archbishop of Venice, the two hundred and sixty-fourth Bishop of Rome and servant of God, do solemnly declare the end of mankind's reign over Christ's church on Earth. I, Peter the Second, shall be the final Pope."

Grace stood dumbstruck along with the rest of the crowd. She imagined stone tablets on a mountaintop, parting seas and pillars of fire. Instead, the tinny words echoed in the foreground of an eerie silence. Hope and anticipation faded from the eyes of the faithful around her. Something much darker took its place.

Marini's voice again cut sharply into the night air. *"I, know this comes as a tremendous shock to the Church, but this is often the case with divine revelation. The prophecies of Saint Malachy were clear that my Papacy would be the last. I too received visions in the past few weeks revealing a new era for the Church. This brings me, regrettably, to the miracle of Fatima.*

"I am saddened to inform the body of Christ that Church

leadership misled us in 1980. Our Holy Mother Mary's third revelation in Fatima allegedly spoke of the assassination attempt on Pope John Paul the Second. However, the truth behind our Holy Mother's prophecy is much different than what was revealed to the world. I have enclosed Mary's actual words, in Sister Lucia's own handwriting, as part of this encyclical.

"In it, Mary revealed a future. A future in which mankind's corrupt rule over God's Church would come to an end. A time when we would no longer drink from the chalice of deceit, from the fruit of the vine of mistruth. A time when there would come forth a new fruit from a new vine, yet one older than time itself. This time is upon us.

Therefore, by way of this Ex Cathedra declaration, I cast a stone into the ocean--a stone whose ripple will never die, creating infinite waves of truth that shall circle the globe.

I leave these words for the joy and exultation of the entire Church, by the authority of our Lord Jesus Christ, the blessed Apostle Peter, and by my own authority. I pronounce, declare, and define it to be a divinely revealed dogma, that the Pontificate of Peter the Second, two hundred and sixty-fourth Bishop of Rome, having completed the course of my earthly life, shall be the last.

Henceforth, if anyone, God forbid, should dare willfully to deny or to call into doubt that which I have defined, let him know that he has fallen away completely from the divine and Catholic Faith. I, Peter II, Bishop of the Catholic Church, have signed, so defining."

As Marini's voice faded into the night, the dancing fire overhead began to pulsate with greater brightness and frequency. The glowing orb renewed its descent, sliding down the side of the obelisk and becoming so bright that Grace had to shield her eyes.

Marini's voice exploded again across the Square. "Just as in the times of our forefathers—Moses, Elijah, Abraham, and the Apostles, I call upon God once again to make Himself known to all. I call upon the one *true* name of God, a name not spoken by humankind since the time of the Prophets. I call upon . . ."

Marini paused for a moment and lifted his arms high above his head. His lips moved, causing one-of-a-kind sound waves to travel acoustically across the Square and electronically across the planet.

Grace's ears tingled and her heart felt as if it would leap from her chest, just as every soul in St. Peter's Square dropped to his knees and fell forward. She found herself face down on the cold stone. And knew—without knowing how—that every person on earth now lay prostrate before heaven.

Chapter 37

In the surrounding silence, Manny's pounding heart slowed, synching with his descent toward the ground. He felt like a caterpillar, ensconced in a chrysalis of light. Below him, thousands lay prostrate on the ground.

And then it happened.

A single, sacred word penetrated the cocoon, separating Manny from his past and triggering billions of dormant brain cells. Without warning, he breathed air imbued with the coppery smell of blood. He heard the sounds of metal pounding metal, ripping flesh, and shattering bone. Indefinable pain roared back in crippling waves as stark memories of a wooden cross exploded across his conscious mind. Then horrific screams. His own.

Beliefs he had held as absolutes liquefied in the intense light surrounding him. The knowledge that death inevitably followed life no longer seemed true. He was no longer slave to the mechanism of time, to its ruthless efficiency that turned everything to dust.

Memories exploded in his mind. He'd been betrayed for thirty pieces of silver and had suffered and died at the hands of Roman soldiers. He had drifted into a deep darkness and re-emerged via a brilliant flash of light—not unlike the one that now emanated from him.

His feet touched the ground next to the obelisk, and the light faded as though reabsorbed into his body. Manny discerned cries of praise and worship in the midst of the verbal chaos. An old man in a crimson robe stood next to him, holding up the burial shroud that had once covered him in death. The man screamed to the crowd, making audacious claims as he welcomed a new dawn.

Chapter 38

Grace slowly pulled herself off the ground and helped her parents up. Together, they stepped around the blanket of worshipers still spread out across the floor of St. Peter's Square and pressed toward the bizarre object as it settled next to the obelisk.

By the time they reached their goal, a team of Swiss Guardsmen had already formed a large circle around it. Marini, Capello, and the other men from the Papal Balcony stood inside the protective ring, along with a CNN news crew, Cardinal Lombardi, and several other men wearing crimson robes. All gazed at the object that had just made contact with the ground.

Grace struggled through a crowd of cardinals until she reached the human chain formed by the Swiss Guard. A muscular guardsman pushed her away from the ring. She would have stumbled if her mother hadn't taken one hand and her father the other. She squeezed theirs tightly and gave each a slight smile.

She turned back to the obelisk just as the glaring light faded enough to reveal the outline of a man. A familiar face followed the familiar outline. Grace's breath caught in her throat, and her body stiffened. She squeezed her eyes shut, trying again to will away that same unwanted vision.

Manny Lusum stood with his arms at his sides, clad in a brilliant white robe. His hair seemed longer than just hours ago. His beard was fuller but his face shallow, as if the bone beneath had given way. The dark skin of his face had become the color of a bruise, and his empty eyes those of a man possessed.

A man dressed like Cardinal Lombardi stood only feet away from Manny, and his powerful Irish brogue pierced the eerie silence. "His return was foretold!"

As the voices of the crowd surged in excitement and volume, a young CNN reporter rushed towards the cardinal, her cameraman hurrying to keep up. "This is Gabriel Luchesi," she said, looking over her shoulder periodically. "Still following the incredible series of events taking place here in Vatican City tonight." She carefully nudged her way past Marini in his wheelchair and stood next to Dougherty, waiting for her cameraman to get in position.

"With me now is Cardinal Patrick Dougherty," Luchesi yelled into the microphone, "a senior advisor to the late Pope Peter the Second and first-hand witness to the spectacular series of events that are unfolding here in St. Peter's Square. Your Eminence, would you comment please?"

The young woman turned to where Dougherty had been standing seconds ago, but he was now on his knees, kissing Manny's bare feet beneath the white robe. Luchesi stepped out of the way to let the cameraman edge closer.

"Cardinal Dougherty." Luchesi slid next to the cameraman with the microphone extended out the length of her arm. Dougherty lifted his head slowly, his hands folded in prayer. "Please, Your Eminence," she added. "The world is watching and listening."

"The world saw what we saw," Dougherty said, not taking his eyes off Manny. "The Messiah has returned to us from the heavens and stands before us now in power and glory. Look at his face. It is clearly the mirror image captured in the Christ's burial shroud. Look at his hands and his feet. Consider the words of His Holiness. The Second Coming is upon us! This is prophecy fulfilled!"

Grace bit her bottom lip, her clasp tightening on the hands she held. The cameraman approached Manny, now standing with arms outstretched from his robe. The massive crowd fell into silence again when the camera zoomed in on hideous scars on the base of Manny's hands and to similar ones on the tops of his bare feet.

Manny shocked everyone within earshot when he spoke. "You will find a similar wound in my side," he said. Then, placing his hands on Dougherty's bowed head, he smiled and added, "You have been a good and faithful servant, Patrick, in whom I am well pleased."

Dougherty fell face down on the ground. "My Lord."

Manny gestured with his left hand toward the Carmerlengo in his wheelchair. "As have you, Tariscio."

Everyone within earshot turned toward the man in the wheelchair. Marini displayed a look of great reverence and lowered his head.

Manny approached Marini and gently placed his hand on his head. "Rise, my son," he said. "Your faith has healed you!"

Grace repositioned herself between the burly guards just in time to see the Carmerlengo lift his head, revealing a look of surprise on his face. An aura swept over him and his hands tightened into fists as his eyes turned down to the lifeless appendages dangling from the bottom of his torso. Suddenly, his dead legs twitched, and a collective gasp went up from the crowd surrounding the obelisk.

Marini grasped the arms of the chair. He pushed straight up until his torso hung above the wheelchair's vinyl seat, his legs draped vertically down. He settled lifeless feet on the ground and, without hesitating, shoved the chair out from underneath him. For a second Marini teetered, and the crowd seemed to suck in air in perfect unison. He steadied himself, took a small, measured step, and, looking up in amazement, threw his arms in the air. "My God has healed me!"

Grace felt her body go limp. As she struggled to keep from fainting, a familiar voice rose above the clamor.

"No!" Cardinal Lombardi screamed as he shoved past several cardinals. His eyes were wide and his body trembling noticeably. "This shall not stand! We know the *truth*. We know—"

"Silence!" Manny boomed, his voice echoing off acres of marble and stone. "Only men of faith shall address my father's church. Remove him."

The Swiss Guard swooped in on a stunned Cardinal Lombardi. Grace looked over her shoulder at her parents and said, "I need in."

Daniel and Kellen nodded, whispered into each other's ears, and rushed the guards protecting the circle on either side of Grace. Two guards turned in opposite directions to push back the invaders, leaving Grace a small gap to slip through. No one seemed to notice her, so it was easy to slide past a few crimson robes. In one motion, she leapt, threw her arms around Manny's neck, and hugged him as tightly as she could.

She felt his muscles tighten and strong arms push back. "It's me, Manny," she cried, staring into lifeless orbs. "Gracie! Grace Barden. I love you. You loved…you *love* me. This isn't who you are."

Manny stood rigid and unmoving. Grace pulled as hard as she could on his neck and pressed her lips to his, trying to penetrate whatever it was that held him captive. She heard footsteps and felt the shadow of the man touch her before his hands did. Cardinal Lucius Capello pulled her away from Manny like she was a rag doll.

"Succubus!" he screamed.

With her feet almost a foot off the ground, Capello's powerful hands dug into her flesh. Forgotten memories from her childhood rushed back so violently that Grace melted under the man's intense glare. She had never met the cardinal, but she knew those eyes, the eyes of a predator, and she recognized the feral odor of the beast that seeped through the pores of his skin.

He threw her backward toward the obelisk with a powerful thrust. Grace landed on her feet, but stumbled and fell, hitting the back of her head on something hard. As her world faded from gray to black, Capello loomed over her. He whispered into her ear, his words rising up as if from a deep pool of venom.

"Where is your Jesus now?"

Chapter 39

Strange. **There seemed to be two of him.**

Both alive apparently. Both conscious, each aware of the other. One was performing on the world stage, fully detached from his former self. That one had left any sense of reason far up in the clouds.

The other Manny Lusum felt like a detached observer, but not drifting invisibly above his body like he had seen so often in movies. This Manny was also inside his body, surrounded by a darkness that pressed in on him.

A young woman lay hurt, and a trickle of blood seeped out from under familiar ash blonde hair, a tiny red river flowing over freckles on a face he was sure he knew. Something lurked just beyond the edges of his awareness, and his lips burned with the memory of hers.

As his mind juggled scrambled memories and realities, faraway recollections surfaced, and a new—yet old—understanding washed over him like a tsunami.

Her name was Grace. He had loved her.

No. He *did* love her.

He began to move toward her. At the same time, a reddish form approached, brandishing a silver dagger. *It was the man who had hurt Grace, and he wasn't done.*

Before Manny could react, cold steel pierced his frail human body. Rather than the pain from the severing of skin, blood vessels, and organs, he felt an eerie sense of déjà vu penetrating him. The man pulled Manny toward him with incredible force, as the warmth of liquid sacrifice leaked from his torn body.

"Consider yourself pierced for *my* transgressions," he whispered into Manny's ear. "You now shed the blood of *our* New Covenant."

Manny stared down at the dagger in his side, at the pink bloom on his robe. He heard a horrific wail. It came from his own mouth.

"Think of this as a benediction of sorts, Immanuel," the man continued under his breath. "The end of what was, the beginning of what will be. As I destroy you, I resurrect me."

He twisted the steel blade in Manny's side and screamed above the crowd. "If he is indeed the Christ, death shall not hold him!"

The man shuddered violently against Manny and staggered backward with the bloody knife in his hand. As Manny slumped to the ground, the old man's face seemed to wake from a deep sleep, and he stared down at the knife as if it had just materialized in his hand.

Manny's body convulsed. Something flashed in his consciousness, and his world faded to a complete and total blackness.

Chapter 40

Grace woke to throbbing pain and probed the gash with her fingertips through her blood-soaked hair. "Where's Manny?"

Her mother crouched next to her and checked the wound. "They carried him away. The cardinal told your father and me—"

Grace looked around. "Where's Father N—where's Dad?"

Rubbing the corner of her eyes with the palms of her hands, Kellen said, "Cardinal Lombardi grabbed your father when they took Manny to the Sistine Chapel. It was on all the video screens." She paused and added, "Manny's hurt, Grace."

Fresh tears rose, and Grace's world blurred again. "Hurt? What? How?"

"After he—" Kellen paused, grabbing her daughter's hands. "After Capello attacked you, he stabbed Manny."

"No! Why? I don't understand."

"Several of the cardinals and some of the crowd were proclaiming him as the second coming of Christ. I guess Capello took exception."

Grace's head pounded as she struggled to her feet. "Is it bad?"

"We don't know." Kellen braced her with a steadying hand. "But he was breathing when they carried him away. I heard the Swiss

Guard calling for a medical team to meet them there."

Grace and Kellen pushed through the crowd to the Bronze Doors, where Grace pounded for entrance. No one came, of course. No one paid her any attention. She slumped on the ground alongside her mother as a single tear coursed down her cheek.

Something dark had risen. A thunderous crack followed a bolt of lightening. Then a small earthquake struck beneath Vatican City, and the thunder rose from the earth instead of the sky.

Chapter 41

Cardinal Lombardi held Manny's limp and frigid hand as the younger man lay on the altar of the Sistine Chapel, his face contorted into a pale mask that rendered it almost inhuman. Anthony pressed his fingers against the side of Manny's neck and found a weak and irregular pulse. The dagger lay by Manny's side, next to a wide splatter of blood that stood out against his brilliant white robe. *So much blood.*

A single Swiss Guard officer stood just inside the doors of the chapel as a contingent of his fellow guardsmen remained at attention behind him. The young man looked confused and fearful. "Bishop Gregorio," he said. "Your orders?"

An old man in a black robe stepped out from amongst the cardinals. "This is not conclave," he said solemnly. "I have no authority here."

The young officer approached Cardinal Lombardi, saluted, and clasped his hands behind his back. "Your Eminence," he said. "The medical team is en route. We must—"

"We have no need for medical assistance," Anthony said.

The officer looked left, right, and over his shoulder.

"This is a spiritual matter, my son." Anthony rested a hand on the man's forearm. "Have the doctors wait outside the chapel until they are called."

"Cardinal Capello?"

"Take him with you," Anthony said, looking over his shoulder at the deflated form. Capello stood hunched over in the arms of Father Daniel Neumann, spittle running down his chin. "Keep him under your control. We will deal with his spiritual needs when we have finished here."

"As you wish, Your Eminence." The young officer bowed his head and saluted once more. He gestured to those with him, and they quickly removed Capello. As the large doors closed, simultaneous voices rose from the College of Cardinals.

Cardinal Luiz Gonzales of Peru pushed through the crowd, his face pale and his eyes large. "He must have medical care, Anthony."

"It is not the knife wound that threatens him, Luiz. You saw Lucius. Do you not understand what has happened here?"

Nodding acknowledgement, the other cardinal stepped up to the altar and placed his hand on Manny's forehead. "Apparently, he bleeds like the rest of us."

"I would not be so sure," Anthony said.

Cardinal Gonzales opened his mouth as if to speak and then closed it. Perhaps he and the others feared their words might again give life to the beast.

"You all know the truth." Anthony's voice rose as he spoke. "The Evil One will not sacrifice his greatest work on an altar of God. Immanuel's body is now the battlefield for his soul."

Suddenly, a loud rumble shook the room as if a dark energy throbbed within its walls. Anthony placed fingers from both hands through the tear in Manny's robe and ripped apart the fabric, exposing the gaping wound. As if Manny's blood carried disease cells, Anthony quickly wiped his hands on his own robe.

"Immanuel is no longer merely a man. I have faced this adversary before, in America twenty-three years ago."

A shudder worked its way through the assembly. The old men inched backward as Father Neumann approached the altar.

"I can smell this adversary," Anthony said. "I can feel him and taste the bile of his very existence."

"He is an innocent young man," Gonzales protested.

Anthony wiped his brow with the sleeve of his robe. "His body was conceived in hell and stitched together by human arrogance, Luiz. He has become a vessel for the unholy one and—"

At that, the lights went out, and the entire chapel pitched and swayed, heaving violently as if about to tumble stone from stone. Hundreds of votive candles in the chapel remained lit but swayed slowly, causing the space to come alive with jumping shadows.

Gonzales leaned against the altar to steady himself. "Look," he screamed. "His wound!"

Anthony grabbed a nearby candle and held it over Manny. He blinked several times as the breath rushed from his lungs. The wound in the Manny's chest was closing up like hot wax running together, the river of blood drawing back into his body.

The Spirit of God nudged Anthony, and he shut out all other thoughts, focusing on what must be done. "I will need assistance." His voice sounded weak. *Please God, strengthen me.* "The Rite must be performed now!"

Daniel stepped up on the altar and knelt in front of Anthony. Anthony blessed him and looked out at the others. "A third?"

The old men glanced at each other, but only the silence answered. Lombardi called out. "Vladimir?"

The elderly cleric stepped forward and silently nodded his head.

"Come. We must prepare." Anthony turned to the others as

Daniel and Svabotka waited. "Brothers," he said, "tie Immanuel to the table while he is still unconscious." He answered their confused murmurs with, "Use your rosaries."

"They are not capable of constraining a small child, Anthony," Gonzales said. "Perhaps we should use our sashes?"

"Show faith, and they will hold."

Daniel and Svabotka followed Lombardi to the table set up for conclave. Anthony handed Daniel a paper cup, pulled the purple skirting of the table, and tore it into three equal sections. He blessed and kissed the fabric, and then draped it around his neck without saying a word. Daniel and Svabotka did the same with the other two pieces.

"We should pray." The sweat on Anthony's neck turned cold. "And gird ourselves for the battle ahead."

Daniel knelt again. Svabotka lowered his head and folded his hands in front of his face.

After a few seconds of silent prayer, Anthony lifted Daniel and said, "The LORD is my light and my salvation, in whom shall I fear? The LORD is the stronghold of my life, of whom shall I be afraid?"

"Amen," Daniel whispered. Svabotka swallowed hard and repeated the word in Russian.

"It is time."

"Should we discuss this, Anthony?" Svabotka said.

"Why?"

"Perhaps a little background on the young man?"

"We will not be dealing with Immanuel."

Svabotka's eyes were pleading. "Then what I am to expect?"

Anthony ushered the other men back toward the altar. "There are four stages to an exorcism," he began. "In the first phase, the demon tries to hide his true essence. We are well past that. The second is when he reveals himself."

"He will give us his name?" Svabotka said.

"There is no need for that," Anthony said. "We are not merely dealing with a demon, but with the prince of demons."

Svabotka halted, and his eyes asked the obvious question.

Anthony accepted Daniel's nod and placed his hands on Svabotka's shoulders. "This is much more than a simple possession, Vladimir. What is happening right now is a battle that has been prophesized for thousands of years."

Svabotka closed his eyes and exhaled heavily. "Matthew twenty-four," he said softly, folding his hands again in prayer. *"For there shall arise false Christs and false prophets, who shall shew great signs and wonders; insomuch that, if it were possible, they shall deceive the very elect."*

Anthony nodded and felt the tightness in his chest ease. God had brought him the right men. "When he awakens, I suspect we will be in the third phase," he said. "The *confrontation* is when we fight for the soul of the possessed. In this case, for the fate of humankind."

"What do you require of us?" Svabotka asked.

"Above all, your strong faith in the power of God, my friends. If we are successful in our battle, the demon will leave Immanuel. After which . . ." Anthony paused.

Daniel whispered, "All hell will break loose."

"I will not fail you," Svabotka said resolutely.

"I know of your difficult times in Siberia, Vladimir. The darkness you faced under Stalin. He knows of these times too. You must not let him manipulate you."

Svabotka's face changed, as if long-forgotten memories suddenly reappeared. He jerked his head, checking to the left and the right before nodding.

Anthony turned to face Daniel. "And he will most certainly appeal to your history with Immanuel. You must—"

"I know with whom we are dealing, Your Eminence," Daniel said with a look of determination. "I do not have a copy of the Rite. I am not sure . . ."

"It will not be necessary." Anthony stood as straight as his seventy-three-year-old body would permit and turned back toward the altar. "The words are forever etched in my brain. What I do not remember will be given to me. I have been prepared."

The cardinals parted for them to approach. Manny was now spread-eagled, his arms and legs fastened to the four legs of the altar with delicate chains linking tiny black prayer beads. Candles lined both sides of his body, and the dagger had been placed near Manny's head.

An inhuman voice spoke, one Anthony recognized. Although the words were unintelligible, the single voice was legion, like an angry mob chanting in rhythm.

"Vladimir, Daniel, we must begin." He grabbed Svabotka by the elbow and nodded at the paper cup in his hand. "Holy water, quickly."

Removing the silver crucifix from around his neck, Anthony kissed it and placed it on Manny's chest. Manny's face was pale and drawn, and his lips were peeled back, exposing blood at the corners.

As Svabotka returned with the holy water, the demon spoke. This time he used Manny's voice. "Clever," the voice said, as blood shot eyes peered out from behind crusted lids. He pulled on the restraints and said, "Where are the wooden stakes, Anthony? Or, perhaps a necklace of garlic?"

"In the Name of Jesus, the Christ, be silent," Anthony said, moving the crucifix from Manny's chest to his forehead.

"I won't make it easy this time, Anthony." The demon's matter-of-fact tone caught Anthony by surprise. "I am not done with this body yet. It is very special to me, and I intend to stay *much* longer than I did with Capello or the little piglet. You don't mind, do you?" Manny's lips bent into a devious grin.

Anthony picked up the bloody dagger near Manny's bound hands. He handed it to Daniel, who shoved it between his robe and sash.

"If you knew the fate that awaited you," the demon cooed softly, "you would turn that feeble weapon on yourself."

Anthony narrowed his eyes and traced the sign of the cross on Manny's forehead with the crucifix. A pounding echoed through the chapel as if its walls beat like a diseased heart.

The demon pulled violently on the fragile rosaries. "Do you think your silly parlor tricks will help you, you old fool?"

Anthony staggered backward at the force of the demon's breath. Righting himself, he pressed the crucifix on Manny's chest. The marble altar shook. As dark, spectral forms climbed the walls of the chapel, the altar slowly lifted off of the floor.

"My God . . ." Svabotka teetered on the top step of the altar. Daniel grabbed the cup with one hand and propped up the elderly cardinal with the other.

"Well said, old man," the demon snickered. "You had better get used to serving your new master."

Several cardinals moved to form a tighter circle around the altar and were quickly joined by the rest.

Anthony cried out. "Our Father, Who art in heaven . . ."

Every voice in the chapel joined in the Lord's Prayer. Moments later, as the prayer came to an end, the legs of the heavy table settled back on the floor with a thud.

Anthony raised his hands over Manny's dormant body and

spoke aloud with great authority. "In the Name of the Father and of the Son and of the Holy Ghost, Amen. Most Glorious Prince of the Heavenly Armies, Saint Michael the Archangel . . ." He paused and closed his eyes, as a familiar warmth rushed over him. "Defend us in our battle against principalities and powers, against the rulers of this world of darkness, against the spirits of wickedness in the high places. Come to the assistance of men whom God has created to His likeness and whom He has redeemed at a great price from the tyranny of the devil. The Holy—"

"Redeemed?" The demon screamed so loudly that it seemed as if the windows of the chapel would shatter. Manny's face had become red and swollen. "You are not *redeemed*. The world has long ago succumbed to me, Anthony. Today is merely the day I have come to collect my prize. You will not stand in my—"

"The Holy Church venerates thee as her guardian and protector," Anthony prayed, his voice powerful enough to drown out the demon's ravings. "To thee, the Lord has entrusted the souls of the redeemed to be led into heaven. Pray therefore for the God of Peace to crush Satan beneath our feet, that he may no longer retain men captive and do injury to the Church. Offer our prayers to the Most High, that without delay they may draw His mercy down upon us, take hold of the dragon, the old serpent, which is the devil and Satan, bind him that he may no longer seduce the nations."

The words of the Exorcism Rite seemed to create their own spiritual substance, like a visible wave of air thicker than water. Manny's body began to tremble on the table. High above, like a monster clawing on the outside of the chapel and struggling to get in, a howling wind spewed rage. Statues began to bleed from their porcelain eyes and dozens of objects in the chapel took flight, whizzing around in a chaotic fashion. The cardinals clung to each other as a hideous swell of images and sounds materialized inside the supernatural tornado.

Cardinal Lombardi raised his voice over the clamor. "Thus, cursed dragon, and you, diabolical legion, we adjure you by the living God, by the true God, by the holy God, by the God who so loved the world that He gave up His only Son, that every soul believing in Him might not perish but have life everlasting."

Something shifted violently, and a powerful surge of cold, liquid air rushed across the chapel, disrupting the swirling imagery. Anthony pressed the crucifix harder onto Manny's chest. "That Thou may crush down all enemies of Thy Church," he cried. "We beseech Thee to hear us. We beseech Thee to save this young man, in Your Son's name."

Anthony's knees almost buckled. He wiped sweat from his brow and nodded at Daniel, who sprinkled holy water across Manny's pulsating body, causing a loud hiss of burning flesh. Anthony again made the sign of the cross.

"God arises!" he called. "His enemies are scattered, and those who hate Him flee before Him. As smoke is driven away, so are they driven. As wax melts before the fire, so the wicked perish at the presence of God. Most cunning serpent, you shall no more dare to deceive the human race, persecute the Church, torment God's elect, and sift them as wheat. The Most High God commands you. He with whom, in your great insolence, you still claim to be equal, He who wants all men to be saved and to come to the knowledge of the truth."

Anthony dipped his thumb in the holy water and traced a cross on Manny's forehead, singeing his flesh. "God the *Father* commands you." As Manny's body twisted, Anthony raised his voice again. "God the *Son* commands you. God the *Holy Ghost* commands you. *Christ*, God's Word made flesh, commands you."

The ground beneath the building seemed to shake.

"God of heaven and earth, God of the angels and archangels, God of the prophets and apostles, God of the martyrs and virgins, God Who has power to bestow life after death and rest after toil. For there is no other God than You, nor can there be another true God beside You, the Creator of heaven and earth, Who are truly a King, Whose kingdom is without end. I humbly entreat Your glorious majesty to deliver this servant of Yours from the unclean spirits . . . through Christ our Lord."

A collective *Amen* rose from the cardinals, Daniel's voice rising above the rest. Anthony took the remaining holy water and threw it across Manny. His body raged in violent spasms, as a thin filament of reddish vapor began leaking from every exposed pore on his body.

A crimson cloud formed, rose up near the chapel's famous ceiling, and swirled into a blood-colored vortex. The cloud spun feverishly, first coalescing into an image of Manny's face frozen in a silent scream and then into alien forms so hideous Anthony had to turn away.

As if powered by an invisible force of impossible strength, the chapel itself seemed to exhale, expelling the crimson mist up the chimney that had been set up for the conclave. Manny's convulsing body collapsed on the table, and the chapel fell eerily silent. The only sound came from rosary beads, skittering across the mosaic tile floor.

Chapter 42

Manny pulled the collar of his sweater up around his neck and tilted the brim of his baseball hat low to protect his eyes from the fine mist. Grace huddled under a hooded poncho. A nervous smile tweaked the edges of her mouth and tears ran down her cheeks. He felt his own welling up.

The ancient cemetery's wrought-iron gate framed a cathedral of trees and creaked on rusty hinges when Manny pushed it open. Trails led away in all directions like spokes on a wheel, and a bright red asterisk in the upper right hand corner of the site map marked his destination.

He tucked the paper back in his pocket and led Grace down a narrow path lined with cypress trees that stood guard over the ornate mausoleums and sculpted monuments. The air was rich with the scents of flowering plants and the remnants of the late spring rain.

A bend in the path brought them to a break in the trees with hundreds of headstones dotting the landscape. They were all stained dark with age, except one.

Grace let go of his hand, kissed him on the cheek, and said softly, "I'll wait here."

He started to object and stopped. She was right. He needed to do this alone. Since his mother had left, his memories of her had faded. But he could see her innocent face again, so unaware of the true depth of evil in the world.

He crouched down in front of the simple white tombstone.

Sister Anastasia
1954 – 2013

No inscription. No last name. No way to know who she was. No way to know she had been loved.

Like the memory of his mother's hand, an unexpected shaft of sunlight filtered down through the gray Roman sky and caressed Manny's face. His heart fluttered. He smiled and said, "Hi, Mom," and basked in the touch until he had to swallow the lump that rose in his throat. "I've missed you."

He caressed the smooth granite. "A lot's happened since you left. Turns out, there was no viable DNA in the blood on the Shroud. They lied to you. My biological father was actually a cardinal in the Church, and they manipulated his DNA to make me look like the face in the Shroud. Oh, and that guy they made you marry? Philip? He wasn't the man you thought he was either. Bet you didn't expect any of that, eh?"

Manny tried to laugh, but the attempt died in his throat.

"You probably knew the guy. Lucius Capello. But he wasn't really Lucius Capello. I mean, his name was Capello, but he wasn't the one orchestrating everything. He . . ." He took a deep breath and bent forward to kiss the cold stone. "Never mind."

He resisted the urge to cry as he pulled a crucifix from his pocket and gently placed it on the ground in front of the tombstone before pushing it into the soft earth. "I know you always wanted me to be a priest, Mom." Manny paused. "But I met this girl."

He glanced over his shoulder, and Grace lifted her hand in a wave. "We're going to get married, Mom. You'd love her."

His vision blurred. He longed for all they'd missed together, all the years they wouldn't have. "I wish you could meet her," he said between choking sobs. "I wish so *many* things could be different."

Eventually he stood, fumbling in his coat for a tissue. He wiped his eyes, blew his nose, and felt a gentle touch on his elbow.

"You okay?" Grace asked.

He nodded. "I was just telling my mother how much I love you."

Grace cupped his chin with the palm of her hand and wiped away the remnant of his tears. "Make sure you tell her how much I love her son."

He encircled her waist, pulled her against him, and kissed her long enough for it to count. He didn't want to let go.

She broke away enough to whisper, "We're going to be late for the consecration, honey."

He drew in a deep breath and let his arms slide down until one of his hands clasped hers. "Bye, Mom," he said. "I'll be back. I promise."

He'd lost so much but had gained even more. He wished he had all the answers to the past or could envision his future.

One thing he knew. Someday, he'd see his mother again.

Chapter 43

Cardinal Anthony Lombardi turned his head at the sound of a knock and a heavy door opening. He turned his head.

Father Daniel Neumann stood at the entrance to the Pauline Chapel. "Thirty minutes, Your Eminence."

Anthony nodded. "Immanuel and Grace?"

"They just arrived."

"Thank you, Daniel."

Anthony bowed his head again as the door closed softly behind him. Breathing in the incense-laden air of the Pope's private chapel, he beseeched God for the wisdom and strength he would need to shepherd the largest church on earth. His heart beat rapidly as he spoke softly into the silence. "I can do all things through Christ who strengthens me."

He wasn't sure how long he had been praying when a tendril of cold air caused him to open his eyes. Something seemed different. Not a change he could see or touch, but something he sensed.

A tiny sound emerged in the silence of the chapel, one no louder than the flapping of a butterfly's wings. It came closer. And there it was, a very small something rolling toward him over the shiny marble floor.

It stopped just inches from the kneeler, and a lump rose in his throat. He picked it up and twirled it between his thumb and index finger. It was a rosary bead. A single, black rosary bead. Anthony slammed his eyes shut. *I will fear no evil, for you are with me. Your rod and your staff, they comfort me.*

He forced his eyes open at another sound. This one approached like a breeze. A single shadow peeled away from the darkness.

A voice spoke, more air than substance. Did he hear it, or did it only manifest in his mind? "No hard feelings, Anthony," it said.

Anthony shuddered and dropped the bead on the floor.

"Think of it as a memento of our time together, old friend."

Anthony mustered his strength. "How dare you enter my God's house."

There was a pause until the voice materialized again, this time coming from the lips of the Bresciano sculpture to his right. "Do you actually believe brick and stone could keep me from you? We have been friends for too long for me to let that happen."

"We are not friends, Devil. You have been mankind's enemy since the beginning of time."

From the sculpture on his left, the voice said, "It doesn't have to be that way, *Your Holiness*, we could be friends. I'm sorry, is it too soon to refer to you as the Pope?"

"In the name of Christ, silence!"

"Peter the Third. I love the name you chose. Makes it much easier than learning a new one. For someone as old as I."

Anthony tried to stand, but an oppressive weight on his shoulders pressed him down.

This time the voice whispered into his ear. "We could accomplish so much together as a team. I could give you everything you have ever dreamed of. Power. Glory."

Anthony brought trembling hands together in front of his face. Now it was he who was under attack.

Or perhaps he was already possessed.....

Or perhaps he was already possessed and talking to himself? Was Mr. Hyde privy to Dr. Jekyll's innermost thoughts? Did he always know what he did in the privacy of his own mind? Was his face the flesh-colored mask behind which hid the face of a demon?

No! He would not succumb to the devil's lies.

Anthony blinked the sweat from his eyes and focused on the crucified Christ hanging over the chapel's altar. "You, my God, are my rock, my fortress, my deliverer."

Instantly, his shoulders relaxed. A familiar warm glow enveloped him, and a peace settled in his bones.

He crushed the black bead with the heel of his shoe. With the growl of an ill-tempered dog, he called out loudly, "In the name of the Lord, be gone you Father of Lies! Once and for all, leave this place, you Cursed Dragon!"

A sudden blast of wind scattered the bead dust and blew open the chapel doors. And then there was silence.

Anthony approached the altar, knelt, and whispered, "Great is Your faithfulness, O Lord."

He stood, bowed his head, and turned toward the back of the chapel where Daniel stood frozen in place. Anthony placed his hand on his shoulder, smiled, and said, "I am ready."

END

Acknowledgements

To Kristine Pratt and Dale Hansen of Written World Communications, for taking a chance on an unknown author.

To Normandie Ward Fischer, for her masterful guidance and professionalism throughout the editorial process. I could not have done it without her. To Robin Patchen for her copyediting skills that helped polish the work.

To my agent Les Stobbe, for his tireless support of first-time authors like me.

To Randy Schrupp, for introducing me to the fascinating history and science behind the Shroud of Turin.

To my children, family, and friends -- who mean everything to me.

To my wife and best friend Lynett, for her unwavering support and love. I couldn't have done it without her either.

To God, for sparing just enough grace to "save a wretch like me."

And finally, to those that purchased and read this book. Thank you.

Jim O'Shea

Jim is a long-time resident of Chesterfield, Missouri, "The City of Sculptures." He is a graduate of the University of Missouri in Columbia and traveled the country and the world for twenty-five years in the computer software industry. Jim now spends his time crafting suspense novels that often tackle the complex relationship between science and religion, stories designed to take the reader places he or she may not have previously considered. His debut novel, *the linen god*, has been called "a wonderfully engaging, page-turning thriller" by Doug Peterson (Award Winning Author of *The Puzzle People* and *The Vanishing Woman*). Jim is currently working on his second novel, *The White King*.

Jim O'Shea lives with his wife and family in the Midwest. Correspondence for the author should be directed to:

http://jimoshea-author.com/main/

CPSIA information can be obtained at www.ICGtesting.com
Printed in the USA
LVOW100951250613

340107LV00002B/3/P